"Abby could use [W9-CTC-205] so don't hurry the job, okay? I need a little time."

"Huh." Old Whitey leaned over to spit his tobacco in the grass. "Thought she wanted her vehicle repaired so she could lay tracks out of Trueheart. Said something about gettin' to Sedona."

"Things have changed," Jack muttered. *Don't make me say what, old man.*

"What?"

Great. Jack rubbed the back of his neck. "Well…Abby would be smart to settle here for the winter." Jack forged on, feeling as if he were trudging head down into a dust storm. "She's never built anything and she thinks she'll build an adobe by the fall? Ain't gonna happen."

"Gal's pretty spunky."

"Yep, but take it from a divorce lawyer, she's smack-dab in the middle of the Divorce Crazies. She'll change her mind ten times in the next ten months. Meanwhile, till she's over this phase, Trueheart's a safer, saner town to raise her son than Sedona'll ever be. Last thing Abby needs is to get lost in a power vortex."

"Hmm." Whitey chewed thoughtfully, then said, "Sure you know which end of the branding iron you're grabbing?"

Jack cocked his head. "Meaning?"

"Meanin' if anybody gets burned around here, it might not be Abby."

Dear Reader,

In this fifth story in my series about the town of Trueheart, Colorado, Abby Lake is a woman caught up in that wonderful/terrifying phase of life I call the "Divorce Crazies." I hope you've never experienced it yourself, but if you have, you know it's a time of extreme vulnerability and extreme creativity.

Since (through no fault of her own) her last effort at making a good life failed, Abby's determined to get it right this time for herself and her young son, Skyler. She's changing *everything*—her job, her home, her attitude toward men, love and marriage. She means to grab life and happiness with both hands before they slip away.

To Abby's wary new neighbor, lawyer Jack Kelton, it seems that Abby "hasn't a clue what she wants—but she'll be flying off in all four directions at once, looking for it."

Jack may have a point. I remember the first year of my own divorce: buying a handyman's-special house on the East Coast one week (I wasn't that handy), then flying to California the next to learn if a man I hadn't seen for fifteen years might be The One. (He wasn't.) Darting back to my new house to buy forty of everything (paper towels! canned beans! flashlight batteries!) as if I could build a wall with all those supplies between me and the cold scary world.

And so forth for the rest of that crazy year, till at last I met someone who taught me to calm down and smile again. So here I give you Abby Lake, on *her* way to learning how to smile again in the town of Trueheart, Colorado. As always, hope you enjoy!

Peggy Nicholson

Other books by Peggy Nicholson set in Trueheart

HARLEQUIN SUPERROMANCE

834—DON'T MESS WITH TEXANS   1025—TRUE HEART
929—THE BABY BARGAIN   1067—THE WILDCATTER

Kelton's Rules

Peggy Nicholson

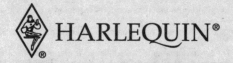

TORONTO • NEW YORK • LONDON
AMSTERDAM • PARIS • SYDNEY • HAMBURG
STOCKHOLM • ATHENS • TOKYO • MILAN • MADRID
PRAGUE • WARSAW • BUDAPEST • AUCKLAND

ISBN 0-373-71119-0

KELTON'S RULES

This edition published by arrangement with Harlequin Books S.A.

® and TM are trademarks of the publisher. Trademarks indicated with
® are registered in the United States Patent and Trademark Office, the
Canadian Trade Marks Office and in other countries.

Visit us at www.eHarlequin.com

Printed in U.S.A.

To Ron, for all the times

CHAPTER ONE

"MO-O-OM, WE SHOULD GO back!" Perched on the bench seat behind his mother, Skyler smacked the Colorado road map.

"Sweetie, I know I took a wrong turn, but see what a gorgeous place we've found. Can you believe those mountains?" Abby Lake took one hand off the school bus steering wheel and waved to the right where distant peaks caught the late-afternoon sun. "Just wonderful, huh?"

Framed in her rearview mirror, Skyler was pink-faced and scowling. He pushed his glasses up his short nose and glared straight ahead at the two-lane country road. "You should've asked me before you turned. I'm the navigator."

"You and DC looked so comfy back there, I didn't have the heart to wake you." Buckled in behind her on the one bench seat remaining in the stripped-out bus, Skyler had drifted off. He'd been smiling in his sleep, hugging DC-3, the enormous white tomcat that lay cradled against his chest.

Abby hadn't seen her son smile like that in two months or more. She'd drunk in the sight, feeling like a wanderer in the desert who'd stumbled upon a stream at last—and knelt to scoop cool, clear water with both hands. Because maybe that smile meant the worst was behind them. Skyler would find his happiness again. And then, please God, he'd forgive her.

Stealing glimpse after glimpse in her mirror, memorizing the tender curve of her child's mouth, the shape of the cat's ear and the spray of his whiskers—she planned to sketch this scene tonight, once they stopped—somehow she'd missed her road, somewhere west of Durango.

"We should go back!"

"It's sort of difficult to turn this beast." Used to a compact car, Abby was still amazed by the huge turning radius of the ancient half-size bus. And it must be leaking power-steering fluid—a tight turn elicited a screeching protest that set her teeth on edge. *Never should've bought this thing.* "Besides, I think we're coming to a town up ahead—Trueheart, if we're where I hope we— Where I *believe* we are. If so, we can angle southwest again toward Cortez." She reached behind her to pat his map someplace in the vicinity of the tiny dot with the charming name of Trueheart. "So we haven't lost too many miles."

"I mean we should go back to New Jersey. We should go home. This is stupid. I hate this place!"

"Oh, Sky, sweetie," Abby murmured helplessly. Beyond the bug-spattered windshield, the road wavered and blurred. She blinked it clear again. "We can't go back." They had no "back" to return to. The divorce settlement had given her the suburban trophy house that Steve had insisted they buy two years ago when he'd left navy aviation to become a commercial pilot. But on a single income, she couldn't possibly afford to keep a five-bedroom minimansion. Didn't want it anyway.

Last week she'd sold it for a profit of twenty-thousand dollars, which would be their grubstake for a fresh start. A new life out west.

A life her ten-year-old son hated already.

"We could! We could be home in four days. Dad's gotta be missing us."

Want to bet? With Chelsea the Super Stewardess—oh,

*pardon me, flight attendant—to fly? And a new family on
the way? He hasn't spared us a thought.* "Of course he
misses you, sweetheart. But he can come visit you anywhere there's an airport."

"There's no airport around here! Nothing but cows
and…and cow poop and grass. It stinks!"

Also a sky like a vast, inverted bowl of blue bird feathers. Cerulean. Indigo. Turquoise at the edges. Mountains
turning to blazing lumps of coal as the sun rolled down
toward a jagged purple horizon. Breathtakingly beautiful
country, if her son would only look. "Okay, but Trueheart's not where we'll be living, you know. Once we
make it to Sedona—"

"I'll hate that, too!"

Abby sighed, reached back to touch his knee, then grimaced as he flinched away. Glancing over her shoulder,
she saw that he was glaring out his side window, mouth
quivering. *Don't cry, sweetie, oh, don't! If I'd had any
choice in this…*

She'd do it all again. Not even for Sky could she have
stayed married to Steven Lake once she'd realized the extent of his cheating. *What a blind, trusting fool I was!* She
should've seen it coming. Any woman with two eyes in
her head—the kind of woman who didn't muddle her maps
and end up blithely wandering off into the wilderness with
the sun going down…

But Abby had never been that kind of woman—a
woman who paid attention. She was always marveling
over a pebble, or a dandelion, or a cloud, when she
should've been turning out her husband's pockets every
time he returned from a cross-country flight.

"And I *hate* this stupid ol' wreck of a bus! The radiator's boiling over again. Didn't you look at the heat
gauge?"

Abby looked—yelped—and took a foot off the gas. "You're right!" They'd filled the radiator only this morning and also the day before around noon. The mysterious leak seemed to be gaining on them with every passing mile.

Coasting to a stop—she hadn't seen another car for ten minutes or more—Abby pulled over to the ragged shoulder of the road and blew out a breath. "Wonderful... Okay, where's the water jug?" They'd used more water than gasoline, it seemed, these past two days.

"It's back—" Skyler unbuckled himself and scrambled into the rear of the bus, which was crammed with boxes and baggage and a washing machine and all the other household essentials they couldn't leave behind. Skyler's model airplanes. Abby's books and easel. DC's litter box. "*Uh*-oh..."

"What?" She'd stopped on a long, gradual upgrade, so Abby shifted the floor lever carefully into first gear, stepped on the emergency brake pedal, then swung around. "What's the matter?"

Sky held up an empty five-gallon jug. "The cap came off. Your sketchbook's all wet."

Abby clenched her teeth on a groan and closed her eyes. Her sketchbook! She'd had three or four drawings in this one that she felt sure were keepers. She'd intended to mat and frame them once they reached Sedona, then use them as samples in her search for a gallery to handle her work. *You couldn't have found a safer place to put the blasted jug?* She managed a shaky smile. "Well... Okay. No big deal." Now what? "We'll just have to find some water." They'd crossed a narrow creek perhaps two miles back, down at the base of this long, long slope. The road had been gradually climbing up from the plains for the last twenty miles.

"I'm sorry." Sky looked as crushed as she felt.

"Plenty more sketches where those came from."

"If we'd stayed in New Jersey it never would've happened."

"Well, we didn't!" She held out her hand for the jug. "We didn't," she repeated, lowering her voice. "We're just going to have to make the best of where we are, kiddo." She swung open her door a cautious inch or two, checking underfoot for the cat, who also seemed bound and determined to bolt back east. "Want to come along? I think there might be a stream down there." The roadside pasture also sloped gently down toward a distant line of trees.

"Uh-uh."

"Well, I'll lock this door then." Not that there was anyone within miles to worry about. In fact, the real concern was how they'd find someone to help them if she didn't locate water. How could a country be so big and so deserted? Not a fence, not a telephone pole, not a house in sight. Just enormous rolling slopes, rising in wave after dusty wave toward the far-off mountains. "I'll be straight down there, if you change your mind."

SKYLER STOOD, staring at the ruined sketchbook, while her footsteps crunched on gravel, then faded away. "Darn. Crap. Oh, *booger*, DC!" He could have found a better place to stow the water. Should have. Had he wanted that to happen, or was he just stupid?

His dad was always telling him to pay attention. Laughing and calling him Spaceshot when he forgot to do something or when he was clumsy doing it. Sky stooped for the cat. "I used to think Spaceshot was good." A name for an astronaut, maybe, or a test pilot. He still remembered how it had stung when the true meaning finally dawned on him.

"Come'ere, luggums." Arms filled with twenty pounds of cat, he rubbed his face through the thick white fur till a rumbling purr kicked into gear. "Like a big ol' DC-3 humming along," his dad used to say. "Fat thing." He wandered forward to sit in the driver's seat, holding the cat in his lap as he stared out through the windshield.

At nothing. There was nothing out there that mattered. "'Cept her," he muttered grudgingly, turning DC's head so they both peered down the hill to where his mom's yellow T-shirt bent for an instant toward the ground. Picking flowers, when she ought to be looking for water. "Or maybe not." Why should he care about her when this was all her fault? If she hadn't gotten so angry at his dad, he'd never, ever have left them. He'd told Skyler that. "But what can a guy do?" Sky muttered, echoing the breezy words he'd heard so many times before.

I can drive us home where we belong.

Skyler blinked behind his thick lenses. He could hijack this stupid bus sometime, when his mom was taking a nap on the mattress in the back, as she did when she got too tired to see the road.

"Drive all the way back to New Jersey," he gloated, picturing it as he ruffled DC's fur, then smoothed it again. "She'd wake up and—zowie—there we'd be in the driveway." Home. His eyes started to water. "Like we never left at all."

If only he could drive.

He leaned over the cat to examine the pedals. Three instead of two like on his dad's BMW and his mom's old Taurus. Which she never should have sold. Not for this hunk of junk.

And this thing had a floor-mounted stick shift. It looked

a lot harder to handle than the gear shift on his dad's car, which he'd been studying all year, practicing in his mind. He'd planned to ask his dad if he'd teach him to drive this summer.

Instead here he sat, in the middle of nowhere. Hundreds and thousands of miles from his dad, his friends at school, his bedroom and his tree house out back. "So first you have to shift." He tried it and was surprised at the big lever's resistance. "Ooof—*move,* you stupid thing!"

DC stood up on his lap, tail swishing in irritation. Sky hooked his left forearm around the cat to steady him. "Help me out here, will you? Why won't it—oh!" *Spaceshot.* Dummy. He'd forgotten the clutch pedal. You stepped on that, *then* you shifted. "Pedal, then hold it, then—ha!" The gearshift moved easily, with a soul-satisfying *clunk!*

"Yeah!" Sky shifted up, down, then over and up again, the way he'd seen his mom do it. Then down again on the other side. "And that's fourth gear, when we're really rolling." Hey, this was easy! He shifted back to the middle.

"Now we have to turn it on."

Did he dare? He stole a glance downhill, but his mom was out of sight in the trees. "She'll never hear us if we run it for just a minute," he assured the cat. Resting his chin on DC's round head, he leaned forward to finger the key. She couldn't possibly hear, but still… His mom didn't get mad often, but when she did…

"Ouch!" Tired of being squashed, DC dug in his claws and slithered down from his lap. His double-wide tail slapped Skyler's glasses, which as usual had slid to the end of his nose. "Hey, stupid hairball, watch what you're doing!"

Cat and glasses hit the floorboard at once, with a clatter and a weighty thump. "If you've broken them—" Sky's mom paid for his first pair of replacement glasses each year, then the rest came out of his allowance. This was pair number three and it was only June. "Crap!"

He couldn't see very well without them. He wasn't blind as a bug-eyed bat, the way that jerk Timmy Ryder at school was always telling everybody, but things got kind of...blurry when he took them off. "Move over, fur brain." Shoving the cat to the left with his foot, Sky squeezed under the steering wheel and cautiously down. "Where are they?"

He patted under the high-set pedals. Nope. "What are you doin', sitting on 'em?" He pulled the cat up onto his knee, ignoring his warning growl. DC was too timid to bite even a mouse.

"Or maybe—ooof—keep *still!*" He twisted around to grope under the seat and— "Yeah, got 'em." Unbroken; for once in his life he was lucky. He jammed them on top of his head, let go of the exasperated tom and, reaching up to the dash, caught hold of something, a handle of some kind, and started wriggling up past the steering wheel.

Thock! The handle jumped in his hand. The bus quivered and groaned.

"What was that?"

No comment from the cat. Ears flattened to his head, DC was doing his best to exit left, wedging his plump body between the driver's seat and the side of the bus in an unsuccessful effort to reach the back. His tail lashed in frustration.

Sky grabbed the wheel to pull himself off the floorboard—and it spun hard to the right. "Hey!" Something felt wrong. The wheel was shuddering in his grasp. Gravel rumbled under the tires. As he squirmed into the driver's seat and pulled his glasses down onto his nose, things swam into focus—and streamed away. No, it was the bus that was moving, he realized, as it gave a horrible lurch.

And kept on rolling.

Backward.

Swerving with a ponderous, dreadful deliberation off the road, then down across the pasture.

CHAPTER TWO

MARYLOU WON'T DO, Jack Kelton told himself, aiming his open Jeep down the road to Durango.

The baby-sitter might be five years older than his daughter, Kat, but she was three jumps behind every time. Missing Kat's straight-faced jokes and veiled warnings. Failing to foresee her pranks, or knowing how to handle them once they'd been played. Worst of all, the girl was gullible, taking Kat at her word when she shouldn't. Apparently they weren't teaching critical thinking in high school these days, or if they were, Marylou was failing.

"And now, shoot me if she's not in love," Jack muttered, scrubbing a hand through his wind-whipped hair as the Jeep topped the hill. A fifteen-year-old in calf-love was useless! Lethally oblivious to the world and her responsibilities.

With Marylou lost in love, Kat would run wild this summer. She was probably contemplating mayhem this very moment, since she'd wanted to accompany him into Durango. She'd pulled a major pout when he refused to let her go to a kickboxing movie alone while he met with an after-hours' client. Right now, back in Trueheart, Marylou was probably sprawled on Jack's couch, bare feet up on the backrest, spooning the last of their chocolate-chip ice cream out of the carton as she giggled on the phone with the Love of her Life. While forgotten Kat was probably somewhere down the street, hot-wiring somebody's car.

She'd pass him any second now with a whoop and a wave and an offer to drag race. Automatically he glanced in his mirror.

Nothing but empty road back there. Still, facts had to be faced. He'd have to find another sitter, and soon. Not that Trueheart had much to offer in the baby-sitting department.

The Jeep crested the next rise and Jack cocked his head. Fifty yards downslope, a bright red, sawed-off school bus was parked by the edge of the road, facing his way. Not from around here; Trueheart school buses were yellow and full-size. Jack's brows drew together as his Jeep closed the distance. Was it—?

It *was* rolling. Backing down the road. Or, no— "What the devil?"

As Jack's foot moved to his brake, the bus curved slowly off the shoulder and trundled out into the field. Some idiot had left it parked without shifting into first! Most likely the emergency brake had let go.

Well, so be it. Whoever the idiot was, he was about to learn his lesson the hard way. The narrow band of brush and cottonwoods at the bottom of the hill screened a twenty-foot drop-off to a nifty little trout stream where Jack sometimes fished. Once the bus had gathered momentum, it would blow right through that fragile barrier.

"Hope to God the moron's not directly in line below, communing with na—" Jack's eyes narrowed. He stomped down on the gas, then spun the wheel. The Jeep swerved off into the pasture, bucked over a hummock and roared in pursuit. There was somebody *in* that bus, a head bobbing above the steering wheel! "Step on the brake, bozo!" Or could the brakes have failed? Swearing out loud, Jack floored the accelerator.

A race between gravity and distance, speed and time.

Eyes sweeping the slope below, gauging probable trajectories and possible outcomes, Jack spotted the woman. Bursting from the trees, a blur of yellow with flailing arms. Pale flapping hair, a mouth open wide in what must be a scream, though he couldn't hear her over his engine's roar. "Get the hell out of our *way,* lady!" What did she think she could do—catch the damn bus like a fly ball? "*Move* it, woman!"

Well, she'd have to take care of herself. The Jeep closed the last few feet, bounding along driver's side to driver's side, and Jack stared up through the open window—into a small, wide-eyed face. Jeez, a kid! "Step on the brake!"

"I can't!" His voice squeaked with panic. "My cat's stuck under the—" He swung back into the bus, yanking desperately at the gearshift.

Jack gritted his teeth at the agonized squawk of stripping gears. So much for the transmission. "Step on the brake and *damn* the cat! Do it *now!*"

The boy shook his head frantically. "He w-w-won't *move!* If I could shift into—"

The bus must've been doing twenty by now. Maybe a hundred yards to the trees—a hundred and three to the cliff. The woman had vanished behind the bulk of the vehicle. "Forget shifting, kid, and *listen!*" Jack yelled, leaning halfway out of the Jeep. "Grab the top of your wheel—*yeah,* that's right! Now slo-owly—*ve-er-ry* slowly—turn it toward me!"

A calculated risk. If the kid panicked and swung the wheel too fast, the Jeep, running parallel, would smash into the bus's left flank. "Good! That's good." Thank God he could take directions.

"Now *slowly.* Turn another inch toward me—*excellent!*" If the bus didn't flip, if they still had room to pull off the maneuver, the kid could steer it in a gentle curve away from the creek, gradually swinging cross-hill till the bus coasted to a halt. "Gimme another inch—good!"

Jack turned his own wheel; they were now running side by side, not three feet apart. He flinched as the bus slammed into something solid—a rock or a log—and the exhaust system peeled away. He glanced back in his mirror as tailpipes and other parts popped into view and clattered along in their wake. "So who needs a muffler?" he assured the kid, sending him a rakish grin.

Yeah, right, we're all under control here. Having the time of our lives!

But the kid actually smiled back at him and Jack laughed out loud. Spunky little devil! "Turn it a little more—ea-aa-sy does it. Yeah!" He sucked in his breath as the bus wobbled, trying to lift onto its right-side wheels—then settled back four-square. *Whew! I owe You one, up there!*

One more in a long list.

"Give it another inch. You're doing great!" And he'd better be—they had forty feet left to the trees and the bus was angled roughly fifty degrees to the fall line. Jack corrected his own course, nodding fiercely. "Now one last time, son—gently—a couple of inches."

As it curved cross-slope, the bus had been gradually losing momentum. It was doing maybe ten when it plowed into the bushes. But hitting them almost broadside, it didn't slice on through. Branches shrieked along steel. Slender tree trunks crackled and snapped. An avalanche of baggage inside the vehicle rumbled to the far side. The bus rocked up onto its off-side wheels for a heart-stopping moment—then, supported by the bushes, settled back again.

As he braked to a halt alongside, Jack blew out his breath. *And thank You!* He stepped out and sauntered on shaking legs over to the kid's window. "That was exciting.'' They measured each other solemnly—then grinned from ear to ear. ''Well done,'' Jack told him, socking his shoulder. ''Very well done ind—''

''*Sky!* Oh, *baby!*''

And here came Momma at last, panting and wind-torn and half-hysterical, clutching a forgotten bunch of crumpled wildflowers. A small frantic tornado, she roared down the narrow gap between the vehicles and actually bumped Jack aside, getting to her child. ''Oh, *sweetie!*'' She wrenched open the kid's door. Jack winced as the edge of it banged into the Jeep. So much for his paint job.

''Are you all *right?*'' But she wasn't waiting to hear; apparently touch would tell her faster. Her fingers flew over the boy's face, his arms, his ribs. Tugging at his clothes, smoothing his hair. ''Where does it hurt?''

Jack met the kid's eyes over her shoulder and gave him a commiserating grin. Sometimes a guy just had to put up with the mushy stuff.

''Aw-ww, Mom! I'm *fine*.'' The boy twisted away as she tried to pull him into a hug, then dived under the wheel. ''It's DC...''

The largest cat Jack had ever seen crouched behind the pedals, tail fluffed to the size of a firehose, eyes like black saucers. Moaning throatily, he slashed at the boy's outstretched hand.

''*Ouch!* He's never done that before!'' The boy— Sky?—brought scratched fingers to his lips.

''Reckon you've never run him backward down a mountain before,'' Jack said mildly. ''Give him a minute.''

Momma swung around, registering his presence at last.

And worth the wait, Jack decided as his gaze dropped from wide green eyes still dilated with shock, down over a lush trembling mouth, over a pair of still heaving, just-the-right-size breasts, to—*oh, boy, forget it!* To a slogan emblazoned across the T-shirt, claiming: A Woman Needs A Man Like A Fish Needs A Bicycle.

Hoo-boy, one of those. A lady with an ax to grind. His eyes flicked back to the bus, filled almost to window level with its assortment of household rubble. Jeez, that thing on its side—could that be a washing machine?

"Been divorced long?" he asked casually.

She blinked. Blinked her long lashes again, grateful smile fading to wariness as she raised her chin. "H-how did you guess?"

Jack threw back his head and laughed.

SHE'D SWORN she'd stand on her own two feet from now on, yet here she was again, letting a man take charge.

Not that it was easy to stand alone when apparently she'd wrecked an ankle, somewhere in that pell-mell, adrenaline-powered chase, Abby reminded herself. Sitting in the topless Jeep, where their rescuer had planted her when he realized—at the same moment she did—that she could barely hobble, Abby clasped still-shaking hands between wobbly knees. She watched with growing uneasiness as he stalked around the bus, hands on lean hips, shaking his shaggy head to himself as he summed up the state of her disaster and decided what should be done about it.

She had a terrible suspicion his conclusions would be the right ones—logical, sensible and therefore impossible to refute, much as she'd rather refute them. She'd already had one sample of his plain-spoken intelligence, with that guess about her marital status.

I don't need this!

Didn't need a disastrous setback, just as she was starting to pick up the pieces of her life and think about rebuilding.

Didn't need someone—another too confident, too brash,

too good-looking-for-his-own-good male—telling her what to do and how to do it.

Except that she did. She was utterly exhausted and confused. *Overwhelmed.* She supposed this was what they called shock. Looking at her son as he smiled wanly up at the man who'd rolled out from under the bus to stand and pat his shoulder, her eyes filled slowly with tears. *Oh, Sky, I could have lost you!*

Losing the life she'd known since she was nineteen was nothing compared to that.

And being bossed around by another know-it-all man— who'd known enough to save her son—was a small price to pay. A price she'd pay gladly again and again. The bargain of a lifetime.

"I haven't even thanked you yet," she said huskily a few minutes later when he came to sit beside her in the Jeep. "That cliff beyond the trees…if Sky'd gone over that…"

He shrugged his broad shoulders. "I couldn't have done it without him. He's a smart kid. Stayed cool when it counted."

"Yes…" Cool under pressure. Steve and his pilot buddies had valued that quality above all else.

Sometimes she wondered if it signified ice at the center. A basic heartlessness. Easy to be cool if you didn't really care. When she'd told him she wanted a divorce, Steve had shrugged, given her a rueful grin and merely said, "Can't say I blame you, babe."

She shook off the memory with a jerk of her head. Who cared if this man was just one more of that type? It wasn't as though she was buying him and taking him home. "I don't understand how this could've happened," she said now, eyes returning to the bus. "I know I left the brake on. And I *thought* I left it in gear."

He glanced down at his boots, then quickly up again—and smiled. "Brakes have been known to fail. My name's Kelton, by the way. Jack Kelton." He held out a big hand and reluctantly she surrendered her own to its shockingly warm clasp, aware of the roughness of his palm. A carpenter, perhaps? Or out here in cow country, with those boots he was wearing, maybe a cattleman?

"Abby Lake," she murmured. "And that's Skyler." She nodded at her son, who'd climbed into the back of the bus and was apparently searching for DC among the tumbled boxes. In the gathering twilight, she could barely see him moving beyond the windows.

"Good enough. So first question, Abby. Do you have any sort of towing service we can call?"

"I'm afraid I—" She'd had roadside assistance, of course, on her car. But in her scramble to close on the house, then move, since the new buyers had insisted on immediate occupancy... What with all the other details of dismantling one's life and carting it across country: changing bank accounts, health insurance, credit cards, mailing address... "I forgot to get it. I just bought the bus last week."

"Ah," Kelton said neutrally, although she could hear his disapproval. No doubt *he* would have remembered. "So question two. I take it money's an issue here?"

A sensible deduction—prodding old bruises and a still-simmering indignation. Three months ago, money wouldn't have been an issue. Now it was survival itself. "It's tight." Budgeted to the penny and now, looking at the bus, she realized her budget was blown. *What am I going to do?*

"Okay, so hiring a tow truck to come out from Durango, then haul a bus forty miles back, isn't practical. And once you get it to a garage, it may need a new transmission, definitely a new exhaust system. I'm not sure about the axles, though they might be intact... Repairs are going to be costly, if you can even scrounge the parts for this old girl. And meantime, while somebody's fixing it for a week or more, I suppose you'll have to stay in a motel. Unless you have friends in Durango?''

''No...'' Abby threaded a hand through her disheveled hair. Tried to find a smile. ''We're from New Jersey. At least lately...'' It was one of the things she'd hated most about being a military wife all those years. The repeated uprootings. The constant farewells. A shy woman like her needed to nest in one place, where she could build and nourish long-term friendships. The kind of support system that sustained you through disasters such as this.

''Anyway, that all adds up to a lot of money,'' Jack concluded, casually reaching across to brush a knuckle across her cheek, where a tear had escaped. He glanced skyward with a comical frown. ''And on top of all that, damned if it doesn't look like rain.''

Reflexively, Abby followed his gaze. Over their heads stretched a vault of cloudless silvery blue, cupping the last of the light, one star already twinkling in the east. She laughed shakily, wiping one hand across her wet lashes. ''Cats and dogs by the bucketful.''

''Well, then...'' Jack folded his arms and leaned back, stretching his long legs, boots braced against the pedals. ''If Durango's not an option, what about this instead? We're three miles from Trueheart. There's an old cowhand north of town, Whitey Whitelaw, who's the best shade-tree mechanic I've ever seen. Cobbling together clapped-out feed trucks and tractors is his specialty, and his prices are pretty reasonable. I imagine he'd cut you a deal.''

''He doesn't know me from Adam. I don't know why he'd—''

"Why don't you ask him and see? I can call Whitey when we get back to town, ask if he'd come out here in the morning, take a look at her…"

Abby nodded doubtfully. She could think of nothing better to try. "I…suppose so. And for tonight, we've got a mattress in back and a camp stove." She could boil enough creek water to—

But Jack was shaking his head. "Don't even think it. You need a real bed and a hot meal—you both do—and that ankle needs some ice to bring it down. You're coming with me. I've got just the place for you."

"You mean, to your…house?" If he was married it would be awful, descending on his surprised, solicitous wife, and if he wasn't, even worse. "Oh, no! We couldn't impose." She'd rather camp for a year in a cow pasture than be forced into that kind of dependency on a stranger, no matter how kindly intended.

"Abby, I never let anybody impose on me. And Kat and I don't have room for guests at the moment."

So he was married. She should have guessed, attractive as he was. He didn't wear a ring, but then that came as no surprise. Steve had shed his within a year of their marriage, insisting it was dangerous, what with all the machinery and electronics a pilot had to deal with.

"But there's an empty rental cottage next door to us set up for mountain bikers and for skiers in winter. It's furnished down to the pots and pans and bedsheets—and I'm sure I can arrange for you to stay there. My landlady owns it."

Abby smiled in spite of herself. He had it all figured out. And she'd bet Jack could sell coconuts to Tahitians, if he took the notion. She should be thankful he was willing to help.

"So what are we gonna do?" Skyler demanded, appearing out of the dark at her elbow, his arms wrapped around a glowering DC-3.

Abby let out a long breath. She supposed she'd never really had a choice in the matter. "I guess we're going with Mr. Kelton."

CHAPTER THREE

"AND HE-ERE WE ARE," Jack announced grandly as he swung the Jeep into an unpaved driveway. Set fifty feet back in a narrow lot, a tiny, two-story cottage crouched under the trees. "Be it ever so humble, you'll find it homey enough. It's basically identical in layout to mine. They were built at the same time for twin daughters, back in the 1880s."

He'd warned her it would be rustic, Abby reminded herself, searching for something to say as she studied the sagging front porch, the weathered clapboard siding that suggested this twin hadn't sprung for a paint job since the 1890s.

Still, whatever its appearance, the price had indeed been right for a week's lodging. On the far side of Trueheart, Jack had left them in the Jeep while he'd negotiated with his landlady, Maudie Harris. He'd loped out of her house minutes later, wearing a triumphant grin while he twirled a key ring around his finger.

"That's my place over—" Jack paused in the act of nodding to their right, across a picket fence hedged by an overgrown border of bushes and waist-high weeds. He scowled. "Over there."

Through leafy branches, Abby could make out the glint of a pickup truck, parked in the shadows beyond an identical sagging porch that ran the width of Jack's cottage.

With lights glowing from the front-room windows, his house looked more inviting than hers.

"Very nice," she said, although a twist of uneasiness coiled through her stomach. Bad enough to be so obliged to the man already. But to have him as her next-door neighbor—ready, willing and able to give his opinion on her every move from here on out... *I don't need this.* "Well..." She swiveled in her seat.

"Hang on." Jack bounded out of the Jeep and around to her side. "You shouldn't put your weight on that ankle. Not till we've had a look at it."

"I can manage."

"I'm sure you can." But his hand blocked her passage, leaving her the choice of shoving it aside—or accepting it.

Used to having his own way, for all his charm and good-will, Abby decided, gritting her teeth behind a close-mouthed smile. She'd learned not to trust charm. She'd found that it was often a substitute for less polished but kinder, more genuine emotions.

"Thank you." Her nerves skittered as those oven-warm fingers closed over hers. Then he took her other arm, supporting her weight as she slithered down from the high seat. They stood for an instant toe-to-toe, Abby looking up—quite a way up—and Jack holding on to her just a heartbeat too long, his fingers seeming to squeeze her a hairsbreadth too tightly.

Or maybe her alarm sprang from her rattled nerves, sensing danger where it didn't exist. There was also the simple fact that she hadn't stood this close to a man—a virile, ruggedly attractive man—in months. "Thanks," she said again.

But he didn't take that as dismissal. Instead Jack transferred her hand to his forearm, a support as hard and muscular as the rest of him obviously was. "We'll get you

settled and then…'' His shaggy head swung back toward
his own yard as they moved carefully across the grass.
Abby could see one decisive eyebrow drawn down in a
scowl. "Then I'll just…''

What was bothering him over there?

But faced with the stairs to the porch, she abandoned
speculation to concentrate on making it up the six steep
steps, then limping across the warped decking to the un-
painted front door.

While Jack fit the key into the lock, Sky joined them,
frowning unhappily, his cat cradled on his shoulder. She
could read his thoughts as if he'd shouted them out loud.
Compared to a brand-new, suburban five-bedroom house
back in New Jersey, this wasn't much. Compared even to
the Motel 6 room they'd slept in last night, this cottage
was outclassed. *And it's all your fault, Mom!*

"It seems very…comfortable," she managed as Jack
steered her inside and switched on the light. If your taste
ran to plaid, broken-backed sleeper sofas. To a La-Z-Boy
chair spilling foam stuffing across a dirt-gray braided rug,
or fluorescent bulbs in a tacky cartwheel chandelier. A
wall-mounted elk head that wore a red bandanna and probably had a case of fleas. A collection of beer cans and
bottles, arranged artfully along the mantel over a small,
ash-choked firebox. "And look, Sky, we have a fireplace!"
Her words came out much too cheery.

"Hmm…'' Jack led her to the couch and lowered her,
oblivious to the fact that she'd stiffened her spine, signal-
ing her resistance to the maneuver. "Haven't been in here
since last fall, when Maudie gave me a choice between
her two places. Looks like those college kids who came
here to ski over spring break were a little…rough on the
decor." He straightened to aim a forefinger at Skyler.
"Now you, kid—you're in charge of unloading your stuff

from my Jeep while I'm gone. Don't let your mom budge, okay?''

He turned to Abby as Sky set down DC and trooped out the door without a protest. ''And you— Let me see if there's ice in your freezer.'' He strode off toward the rear of the house and returned in seconds. ''Nope, no ice. So sit tight, let Sky do the work—I mean *all* the work, Abby—and I'll be back soon as I can. There's a few things I have to…''

He was gone before she could open her mouth to tell him thank-you, but from here they could manage alone.

BY THE TIME Sky returned with their sleeping bags, Abby had hobbled into the kitchen. Propped against the back of a wobbly kitchen chair, she surveyed the vinyl floor with its missing tiles; that had to be pre-World War II. The dingy cabinets, the ancient, grease-caked gas stove and narrow refrigerator with its rusty door, to which somebody had taped a poster of a snow-boarding ski bunny, wearing nothing but a bikini and a wet-lipped smile.

Lemons into lemonade, Abby chanted inwardly. *You get lemons, you make lemonade.* There was no reason to cry, no real reason at all. This dreadful kitchen *wasn't* a preview of the rest of her life. Wasn't the top of the slippery slide to poverty and despair and loneliness. This was only a temporary setback, something she'd be laughing about six months from now—even a week from now, when they reached Sedona.

Surely.

Tonight she was simply…tired.

''Mr. Kelton just put a guy in a truck,'' Sky said, dropping his load on the oilcloth-covered kitchen table.

She rubbed her lashes and turned with a puzzled smile. ''Put who, honey?''

"A guy with a cowboy hat. And boots. Into that truck over there. He sort of carried him by his belt and his collar and…threw him."

"Ah… Oh…" *Wonderful.* "Well, he's very helpful, sweetie, isn't he?" And just who had Jack been helping out his door? His wife's lover? *Oh, we don't need this at all!*

"Then the guy drove off like a bat out of hell!"

So that was the roar and rumble of gravel she'd heard a moment ago. "Don't swear, Skyler."

"Dad says hell."

"Your father's a grown man." Physically, if not emotionally or mentally. And now were they stranded next to another overgrown adolescent with his own amorous troubles? They ought to leave first thing in the morning, but how? Even if Maudie would refund their money, renting a car for even a week would deliver the coup de grâce to her tottering budget. "When you're grown up—"

"I'm moving back to New Jersey."

A brisk knock on the front door saved her from a retort she might have regretted. Jack strode into the kitchen, his hair no wilder than it had been before, his clothes untorn. He didn't appear to have been brawling, though the color across his craggy cheekbones might be a bit higher. With the fluorescent lighting, Abby couldn't be sure. Perhaps Sky had misinterpreted whatever he'd seen.

"Let's check out that ankle." Jack set a loaded tin soup pot on the counter, then swung out a chair for her. "And, Sky, hustle the rest of your gear out of my car, will you? I need to take off in a minute."

The fastest way to get Jack out of their lives was to let him follow his own program, Abby concluded, giving up and sitting. When he'd gone, she could lock the door, re-establish control. By tomorrow, once she'd caught her breath, she'd be able to cope with him. Enforce her boundaries. Resist his plans without rudeness.

Tonight—for a few more minutes—she just needed not to scream.

She bit her bottom lip as he lifted her foot to another chair and then, with surprising gentleness, pulled her sock down over her—shockingly swollen ankle. Which was already turning a fine shade of mottled eggplant.

"That hurt?" He glanced up as she made a tiny sound of dismay.

"Not...much."

"Hmm." Frowning, he drew one fingertip from her ankle down the top of her foot to her toes.

A line of ice and then fire sizzled behind his touch. She blinked back tears, focusing fiercely on his big blunt fingertip with its well-tended nail. On work-roughened hands that were very clean. On the top of his down-bent head. He had thick, straight hair of that color men call dirty-blond and women call wheat or tawny. His eyes were gray, she noted, as he peered up at her from under bristly brows, two shades darker than his hair.

"I'm no doctor, but I'd guess it's a sprain." Idly, absently, his finger returned up her foot as he held her gaze.

For too long.

He looked into her too deeply.

Something leaped between them before she could lower her lashes. Awareness. It triggered an echoing flutter in her stomach, a flow of warmth. Between one breath and the next, Abby felt as if they were toppling toward each other. Gripping the sides of her chair, she fought down the urge to smack his hand aside. *I don't need this. Don't want it.*

"I seem to be able to—*oo-oh*—move it. Sort of."

"Your call, Abby. I'll be happy to drive you into Durango if you want to go to the emergency room. Or I suppose I could ask Doc Kerner, our local vet, to come over, give us his opinion.''

Was he kidding?

He wasn't. The town of Trueheart, what she'd seen of it, seemed to be less than a mile square. No motel. Apparently no real doctor. "Why don't I give it till morning?'' Forty miles to Durango and back again in Jack's unnerving company was more than she could face at this point. He'd been coming on to her, hadn't he?

"That's what I'd do,'' he agreed with a relief that assured her she must have been mistaken. Rising with an easy grace that belied his big-boned build, he reached into the pot. "I was a bit low on ice cubes myself, but I've got frozen peas and corn a-a-nd wild mountain blueberries.'' He draped a plastic bag of each across her ankle as he spoke. "Give it half an hour, if you can sit still that long.''

He was a fine one to talk. Jack was halfway to the exit already, speaking as he moved backward. "I've got to drive this little, um, a baby-sitter home and then I have to find Kat. But after I've rounded her up, can we take you and Sky to supper? Nothing fancy—Michelle's will be closed by then. But Mo's Truckstop has the best steak-burgers in a hundred miles and Mo keeps the grill fired up all night.''

A baby-sitter. So Jack and his wife had a child or children. And the banished cowboy with the truck is the baby-sitter's boyfriend, Abby hazarded a silent guess. That was a better scenario than her first one. Meanwhile Kat, Jack's wife, must be out on the town. This was too many players to follow. "That's awfully kind of you, but please don't trouble yourself. We've got sandwich makings right here.'' She nodded at Skyler, edging past the man with his arms full of a big plastic cooler. "I think we'll eat in, then go straight to bed.''

"Probably just as well," Jack said readily. "In that case, sleep tight, and don't worry about the bus. Whitey and I will look after it first thing tomorrow."

And he was out the door before she could make the man see that she'd rather handle her own problems.

SUNLIGHT and the sound of birdsong awoke her the next morning, cool pine-scented air wafting in an open window. Abby smiled, stretched luxuriously…and let out a yelp as her injured foot brushed the footboard.

"Oh!" She lurched to a sitting position, memory tumbling back in a jumble of sharp-edged images. Her ruined sketchbook. Steve's infidelity. A blue columbine she'd picked somewhere recently. Her mother's fretful face, matching her querulous voice on the phone. Steve's new wife, Chelsea—pridefully, astoundingly pregnant when Abby had run into her at the mall. The plunging crimson bus. The pain in her side as she chased it.

A man's hand on her aching foot.

Piece the puzzle together, and here she sat on a lumpy bed in the middle of nowhere. Her wincing gaze swept the tiny bedroom with its minimal furnishings. A scratched maple bureau and an ancient pine wardrobe; she'd bet there was a twin to that piece next door. And what time was it? Her faithful old wind-up alarm clock must be ticking away back in the bus.

If it hasn't been stolen by now.

A second wave of panic washed through her. All their belongings out there on a mountainside! Jack had promised her they'd be safe, but Jack struck her as the type to whistle through hurricanes. Hardly a worrier.

Shower. Coffee. Get out there, girl! Abby threw off the covers.

TWENTY MINUTES LATER, she stood lopsidedly at the kitchen sink, washing dishes. There was a jar of instant coffee tucked in her cooler for waking in motels. But there was no way she'd boil water in any of the utensils she'd found in the cupboards before she'd thoroughly scrubbed them.

Meanwhile, where was Jack? He'd said something about helping her early this morning. But when she'd looked out her front door and across their adjoining fence, she'd seen no sign of his Jeep.

Maybe he'd forgotten his offer? Went off to work, wherever and whatever that was? He seemed to be a short-attention-span kind of guy, superb in a crisis, too restless to be good with the follow-through.

Or possibly he'd sensed her discomfort last night and had left her to handle her own affairs.

"Careful what you wish for," she told herself wryly. Without his help, how would she get out to the crash site? A town with no doctor would hardly have a taxi service. And then how to contact this Whitey person, the mechanic?

"Coffee first," she decided, then she'd cope. Somehow.

"Arrrr…" Skyler trudged into the kitchen, DC tiptoeing hopefully at his heels.

"Morning, love." She smoothed his pillow-tossed hair, the same pale ash-blond shade as her own. "Sleep well?"

"Mmmph." He took after her in appearance, and in most other ways, as well. But unlike her, Sky was no morning person. He sat heavily at the table, his glasses wobbling on the end of his nose, the cat winding around his bare shins. "What'sferbreakfast?"

Abby tried for a note of enthusiasm. *Think of this as an adventure, will you?* "Tuna fish sandwiches." All that was left. She'd meant to replenish their traveling snacks when they reached Cortez last night.

"Yech-hh! Why can't we have oatmeal?"

As she usually gave him back home, was the unspoken accusation, but if Sky mentioned New Jersey one more time, she'd throw something. "When we get to Sedona I'll buy some, sweetie, but this morning—"

Knock knocka knock knock! A cheery rap sounded on the back screen door, which Abby had opened to air out the kitchen.

Relief surged through her chest, mixed with an odd sense of wariness. She hobbled across the room, wondering: Could the man have half the impact in daylight that he'd had on her last night? Or had the shock and disorientation of the bus crash made her unusually—and temporarily—vulnerable?

She'd have to wait to find out. Their visitor was a child—a girl roughly Skyler's age—all long spindly legs and reed-thin golden arms. She stood on the back stoop, fist lifted to knock again. "Um, hi."

"Good morning." Her ponytail was two shades lighter than the wheat color it would probably be when she was grown. Still, Abby knew who'd bequeathed her that tiny cleft in the chin. And those enormous gray eyes. She opened the screen door with a smile—and blinked. The child had Jack Kelton's eyes, but how to explain her lack of eyelashes? Her eyebrows frizzled to kinky ash? The crinkled hair along her forehead that had obviously come too close to a flame?

"Dad said to bring you these." The girl clutched a pile of bright packages to her skinny chest with a clumsily bandaged hand. "He said you'd want breakfast."

"He didn't need to do that, but please, come in." Abby stepped aside and had to smile as the two children spotted each other. The girl stopped short and scowled. Skyler looked up—and whipped off his glasses, which rendered him utterly blind. He turned them nervously in his hands, torn between seeing and being seen, squinting up at her.

"Waffles," announced Jack's daughter, dumping her packages at Sky's elbow. "Dad said you have the blueberries to go with 'em already. And these are burritos." She placed another frozen package on top of the first. "And a pizza."

This was Jack's idea of breakfast?

"And coffee." A package of ground coffee—now here at last was something useful—was added to the stack of offerings. Jack's daughter made a rueful face as she turned toward Abby and pulled a crumpled envelope from the pocket of her ragged blue jeans cutoffs. "And this is for you."

As her name, printed in a bold, slashing script, attested. Abby leaned back against the counter, opened the envelope and read.

Hi, neighbor!
Whitey and I are checking out your bus. Meanwhile, this surly outlaw is grounded from here to eternity and I'm down one baby-sitter. Mind keeping half an eye on her, just for the next hour? There's a fire extinguisher next to your stove.

Thanks.
Jack

Surely that last line was a joke? Had to be. And asking Abby to pinch-hit for his baby-sitter was certainly reasonable, given all he'd done for her. Now Jack was doing even more, taking time out from his own day to look over her bus with the mechanic. Still, she wished he'd taken her along. She hoped he didn't intend to commit her to a course of action without consulting her first.

At the table, curiosity had overcome Sky's vanity and he'd put on his glasses. Studying his counterpart, he demanded, "What happened to your eyebrows?"

"Burned 'em off, welding." Apparently some decision had been reached. The girl pulled out a chair and sat, scooping up the tomcat to drape him over her lap. "I never saw a cat with one green eye and one blue before. What's his name?"

"DC-3."

"Huh!" She nodded gravely. "I'm a Kat, too—Kat Kelton. Who are you?"

Kat. So *this* was Kat? Abby sucked in a breath, suddenly feeling that the walls had flexed inward half a foot or so. She limped to the screen door and stood there, seeing not the house beyond the fence but a big, blunt fingertip gliding down her ankle. She felt something oddly akin to panic....

Good grief, what was this, a goose waddling across her grave? Or caffeine withdrawal—what time was it, anyway?

Gradually the sensation faded; her eyes refocused on the house next door, her ears on the halting conversation behind her.

There might be a Kat Senior, as well, she told herself with a surge of relief.

Which dropped as swiftly as it had spiked. No. There couldn't be. Had there been a mother in residence, she'd already have trimmed that fire-frizzled hair. And Kat's bandage needed redoing. *Coffee first, then I'll see to it.*

So Abby lit the oven, put the water on to boil, washed three plates, three glasses, three sets of silverware. Picked up one of the packages and wrinkled her nose as she read the directions. Frozen pizza for breakfast; that should've told her everything she needed to know.

One week, she reminded herself. No more than a week.

CHAPTER FOUR

PIZZA FOR BREAKFAST wasn't such a bad idea, after all—if you ate it outside on a blanket, on a glorious sunny morning in southwestern Colorado.

Picnic completed except for a last cup of coffee, Abby limped along the weed-choked perennial border between her cottage and Jack's. Once upon a time an ardent gardener must have lived here. The remnants still bloomed: several sprawling rambler roses, a late lilac of an exceptionally gorgeous shade of violet, a clump of daisies splashed white against the rioting green. Blue flag irises unfurled their petals to the sun, while at their feet, ruby and white alyssum duked it out with the dandelions. A bit of unkempt heaven just begging her to reach for pen and ink and watercolors.

Kat and Skyler had insisted that DC-3 should join their feast, and now Sky lay on the blanket with the tomcat crouched on his chest like a rampant lion. Abby cut another branch of blowsy pink roses, arranged it in a chipped blue stoneware pitcher she'd filled with water, then glanced around. "Where's Kat?" Just a minute before, the girl had been perched on the old swing that hung from the branch of the gigantic oak tree shading the back of their house.

"Went to get something at her place," Sky said as he stroked a knuckle down DC's outstretched throat.

How close an eye was she supposed to be keeping on

this girl? Normally, Abby wouldn't have thought twice about allowing a visiting neighbor's child to wander back home, back in suburban New Jersey. But here in Trueheart she didn't know the rules or the dangers.

As far as she'd been able to see last night, the town was safe as could be, near idyllic. Small enough that strangers, good-intentioned or otherwise, would be instantly noticed. So small that any adult would know all the children—and more to the point, their parents. Her cottage was on a narrow road serving perhaps twenty nineteenth-century houses set on deep, old-fashioned lots that had been laid out at a time when each family probably tended a vegetable garden or kept chickens and a milk cow out back.

"Maybe you should go find her," Abby suggested. She wouldn't have dreamed of entering Jack's domain uninvited, but somehow Sky wouldn't seem quite such an intruder.

"Don't need to." Her son nodded at the fence, where Kat was just now wriggling between two missing pickets. Abby swallowed a laugh. The girl hadn't bothered to deviate thirty feet out of her path toward the street, to where a garden gate stood ajar under an arching, rose-smothered trellis. Kat was a straight shooter in every sense of the word, Abby was finding. Another trait she'd inherited from her blunt-spoken father.

And where is her mother? Abby had wondered that several times already this morning. Not that it was any of her business. "Oh…Kat," she murmured helplessly as the girl arrived beside her to offer a pair of garden shears.

"Do you want to use these? They were in our junk drawer."

"Much better than this old knife," Abby agreed, accepting them. "Thank you. And I see you…fixed your eyebrows."

Kat's brows had been scorched to ash in whatever fire had burned her poor little hands in several places. Abby had attempted to question her while she'd smoothed antiseptic cream on her burns then rebandaged them. But beyond claiming that she'd been welding last night, Kat had scowled and refused to elaborate.

"They were so icky I figured I'd shave 'em," Kat confided now.

She had. She'd shaved them off entirely—then redrawn them, with what looked like black ink from a felt-tipped pen. She'd drawn them the way a child usually pictures eyebrows, in continuous arching lines rather than short, hairlike strokes. Worse yet, she'd placed them a quarter-inch too high and given the left one a zany, quizzical slant. She looked like Groucho Marx, astounded.

"Yuck!" Skyler had come to join them. "You look weird! Loony!"

Kat bristled. "No loonier than you, goggle-eyes!"

Sky went as pink as the roses, and Abby fought the urge to rush to his rescue. His weak eyesight was a constant source of woe. Bullies at school had singled him out for attention, using his thick lenses as a point of derision, even snatching his glasses off his face.

But on this occasion, Sky had been the first to make a personal remark and so should pay the price.

"Least I didn't burn off all my hair," he retorted, unrepentant.

Oh, Lord, if he gave Kat the idea of shaving her head! "I wonder what *Kat* would look like in glasses?" Abby intervened hastily.

"Yeah." Sky whipped them off and held them out. "I dare you! Let's see if you look any better."

Apparently "dare" was the magic word. Kat settled them on her nose and gave him a haughty glare.

Skyler smirked. "Now you're a *goggle-eyed* loon."

"And you're another!" But Kat wriggled her brows, made a maniacal face—and Sky burst into giggles.

"If you c-could see what you look like!"

They trooped off into the cottage in search of a mirror and Abby let out a sigh of relief. Storm averted for now, anyway. Life would be so much easier this next week if those two got along. And Sky had been dreadfully lonely these past few days, mourning the loss of his friends on the East Coast. He was a bad mover, as she'd always been, shy and therefore slow to reach out, to make new friends.

Another reason Abby felt guilty. Was she totally crazy—utterly selfish—dragging him away from his hard-won pals? From the only town he'd ever lived in for more than a single year?

But what about me? She'd hadn't chosen a new life; she'd been launched into it willy-nilly when Steve had left her for a young woman who was determined to bear his children.

But once he'd done that, didn't Abby have the right to make the best life she could, someplace fresh and new and unencumbered by old hurts and worn-out dreams? Where she wouldn't have failure rubbed in her face each time she encountered her replacement? Biting her lip, she cut another spray of roses, a handful of daisies, and shoved their stems into her pitcher. Then she stood, hugging the bouquet of flowers to her breast, staring vaguely around her at the overgrown yard and woebegone cottage. *I wanted a new life for us, but look at this! This wasn't part of the plan.*

She raised her head at the sound of distant engines coming nearer. Then a parade of vehicles burst from beyond her far neighbor's pine trees and came rumbling down the street. In the lead rolled an enormous, open-backed truck

whose drab olive color and rugged design suggested some
sort of military surplus. It towed a crimson bus—her bus—
effortlessly behind it. Jack Kelton's Jeep brought up the
rear, a pile of lumber angled up over its stern. He lifted
his hand in a jaunty wave.

*Didn't even think to ask me if I wanted my bus here—
or somewhere else,* she thought, half vexed, half amused.
He'd simply decided what was best for her and forged
ahead.

The truck turned down her driveway, while the Jeep
continued on to Jack's. When the vehicle stopped beside
her, Abby stood on one wobbly tiptoe to peer into its cab.

"Ma'am." A weathered old cowboy touched his battered Stetson. "Reckon you'd be Miz Lake?"

"Abby." She stepped onto the running board to accept
his extended hand, dry and gnarled as a knot of driftwood.
"And you're Mr. Whitelaw?"

"Whitey, and this ol' cuss is Chang."

In the dimness of the cab, Abby had taken the lump of
white and orange at his side for a heap of rags. But now
a rounded head reared up; two rheumy-brown pop-eyes
considered her with an air of jaundiced malevolence. An
ancient Pekinese. The dog lifted his black lip in a toothless
snarl as she stretched out a hand to pat him—then changed
her mind. "Pleased to meet you both, Whitey, but however
did you drag my bus up that hill?"

"Huh! This truck could yank that oak out by the roots,
if I asked it to—" He jerked a thumb at the swing tree.
"Now, where'd you like your bus?"

JACK JOINED ABBY and the children to watch Whitey maneuver the bus farther into the backyard, working it around
so that it was finally parked, hood toward the street, tail-
lights a few feet from the listing toolshed that stood near

the back fence. The bus was nicely shaded by trees, with a strong limb overhanging the engine, in case Whitey needed to set up a block and tackle.

Jack nodded approval, then glanced down at his daughter and flinched. "Katharine Kelton, what am I going to do with you?" To look at her, you'd never guess that her mother had been—was—a beauty. As feminine as a pink powder puff or a feather-trimmed, high-heeled mule.

Kat stuck out her stubborn chin. "I like 'em better this way."

"Glad to hear it, 'cause if that's my pen you used, it's permanent ink." He sent Abby a rueful look, meant to show he had no hard feelings. You watched the Kat every minute of the day, which, of course, was impossible, or you learned to live with the consequences.

"Oh, I'm sure we can get it off, whenever she likes," Abby murmured, laying a slim hand on Kat's shoulder.

The lightest of touches, but it seemed to align woman with girl, consigning Jack to the outside of an invisible circle. *Leave her to me,* said that gesture.

Fine; so he would. He hadn't a clue what to do with Kat and it got worse every year. He turned to Sky for some masculine support—and groaned out loud. The kid gave him an embarrassed smirk from under an inked-on mustache, à la Adolf Hitler. "Whatever." Too much to hope for that Abby would bring a note of sanity to the neighborhood. She was just a new kind of craziness.

He pulled her aside, noting as he did that her ankle was still swollen but apparently functional. "Whitey says the gears are stripped. That means a new transmission, plus the new exhaust. And he thinks your radiator is shot—rusted through at the bottom."

She'd crossed her forearms under her breasts, as if to hold herself together. "Yes, I knew about the radiator."

It took real effort to keep his eyes focused on her face. "He can work on it for fifteen dollars an hour plus parts, if you like. That's less than half of what you'd pay a city mechanic. But he thinks maybe you should junk her. Sell her for whatever you can get."

"Darn…" Abby tried for a smile. "What a sucker I was. If she hadn't been such a wonderful color…"

Jack frowned. "Come again?"

"I fell in love with that crimson. It's why I bought her. I could just picture her parked in front of those red-orange cliffs you see in *Arizona Highways* with that blue desert sky. I even brought along some green-and-purple striped canvas to make an awning for her."

"That would've been…bright," he allowed. *You're losing me here, Abby. You make life decisions based on color?* Still, he felt himself leaning toward her, she looked so little and lost. "But maybe it's time to let her go. Buy something a little more practical." Like a car. "You could rent a truck to get you and your belongings to wherever you're going, then—"

"Sedona. That's where we were headed."

Sedona. He should've guessed. Sedona, Arizona, where all the hippies and mystics and misfits and tofu-eaters and New Age scam artists congregated, drawn by power vortexes and drumming circles and too many juice bars. *Well, that explains a lot.*

"I have a friend out there, a Feng Shui consultant, who owns some land. She was going to let us park our bus on her property. We were going to live in it for the summer while we built something permanent. An adobe, I was thinking."

Ah, yes, he'd seen this so many times before. A clear case of the Divorce Crazies. "Have you, um, ever built a house before?"

"Well, no, but how hard can it be?"

Jack turned with relief to Whitey, who'd been unhitching the bus and now stumped over to join them, his moth-eaten Pekinese waddling at his worn-down boot heels. "You tell her what I said?" He leaned aside to spit a stream of brown tobacco juice, then pulled out a yellow bandanna to dab primly at his mouth. "Gettin' the parts is gonna be the hardest thing. Might take some fancy scrounging. There's a yard over on the reservation. Seems t'me they had an ol' bus or two."

"Do you…have any idea how many hours it would take…to fix her?" Abby asked.

How much it would cost, she meant. Jack wondered what kind of settlement she'd gotten. Whether she'd had a competent lawyer. Dithering soft women like this one always seemed to hire kindly bumblers, while their husbands hired sharks.

"There's no telling. I'd put one foot in front of t'other till she's done or till you say 'whoa.'"

She stood, arms clasped tightly around her middle. "Could you tell what caused the brake to fail in the first place?" she said at last. "Or how it popped out of first gear?"

Whitey and Jack exchanged a quick, wry glance, then the old man shrugged. "Driver error."

"But I wasn't—" Her eyes widened. "You mean, Skyler? *Sky* did this? I know he tried to stop it, but you think he—"

"He's a boy, ain't he? When I was his age, anything on wheels was fair game. How else is he s'posed t'learn?"

"Driver's Ed when he's of legal age!"

"Pshaw! Most ranch kids're driving by the time they can see over the steerin' wheel."

"But he's not—" Abby swiped a lock of hair behind

her ear and blew out her breath. "Okay. What's done is done. About fixing it, though. Whitey, you really can't give me an estimate?"

"None that I'd care to stand by." Whitey shifted from his good leg to his bad and back again. "You know, you might want t'chew it over, Miz Lake. I'm in no hurry. Can't work on her anyways, 'cept Saturdays and Sundays. We're pretty hard-pressed out at the Circle C, since Kaley dropped her twins this spring, smack in the middle of calving season. Been up to our ears in puke and diapers ever since, ain't we, Chang?" He looked down at his feet, then quickly around when he didn't see the dog.

A feline screech and a flurry of barks dragged everyone's eyes across the yard. DC shot out from under the truck with the Pekinese snapping toothlessly at his heels, bellowing blue murder.

"Dad*blast* you, Chang!" Whitey yelled, "Get on back here!"

The tomcat swarmed up the swing oak and disappeared beyond the leaves. Chang hopped twice, scrabbling frantically at the bark—then collapsed in a wheezing heap at the base of the tree.

"Gonna give yourself a stroke someday," Whitey scolded, though Jack could tell this was for Abby's benefit. The old man's face was pink with pride. "I'm mighty sorry, ma'am. If a cat looks at him sideways, he can't control himself."

The kids had hopped out of the bus at the first sound of mayhem. Sky leaned against the trunk, staring upward. "DC? DC! What if he falls, Mom?"

"He's not an outside cat," Abby explained to Jack. "I don't think he's ever been up a tree before. Certainly not a high one."

He was an hour late for work already and his ladder was

across town at the building site. Jack clamped a lid on his instinct to ride to the rescue. For Abby, anytime, but not for a cowardly hairball. "Not bad for a beginner." And what goes up must eventually come down. No use breaking his own neck speeding the process along. "Once Chang goes away…"

"He's leavin' now. We gotta get a move on." Whitey whisked his snarling companion into the truck, clambered up, then poked his head out the window. "You sleep on it, Miz Lake, and give me a call, okay?" With a wave to the children, he rolled off toward the street.

"I can get him," Kat declared, peering up into the branches. "If I had spiked boots like a lumberjack it'd be easier, but if somebody'd boost me up to that first limb…"

"*Uh*-uh." Jack tugged on her ponytail. "You're grounded, kiddo, and that means what it says. Both feet *strictly* on the ground."

She gave him a disdainful look, or it would have been, except for those funhouse eyebrows. "Aren't *you* supposed to be at the office?"

He showed his teeth. "I am. Soon as I set you up. Go get the extension cord out of the Jeep and plug it into the carport plug. You've got some sanding to do. *Lots* of sanding."

Kat made a terrible face, but she knew when to stop arguing. Off she trotted.

Sky looked from the tree to the departing girl squeezing through the gap in the pickets. "Don't you try and climb this, either," Jack warned him. "He'll come down when he's hungry."

"DC's always hungry."

"Then we'll see him soon."

Sky nodded doubtfully, then brightened. "Can I help Kat, Mr. Kelton?"

"Not for a minute. I suppose you can watch, but don't let me hear that you helped, Skyler. Kat earned every inch and splinter of this job and now she pays up."

They watched the boy hurry down to the gate, then through. "There was a fire?" Abby inquired after a pause.

"Mmm." Jack hooked his thumbs in the pockets of his jeans and braced his back against the tree trunk. "She snuck out on her baby-sitter last night, then went over to where I'm building a house, across town. Played with my butane torch and somehow set a can of kerosene on my workbench—and then the bench itself—on fire. Luckily Sheriff Noonan happened by while she was trying to beat out the flames." *And if Noonan hadn't?* His shoulders jerked in a shudder. "At this rate I'll have white hair before I'm forty. I had a pet raccoon when I was a kid that could open any drawer, any cabinet, any package a human could, but Bandit wasn't half this much trouble."

"She is rather…high-energy." Abby laughed softly. "What's her punishment?"

"I stopped by my site and collected enough rough lumber to build a new bench. But it all needs sanding, then painting. Her eyebrows will grow in before she's done with the eighty grit.

"And that reminds me." He caught Abby's arm—blinked at its silky warmth and slender definition—then eased her toward the gate. "I've decided to give her baby-sitter, Marylou, one last chance. But if you happen to see a red pickup parked outside my house anytime today—anytime this week—would you let me know? Marylou can entertain her boyfriend on her own time, not mine."

"Of course."

They'd halted, facing each other as they reached the gate. His fingers were strangely reluctant to leave her skin.

Been too long, Kelton. He'd been too busy this spring, working every weekend, to chase women. "Well…"

"You're headed to your office," she murmured helpfully. "You're a…contractor?"

He laughed and shook his head. "I build on my own time. Weekdays, I'm a lawyer—family law. Wills. Custody squabbles. Divorce."

"Ah." She took half a step backward, out of his grasp. "Oh, I—" If he'd announced he slept with snakes in the bed and ate kitty cats for breakfast, she'd have looked at him in much the same way.

Jack gave her a steely smile. Lots of people didn't like lawyers. Just as well that Abby was one of them. Last thing he needed was to chase a woman in the midst of the Divorce Crazies. *Been there, done that, honey, with the scars—and the kid—to prove it.* "Have a nice day, Abby."

"You, too. And…thanks for retrieving my bus." She turned away before he did.

A lesser man might have slammed the gate. Jack closed it with a precisely calibrated firmness. The top hinge tore away from the post.

CHAPTER FIVE

IT WAS *BO-O-ORING* sanding the planks. Kat had enjoyed the feel of a big, vibrating block sander in her hands for maybe five minutes—then it got old. And she'd felt kind of superior at how impressed Sky was that she knew how to use power tools, but then that good feeling had faded, too. Now it was nothing but rumble up the long plank laid out on two sawhorses in her yard, then buzz back the other way.

Each time she turned and faced Sky, who sat on the kitchen steps, she made a horrible face. Since she was using the enormous earphones her dad had insisted she wear to protect her hearing, she couldn't hear Sky's resulting laughter, but she could see it.

By the third time, he was making faces back at her. From then on it was a contest: who could make the grossest, most terrible face?

After what must have been hours and hours, Marylou came out on the stoop—her soap opera had probably stopped for a commercial—so Kat made faces at her.

Mushy, gushy Marylou. Kat had actually seen her stick her tongue—*her tongue!*—in Peter Sikorsky's mouth last night. They hadn't realized she was sitting at the top of the stairs while they were on the couch. Revolted by that disgusting spectacle, Kat had decided it was time to go. She'd crawled out her bedroom window to the branch of a tree, then to the ground and away.

And why don't you go away, she silently told Marylou. Marylou was gooey nice to her when her dad was around. Other times they did their best to ignore each other. Kat touched the tip of her tongue to her nose, well, nearly to her nose, crossed her eyes and wobbled her head back and forth like a dizzy duck.

Marylou shook her head pityingly and went back indoors. Sky almost fell off the steps laughing.

The next time Kat completed her dreary circuit and looked his way, she stopped short and grinned. Sky was standing on his head on the top step, with his mouth twisted into a sneer, which looked like a loony smile upside down.

She switched off the sander. "Not bad." She would have to try a headstand like that, with her forearms down on the ground. If he could do it, surely she could, too. "Where'd you learn that?"

"My mom does yoga."

"And she does that?" Kat was impressed.

While she changed to a fresh square of sixty-grit paper, Sky turned right-side up again and came to stand beside her, running his palm gingerly along the board. "Still pretty rough."

"Yeah," she agreed glumly. "I have to sand 'em all—" she nodded at the stack of planks "—with sixty grit, then eighty, then Dad's still deciding about one hundred. I'll be sanding till I go back to school in September. Till Christmas!" Or maybe she'd die of boredom first.

"He's pretty tough," Sky observed.

"Yeah." But he was fair. Like Justice, the blind lady with the scales that he always claimed he was dating on those rare occasions when he dressed up and went out at night—leaving Kat stuck with Marylou.

"Tough is good," she defended him when Sky looked too sympathetic. "Navy SEALs are tough."

"Not as tough as navy aviators."

"Huh! They're *much* tougher." Someday she'd be a SEAL, just like Demi Moore in that movie, if she didn't become—

"No way! Pilots have to handle terrorists and thunderstorms and icing on the wings and—" He shrugged. "They take care of people every day. My dad's a pilot."

"Really? In the navy?" Kat felt a twinge of envy. Her dad only worked in a stupid office.

"Um, no," Sky admitted, fiddling with the sander. "He used to be, but now he's a commercial pilot. Flies for American Airlines. He flies all over the country."

That was still way cooler than sitting in an office, filling out forms. "Is that where he is right now, flying?"

"Yeah…" Sky didn't look up. His hands had stilled on the sander. "That's…why he couldn't come with us. But he'll catch up with us later on. Sometime soon. He can fly to meet us just about anywhere."

"There's an airport—a little airport—here, outside of town. But I guess he couldn't land his jet."

Sky shrugged. "That wouldn't stop Dad. Sometimes for fun he rents a twin-engine plane, a Cessna. I was—I *am* going to learn to fly. He'll teach me when I'm older."

Kat could think of nothing to match that. So she put her earphones back on, crossed her eyes and twitched her upper lip and nose like a chewing rabbit, then sanded away.

The next time she swung around with an even better face, Sky had wandered off to the carport and stood kicking the tires of her dad's winter car, the Subaru he'd accepted in trade for some legal work. Sky looked as bored as she felt. If only she weren't grounded, she could take him around Trueheart. Show him the creek that ran through the center of town and how she could catch fish with her hands. They could buy ice cream at Hansen's.

It would be nice to have a friend in Trueheart. She and her dad had only moved up here from Durango last fall. The girls were all mushy and prissy and talked about nothing but boys. The guys were more interesting, but then she'd tackled Sam Jarrett, a really *big* eighth-grader, in a football game last October. She'd sat on his foot and wrapped her arms and legs around his calf and ridden him almost to the goalposts before she'd brought him down. But instead of being impressed, the other boys had fallen all over themselves laughing. Ever since then, they just smirked when she asked if she could play. And Sam flat-out hated her. She sighed, realized her sandpaper had gone dull and stopped.

Sky appeared beside her with another square all cut to size and ready.

"*I'm* going to sail away on a tall ship someday soon," she confided as she fastened it into place. "Like Rafe Montana's daughter, Zoe. She sailed all over the ocean counting whales and dolphins. I'm going to be a ship captain someday, for Greenpeace, and I'll save the whales." If she didn't become a navy SEAL; it was a hard choice.

"Cool." Though Sky didn't sound very interested.

But maybe he had a stomachache or something. He looked sort of funny and distracted, the way her dad had the time he'd eaten the bad taco. Her stomach rumbled at the thought of food. Or maybe Sky was just hungry.

The next time Kat stopped, she opened her mouth to ask if he'd like a peanut butter and jelly sandwich, but he spoke first. "You know how to weld?"

"Uh-huh. Um, well, sort of. I'm teaching myself." She'd learned the most important lesson last night. You should never leave your torch on, then set it near a can of kerosene while you crouched down for the piece of steel you'd dropped.

"Cool. What are you going to weld?"

"I'm making—I was trying to make—a brand. But the metal wouldn't bend. Guess I didn't get it hot enough."

"Guess not." Sky nodded judiciously. "Why do you want a brand?"

She gave him a mysterious smile. "I've got something needs branding."

"SO IT'S…going to need a little work," Abby finished her carefully edited tale, trying for a note of brisk optimism. She never should have called her mother, but she'd promised to stay in touch. Phoning her friend Lark in Sedona to report their delay had given her the momentum, but it was now fading under her mother's grilling. Seated in the swing, she held the cell phone to her ear and glanced overhead. Forty feet up, looking like a snowy, feather-fluffed owl perched in the crook of a branch, poor DC returned her rueful gaze. His rounded eyes were black pools of dismay. He could no sooner climb down this tree than he could fly.

"How much is 'a little work'?" her mother demanded, as usual going straight to the bottom line. "And how much will this cost?"

"Oh, possibly a week's worth." Or more, if Whitey could only work weekends. And how long would it take him to scrounge the parts? "I've found—my neighbor found—an excellent mechanic, whose prices are very reasonable." She hoped and prayed. Though Whitey moved about as swiftly as his Pekinese. If he cost half as much as a garage mechanic, but took three times as long to…

No. Surely Jack wouldn't have recommended him if he couldn't—

"What's he do?"

"The mechanic? He's a cowhand, I believe, at a ranch north of—"

"Your neighbor. The nice man who drove you into town. What does he do for a living? And please don't tell me he's a cowboy, because if he is, I understand that cowboys never settle down."

"He's a lawyer, Mom, not that it matters in the least."

"*O-oh*... Lawyers are very good. They always make a living. The worse times get, the better they seem to do."

Abby sighed softly. Her late father had been a portrait painter, a really wonderful artist, whose hobby was painting houses, as he'd always put it with a wink and a grin. They'd had enough money, but not a penny more, while he was able to work.

After he'd fallen three stories off a ladder and was no longer able to pursue his "hobby," times had gotten much harder. But he'd stayed happy to the end, painting his portraits of their friends and neighbors and even getting the odd paying commission. He'd have been so proud to know that, seventeen years later, his work was starting to receive critical acclaim.

To Abby's mother, who'd sold all but one of his portraits years ago, this was the final drop of frustration in a bitter cup.

"Is he a trial lawyer? Or perhaps corporate. They do extremely well."

"He's in family law, Mom. Small-town stuff, I imagine, but—*listen to me*—it doesn't matter. I'm not shopping for a lawyer, a tailor or an Indian chief. Really, I'm not. I've only been divorced since March."

"It's never too early to plan."

Abby bet she could hit the bus's side mirror from here, if she threw the phone. She took a deep breath instead.

"Mom, please try to understand. I'm not in the market for a man.

"And if I was, the last man on earth I'd choose—the very last—would be a lawyer. I've had it up to here with lawyers."

She was only beginning to realize what a poor choice she'd made in a divorce lawyer. When she'd first hired him, Mr. Bizzle had seemed kindly and wise and avuncular. He'd agreed with her completely that two people who'd once loved each other shouldn't try to snatch and maim when they parted. That the high road was always the best road.

Meanwhile, Steve had found a lawyer who was considered to be the best divorce specialist in northern New Jersey—a smiling, hard-eyed man who could smell a wounded wallet a mile away. Who thought the high road was for losers and fools. Who knew how to turn caring into weakness, selfishness to strength.

Under his cynical tutelage, the Lake family assets had melted away like dirty snow in springtime.

Abby had protested that only months before they'd seemed to be doing quite well, that between Steve's income and her teaching salary, they'd amassed a reasonable cushion of stocks and savings. Where had that all gone? she'd wondered. Mr. Bizzle had patted her hand and sworn he'd get to the bottom of the mystery—well, he'd hire a couple of two-hundred-dollar-per-hour accountants to get to the bottom of the mystery—and then he'd squeezed her shoulders, walking her out of his office, and asked her for a date!

By the time the whole miserable process was finished, Steve's lawyer had done magnificently for himself. And quite handsomely for Steve and his new family. Mr. Bizzle's fee had taken a hefty slice of what remained, which seemed to console him for Abby's inexplicable coolness to his advances.

So Abby had walked away from twelve years of marriage with twenty-thousand dollars that must be carefully hoarded for the coming year.

And a lifetime loathing of lawyers.

"You feel that way now, dear, but later on I'm sure you'll—"

"Not now." Abby shook her head emphatically. "And not later. I've learned my lesson." About lawyers. About men in general. "You build your entire world around a man…" *The way you did yourself, Mom, and look what it got you.*

"You make him the almighty center of your world, and then one day he up and goes? Then you have nothing left." Nothing, nothing. She was hollowed out—an empty echo where her heart used to be.

And when she gathered the strength to fill that hollow again, it would be with something other than the love of a man. Something more trustworthy and enduring. Something she could always count on—herself, happily and capably living a life she'd shaped to her own design. Meanwhile… Abby swallowed and found that the ragged lump she'd carried in her throat all this past winter had returned. *Dadblast it, Mom!* as Whitey would have put it.

"You have Skyler," her mother pointed out.

Who blames me for leaving his dad! Abby's eyes blurred; she tipped her head back and focused desperately on the blue patches beyond the leafy green. "Yes, Mom, I have Sky. And come to think of it, he must be starving by now. Why don't I call you back in a day or two?"

JACK WAS SHARING a late in-house lunch with his friend Alec Fielding, a defense attorney who rented an office suite down the hall, in a three-story building in Durango. They ate together once a week or so, when whoever had lost their latest bet paid up with Reuben sandwiches and barbecue potato chips from the deli down the street.

This week Jack in his wisdom had bet that Lena Koo, the assistant district attorney, would not press criminal charges against Councilman Ferulli's son, an impetuous youth who'd been injudicious enough to drink two six-packs of Coors, then sic his pet macaw Geronimo on an unfortunate girlfriend.

Instead, true to Jack's prediction, assault charges had been dropped in favor of an agreement that young Ferulli take a course in rage management—and that he pay all plastic surgery fees for the young lady's new and greatly improved nose.

"Food of the gods," Jack proclaimed, more by way of self-congratulation than thanks as he waved his last half sandwich at his friend. Leaning forward over the ostrich-skin boots that he'd propped on his desk, he grabbed another chip.

"I really wanted that case," Alec mourned, his own custom-booted feet resting on the coffee table in the conversation area at the other end of Jack's office.

"Winning cases for councilmen's sons is always good," Jack allowed. "Political capital in the bank."

Alec snorted. "That junior thug? I always looked on the bird as my client. I had three credible witnesses ready to testify that he'd been regularly and unduly provoked by the plaintiff."

"And if you could've put the parrot on the stand..." They grinned at each other. "Polly wants to whack her?"

Alec toasted him with his can of root beer. "Self-defense all the way." He reached for his chip bag. "So what's new on the home front? The enchanting Kat robbed any banks this week? Shot any cowboys yet?"

A confirmed bachelor himself, Alec found tales of Kat's escapades endlessly entertaining. He'd gone along this spring when they'd been invited to a branding party at Suntop Ranch. Kat had been horrified—outraged—when she realized they were actually ''burning'' the calves.

When her protests had been ignored, she'd offered to brand several of the highly amused cowhands to show 'em how it felt. At last Jack had given up and hustled her home and she hadn't eaten meat since that day. Which was a problem, since her father had an extremely limited repertoire of meals to cook—and none of them featured tofu or soy milk.

''She scorched her eyebrows last night. But the real news is, I have a new neighbor.'' Jack found himself describing the bus rescue. That led to a long and involved discussion of transmissions, then the best junkyards for used parts in southwestern Colorado.

Finally, as Alec stuffed his trash in a deli bag and rose to go, he asked casually, ''So what's she like?''

''Who?'' Jack said, instantly on the defensive.

Alec smirked. ''That good?''

''Oh, *her.* Um, nothing special.'' Small, with dangerous curves and a mouth that quivered when she was upset. Warm velvety skin. ''Lots of frizzy, mousy blond hair.'' Almost but not quite the color of cornsilk, and it was rumpled and ripply, rather than frizzy, but why tell Fielding that?

''Hot?'' Alec insisted.

Jack gave an irritated shrug. ''Wouldn't matter if she was. I've got my rules.''

''Yeah?'' Alec folded his arms. ''What are they this week?''

"This week and forever. Kelton's Rules of Survival."
Jack held up one admonishing finger. "Rule One. Never
marry."

"Honored in the breach!" Alec jeered.

"And Rule Two," Jack continued, ignoring him. "If
you're stupid enough to ignore Rule One, then never,
NEVER marry a newly divorced woman. She's in the midst
of the Divorce Crazies. She hasn't got a clue what she
wants, but she'll be flying off in all four directions at once,
looking for it. And no doubt she hates men—temporarily,
which'll be just long enough to make your life hell.

"Or she hates men permanently—which means you'll
spend the rest of your miserable marriage atoning for her
last husband's sins."

"But if she's hotter than hot?" Alec teased, pausing in
the doorway.

Jack flipped up his hands. "Then have a fling. Have a
hot, short, sexy affair with her if you must. Be her Transition Man between her last cad and her next husband.
Teach her how to smile again—then *run for your life!* But
NEVER get serious about the newly divorced."

Alec flashed that coming-in-for-the-kill grin he usually
saved for hostile witnesses. "Who's talking about marriage, old buddy? I was asking if the lady was bedworthy."
Seizing his exit line, he turned and walked.

Leaving Jack standing, mouth ajar, hands frozen in midair.

CHAPTER SIX

AROUND FOUR that afternoon the phone rang and Jack glanced up from a client's divorce petition, which he'd been reviewing. The second button on his phone began to blink, meaning the caller was on hold.

A slender hand with lime-green fingernails curled around the edge of his door and cracked it open to reveal Emma Castillo, his quasi-legal, as Jack thought of her. She was wearing a tiny turquoise stud in her nose today, to match her blue-green jumpsuit and that one blue streak in her raven hair. "Are you in?"

"Depends on who's calling." He was about ready to wrap it up for the day. The whole point of working for oneself was the hours. Jack had slaved six years in a big-city law firm, struggling to make partner, before he'd seen the light and opted for a saner, less lucrative lifestyle in ski country.

"A woman with a sort of scratchy, stop-and-start voice. Um, Annie Leek? Locke?" Emma could be hopelessly preoccupied, when she was writing songs on the sly instead of filing.

"Abby Lake." Jack grabbed for the phone, nodded his thanks to Emma, then turned halfway around in his swivel chair. "Kelton, here."

"Oh…I was hoping you'd still be in," Abby murmured, sounding not all that happy to find him.

He smiled in spite of himself. She did have a voice that

scratched pleasantly along a man's nerve endings—low
and a bit breathy, as if she'd been nudged awake in the
moonlight. Had just rolled over on her pillow and opened
those big green drowsy eyes. "Hello, Abby. How'd you
find my number?"

"Kat. She's the reason I'm calling, actually."

He groaned. "What's she done now?"

"Not a thing. The poor kid's been sanding all day, except for a lunch break, where we ate your burritos. But I
was wondering, could I ask you to drop by a drugstore on
your way home? If you bought an eyebrow pencil, I think
I could improve on the clown face."

An odd little glow started under his rib cage, if that
wasn't the corned beef returning to haunt him. "I could
do that. What color?"

He listened carefully as she dithered, stopping and starting as Emma had noticed, deciding at last that perhaps two
closely related shades of light brown and taupe—whatever
that was—would give the most natural effect. "I can do
that," he repeated finally. Or rather, he could report the
request word-for-word to any female clerk at a drugstore
and likely come back with what was required.

"Oh, good!" She started to speak, paused, then added,
"And I was wondering. About her hair. Do you ever take
her to a hairdresser?"

"She always insists on my barber when she needs a
trim."

"Ah. Well, then. How would you feel if I tried to do
something with that frizzled hair on her forehead? I was
thinking bangs."

Relief, that was what this sensation of warmth must be.
To hand Kat over to somebody who knew what she was
doing, for even a week... "As long as she'll let you, cut
away. Or you can wait till I get home to hold her down."

"Oh, she'll sit still for me." On that score, Abby apparently had no doubts.

"Fine, have at her." As Abby made sounds of imminent farewell, he added quickly, "Besides which, I'm glad you called. I forgot to ask this morning if you could use some groceries—cereal or juice or whatever. I'll drive you into town for a real stock-up this weekend, but in the meantime?"

"Oh, I couldn't ask you to…"

"Of course you can." What had she planned to do, hobble down to Hansen's on that ankle? "You can ask me for anything you need. You're out west now, remember? Where the sky is big, the dogies are bold and the neighbors are neighborly, neighbor."

She had a shy, husky laugh. Funny how a phone freed a man's imagination, allowed him to draw his own mental pictures. New and improved pictures. He could see her swiping a soft tangle of hair out of her eyes when she laughed like that. Imagine her stretching sleepily beside him so that the covers rustled.

"Okay, neighbor, if you put it like that." Abby paused, then murmured, "Milk?"

God, but she was sexy. "Skim, one percent or whole? Goat or cow? Quart or gallon?" He reached for a pad and pen. *And how do you feel about T-bones?* Because he was cooking tonight. Suddenly company seemed like an excellent idea. Best idea he'd had in months. "A gallon of skim—fine—and what else?"

JACK HAD ROLLED blithely over Abby's protests that he must be tired after a day at work. Also that he shouldn't feel the least responsibility to entertain the Lakes simply because they'd landed next door to him for a week.

Never once had it occurred to him that she'd really

rather eat alone with Sky. That making dinner-table conversation with a stranger—an exuberant, overwhelmingly
male stranger and a lawyer, at that!—was an ordeal she'd
just as soon skip. A quiet meal, followed by a book and
then bed would have suited her better.

But Sky's face had lit up at the invitation. And she simply didn't have the force of personality to refuse Jack once
he'd gathered momentum. So Abby had smiled and gone
along. In the end, she was glad. It hadn't been such an
ordeal, after all.

Abby had whisked Kat off to the Kelton's upstairs bathroom, where she'd recreated the girl's eyebrows, then cut
her bangs while Jack and Sky prepared the meal.

The first half of the feast had been a rowdy foursome
with the kids and Jack doing most of the talking, allowing
Abby to sit back and applaud or tease or ask the odd question. And savor steak cooked to medium-rare perfection on
a gas grill by the back door, then served in Jack's kitchen
along with deli potato salad, baked beans and coleslaw.
Savor, too, the luscious light, since Kat had insisted they
put out the overhead bulb and eat by the glow of a kerosene lantern, which she and her father used on camping
trips.

"Which means this rates as a special occasion," Jack
had translated as she ran to get it. "We haven't lit it since
my birthday in April."

Lemonade for the kids. A glass of dry zinfandel each
for the adults. As the evening flowed on, Abby felt as if
the clock spring inside her that had been wound to the
breaking point all winter had loosened half a turn at last.
Jack's kitchen was comfortably messy rather than hopelessly shabby like her own, charming by lamplight. Every
which way she gazed, she found scenes that needed sketching. Kat's delicate profile as she whispered wickedly in

Sky's ear. The powerful lines of Jack's flame-gilded throat when he threw back his head in laughter. The miracle of Skyler smiling again.

Sky arranged his fork and knife along the top edge of his plate. "Could we be excused, Mom? I've gotta go check on DC."

Throughout the day the tomcat had descended perhaps five perilous feet to a wider limb, but there he'd lost his nerve and stuck. Abby had a nasty suspicion that Trueheart didn't have a fire department with cat-rescuing firemen, either. "Ask your host, sweetie."

Jack bent his shaggy head. "Off with you both, but *no* climbing. Understood?" They vanished with a clatter of chairs and a bang of the screen door.

Sooner or later, she was going to have to do something. If her ankle hadn't been twisted, she'd have gone after the big softy herself. Abby speared a potato slice and contemplated it with a worried frown.

"If he's not down by morning, I'll get him," Jack assured her as he refilled her glass.

"You've done so much already…" Too much. The last thing she wanted was to feel obligated.

He waved a dismissive hand. "For the woman who gave my daughter back her eyebrows? Nothing's too good."

She laughed quietly. "They'll do by lamplight, anyway." Actually she'd made a pretty good job of it. And somehow the bangs softened Kat's intensity. Now she looked like a warrior princess, rather than a prince. "I…couldn't help noticing tonight, Jack, that she doesn't eat much." Kat was still in the prepubescent stage—all slender limbs, not an ounce of fat—but still…

"Mmm. She's gone vegetarian on me, since this spring." He told her about the branding and Kat's indignation. "She's been picking the pepperoni off her pizza ever since. I don't think it's occurred to her yet that frozen fish sticks come from fish, but other than that…''

"You're not, um, worried?'' His daughter was at an age when calories and nutrition really mattered. But Abby knew how she hated it when her mother criticized her own parenting decisions with Skyler.

"Not yet. I find, generally speaking, that the less I push her, the more yardage I gain. And so far she seems to be thriving on ice cream and peanut butter. Plus I convinced her that all Olympic athletes and navy SEALs take two scoops of protein powder in their fruit smoothies every day.''

"Do they?'' He had a wonderfully whimsical smile by lamplight.

"Cross my heart and hope to choke.'' He raised one big hand over an imaginary Bible. "Besides, this strike's only been going on since May. Kat tends to practice her passions pretty fiercely, then drop them when new ones come along. With any luck, by Christmas she'll be shooting elk and dragging them home for me to roast.''

Meal finished, Abby offered to do the dishes, but Jack shook his head. "Don't worry so much about the *quid* for the *quo*,'' he teased her, collecting their wineglasses. "Who's keeping count?'' He nudged the screen door open with a shoulder. "Let's see if the moon's risen yet.''

It had.

Hard to believe this was the same cold, pinched and saddened sphere that had pursued her every night of the drive from the east coast. This was a big, boisterous jack-o'-lantern moon, dancing over the trees to their east. She and Jack settled on the top step of the back porch to watch it climb.

"So what did you decide about the bus?'' Jack asked after a while.

She sighed. "No choice, really. We'll still need some-place to live once we get to Sedona. Lark doesn't have enough room for us in her own adobe." She ran the cool rim of her wineglass along her bottom lip. "I had it all perfectly figured out. The bus would save us the cost of a moving van across country, then rent when we got there. Once we'd built our own place, I could sell it—recoup our money. Seemed like it would work." She shrugged her mood aside and sipped. "I'll still make it work." She had to.

"Sure you will," Jack said comfortably. "And I sup-pose you'll get a job. Do you have any particular, uh, something you do?"

"I've been a teacher—high school art—these past two years." It had taken her forever to finish her degree and gain a teaching certificate. First she'd become pregnant with Sky, and she'd let her own education lapse while she found her feet as a mother. When Sky reached kindergar-ten age, she'd begun again. Still, with all their moves from base to base, she'd needed years to complete her degree.

"Oh, well, that's all right then," Jack said. He seemed relieved. "Teachers can always get jobs."

She hunched her shoulders. "Except I don't want to teach anymore."

"Burned out already?" He'd used a light, humorous tone—but the wrong words. Steve had taunted her with those same words on more than one occasion.

She stiffened. "Not that, precisely, but I'm afraid teach-ing was a mistake from the start. I loved the kids but not the discipline—forcing them to work when they weren't in the mood, and at that age, they're never in the mood. I'm not much good at forcing anybody." Plus the endless paperwork: the grading, the testing, taking attendance.

And—oh, Lord—the lectures! Steeling herself day after

day to face a roomful of squirming bodies, tapping feet, twenty-five bored or sympathetic or even hostile teenage faces. Shy as she was, she'd always been better dealing with people one-on-one rather than in groups.

"It just wasn't what—" Why she'd ever dreamed she could… Angrily, Abby brushed her hair back from her brow. She didn't have the words to explain her dismay. *All those years I wasted—what a dope I was!* "It just wasn't what…I'd imagined. Teaching art isn't the same as *making* art." She didn't want to watch others create, she'd quickly realized; she needed to do it herself.

"Ah," Jack said, sounding more disapproving than enlightened. "Okay, so what will you do instead?"

She felt a flicker of irritation. Since when was she required to give him a report? She edged away from him on the step, stared up at the moon and muttered, "I'm going to write a book and illustrate it. A children's picture book."

"Ah." His voice was blank, carefully neutral.

"Then I'll do another…and another." And another. She had ideas to burn.

"And you plan to sell them?" he inquired.

"Well, of course I do!" She got restlessly to her feet. "I know it sounds crazy, but don't you see? This is my chance—maybe my last chance to get my life right. To find what works for me and commit myself to it." *To meet nobody's expectations, this time, but my own.* Not Steve's, not her mother's, not her principal's. "To become the artist I've always wanted to be." *Even when I was too scared to admit that's what I wanted.*

Last chance to shape a happy life. It's now or never.

Steve might have kicked her off his magical airplane, but she was darned if she'd fall.

She meant to fly. No wings, no man, just…sheer determination. And terror.

"Hmm." Jack rubbed a knuckle across his mouth. He might have been erasing a skeptical smile.

At least that was what she thought—and she bristled. *Think I can't do it? Well, who cares what you think?*

"So the bus is part of that plan," she continued. "I made enough selling our house to carry us for a year, while I create my first book and find a publisher to buy it. But there's not a penny to spare. So I hope Whitey can fix our poor bus, and soon."

Jack tilted back his glass to finish his wine in a gulp. "Assuming he can find the parts, Whitey's your man." *And I wash my hands of you,* said his tone and that gesture.

The moonlight wavered and she realized her eyes were watering. Odd how her courage never lasted for more than five minutes at a stretch. "Well. I guess I should be heading home." She grimaced. To a cottage with a moulting elk head in the living room.

"I'll walk along. Collect my hotshot."

But the kids came running to meet them as they neared the gate.

"Mom, it's DC!" Skyler yelped. "He's missing!"

CHAPTER SEVEN

THE NEXT MORNING was Friday, thank God, Jack reflected as he tossed his briefcase into his Jeep. Saturday was trudging into view on leaden feet, but at least it was coming. Or maybe his were the feet of lead. He'd helped Abby search for her damned cat till midnight, driving slowly around and around Trueheart. Then he'd taken her and the kids home, but haunted by her stricken face, he hadn't been able to sleep.

At 2:00 a.m. he'd given up the battle and gone out to walk the neighborhood, softly calling, "Here, kitty, kitty" till, over on Polaris Street, old Clay Abbott had almost shot him for a prowler. At which point he'd staggered home and caught at least a couple hours of shut-eye.

Not nearly enough. He slid behind his wheel, then blinked stupidly at the paper he could see through his windshield.

A note from Abby, which she'd tucked beneath his wiper. "Jack, could you please see me for a second before you go? A."

When he came through the garden gate, she was huddled, looking very small, on the top step of her front porch. She set a mug of coffee aside and smiled at him wearily. "Thanks for stopping by."

"My pleasure." She had shadows under her eyes to match his own, and guilt stabbed him again. Abby had taken enough losses lately, something told him. She didn't need to lose that tomcat, however worthless he was. Wouldn't have, if Jack had followed his first instincts and climbed to the rescue. So much for being sensible. Practical. "I take it he didn't return?"

Abby had left her kitchen door propped open, with a bowl of the beast's favorite food just inside, but her face told him the ploy hadn't worked.

"'Fraid not. So I was wondering, could I ask a favor? Is there a print shop anyplace near your office where you could drop this off? Ask if they'd make fifty copies?" She handed him a manila envelope, stiffened with cardboard.

"Sure. May I?" When she nodded, he slid the single sheet of paper out—and gave a grunt of surprise.

He held a portrait, a Wanted poster of DC-3. Seated upright, with his big tail curled primly around his toes, the white tomcat was depicted in a few lovely loose strokes of black ink. The effect was as fluid as a Japanese brush painting. Comical. Not meant to be camera-realistic but, all the same, DC to his owl-eyed life, whiskers bristling, somehow looking the tiniest bit sheepish and homesick.

"Wanted!" Abby had lettered in big block letters above his ears. At the bottom of the poster, she'd inked in the rest of her plea: name and description of the cat, her cell phone number, a one-hundred-dollar reward for his return.

Jack opened his mouth to tell her that to cover Trueheart, she'd need maybe five copies, if that. But he changed his mind. This poster was eye-catching. Framable. He wanted one for his own wall. Even in law-abiding Trueheart, people would be swiping this as soon as it was tacked to a tree. *Well, well, well, Ms. Lake.* Maybe she wasn't quite as crazy as he'd feared last night when she'd told him of her plans. Not that one illustration made a book. And certainly not a publishing career, but still…

"I didn't have a photo of him that I thought would blow

up worth a darn,'' she explained as she pulled a cloud of pale hair back behind her small shapely ears. ''Do you think this'll do?''

''Oh, this'll get their attention, all right. As will the money. That's a mighty handsome reward for these parts, ma'am.'' More than Abby could afford, he suspected.

He'd won a smile with his cowboy drawl, but it faded away. ''I've *got* to get him back. He's Skyler's and Sky...he's lost enough.''

Jack did a ten-second review of his day's engagements and concluded regretfully that he couldn't play hooky, couldn't spend the day finding Abby's cat for her. He needed to be in court in an hour. ''He'll turn up,'' he assured her, wondering if the Durango pound—heck, he'd drive to Denver if need be—might have a white tomcat of the precise weight and size and eye colors as the one she'd lost. Or would Abby know the difference?

''Meantime, I'll make your copies on one condition.'' He pointed a finger at her nose—and a very nice nose it was, he realized for the first time. Generally her mouth grabbed most of his attention, with her eyes claiming the rest. ''You take it easy today, and don't go gimping around town.''

''But I—''

''I mean it, Abby. You want that ankle to heal, which means stay off it. Let Sky and Kat do your legwork. I've ungrounded Kat for the duration and told her she has to report in to you every two hours. Is that all right by you?''

''Of course, but—''

''No buts.'' He waved the envelope to remind her. ''That's my condition. Tomorrow's Saturday and we'll flood the town with your posters, if the kids haven't found him by then. Today, the one useful thing you can do is call Josie Hansen at Hansen's General Store and tell her you've lost a cat. Then sit back and don't worry. Everybody in Trueheart will know inside half an hour. Somebody's bound to spot him. Now…'' He glanced at his watch and winced. "Gotta run."

He had the weirdest damn impulse to lean over and plant a farewell kiss on the corner of her mouth, there where it tucked in and tipped up, even when she was sad. Instead he sketched her a jaunty salute. "Catch ya later, kid."

Or maybe he'd caught her already. Like one of those summer colds. One sneeze and your temperature starts to rise.

THEY'D CANVASSED all the houses on their own street, which was named Haley's Comet Street, according to Kat, although there was no sign anywhere to prove her claim and Sky wasn't sure he believed her. But nobody had seen a trace of DC. "Not a tail, not a whisker," insisted that nice old Mrs. Connelly while she fed them chocolate-chip cookies hot from her oven.

After that they'd knocked on all the doors along the next street down the hill toward town, tiptoeing through the backyards when nobody was home to ask permission. They'd waited patiently for half an hour by a chicken coop in the Butlers' yard. Kat had been convinced that sooner or later DC would come to hunt the plump, dirt-pecking hens, although Sky tried to tell her that DC thought food came packed in cans, not feathered and clucking. He wouldn't have a clue how to feed himself. Had to be starving by now.

Discouraged, they'd wandered down to the junior high school, their "kitty, kitty!" echoing up and down its ramps and corridors. They'd pressed their faces and cupped hands to a window while Kat showed him which classroom would be hers next year—the terrible Mrs. Callahan's, who was said to *yell* and sometimes even *throw* things.

"But if she throws anything at me, I'll throw it right back," Kat growled, nose to the glass.

"Glad I won't be there to see that," Sky said fervently.

Kat turned to study him. "Where will you be?"

"Uh…back home in New Jersey."

She cocked her head at him, the same way her dad did it. "You're on vacation?"

He shrugged and looked away. "Yup. That's right."

"Then why'd you bring your washing machine?"

He set off across the schoolyard, not bothering to see if she followed. "Mom likes lots of clean clothes."

"And your model planes?"

He broke into a run.

When Kat caught up to him a block later, she tugged at his T-shirt sleeve, dragging him toward the nearest corner. "We've got to go to Hansen's now."

"Why?" He was sick of this whole stupid town. They'd never find DC. Never. He was as lost as Skyler himself.

"'Cause when I'm sad, ice cream always helps."

He felt his face go hot as he glared at her. "Who's sad?"

Her drawn-on eyebrows pulled together and for a second it looked as if she'd snap back, but she only said mildly, "Well, you've lost your cat. You must be sad. Though Dad says he's only temporarily misplaced."

They turned downhill at the corner and Sky glanced upward. Finally a street sign. "This is Arcturus Street?"

"No, that one back there is Arcturus. The children around here are always turning the street signs around. Baby stuff."

"Arcturus is a star."

"Uh-huh. All the streets that run east and west are called

after stars and planets and sky stuff. The north-south ones are named for birds. Like this is Chickadee.''

''My dad taught me all the stars you use to navigate by if your instruments ever go down.'' His misery deepened. ''When I'm a captain I'll steer my ship by the stars.''

''Girls can't be captains,'' he said nastily, though he knew it wasn't so. His dad even knew a lady pilot.

''Oh, yeah? Zoe Montana said, last year at the Christmas party at Ribbon River, that she saw lots and lots of women captains—well, two—in the Caribbean.''

So what? Big deal. But he gritted his teeth on the words till they got to Hansen's, where the old lady behind the counter, Mrs. Hansen, somehow already knew they'd lost a white tomcat. That made him feel better, but when he tried to order Rocky Road ice cream, his heart sank to his sneakers.

Mrs. Hansen looked at him over her horn-rimmed glasses, as if he'd burped out loud. ''Vanilla, chocolate or the special is all we ever have, young man. Today's special is lemon-banana.''

''Gimme the chocolate,'' he muttered. He couldn't wait to get out of this town!

Mrs. Hansen rose up on her tiptoes and leaned over the counter. ''I *beg* your pardon?''

''Could I please have the chocolate?'' he mumbled as Kat stuck a hard little elbow in his ribs. He gasped as she jabbed him again and added, ''Ma'am?''

That earned him a baleful look and a loaded cone, then it was Kat's turn to sweat. ''I hear you tried to burn your father's house down,'' said Mrs. Hansen as she scooped lemon-banana.

''Did *not.*'' Kat stuck out her chin. ''I was welding.''

''*Humph.* Not what the sheriff told Mo.''

Kat simply shrugged, took a cautious lick of her bright-yellow ice cream, then asked, "May we please use the phone?"

"That'll be ten cents." Mrs. Hansen brought an old black dial phone from under the counter, smacked it down, then bustled off to help a man in a cowboy hat, whose boots rang loud as horse hooves on the plank floor.

They called Sky's mom and received permission to stay out for another two hours, then they escaped out the screen door—where Sky stopped short. "We forgot to pay!" The old witch would kill them!

Kat managed to shake her head with her tongue attached to her cone. "No, we didn't. I have an ice-cream account. She makes Dad pay whenever he stops in for milk."

"Oh." Trueheart was a very strange place.

ABBY SAT ON THE TOP STEP of the back stoop, her eyes fixed on the crimson bus as the number Jack had given her rang half a dozen times. She had her finger on the disconnect button when a feminine voice cried, "Don't you *dare* be a telemarketer!"

"Um, hi. No. I'm not. This is Abby Lake calling," she said, raising her voice since a baby was lustily howling at the other end of the line.

"Oh—sorry! Yes, you're Jack's friend. The one with the red bus," said the voice, adding in an undertone, "*Hush,* sweetie."

"I'm afraid I woke you."

"Oh, not really. We were just dozing on the couch and I'd forgotten to take the phone off the hook. I'm Kaley, by the way, Kaley McGraw, and the hallelujah chorus you hear is Shannon and Shea."

Twins, Abby remembered Whitey saying. Born in calving season, whenever that was. "I'm sorry to have both-

ered you. I remember I would've killed for an hour of
sleep when my son was young.''

"At least they're both up at the same time for once,"
Kaley agreed on a note of weary amusement. "Usually
they work in shifts. One snoozes while the other yells."

They traded first year stories for a couple of minutes,
then Abby asked for Whitey, only to learn he was out
dosing cattle with pinkeye ointment. "I was hoping he
might be able to work on my bus sometime this weekend,"
she said apologetically. "That is, if you don't have plans
for him?"

Kaley laughed over her babies' wails. "Don't let Whitey
hear you say that! After forty years at the Circle C, he's
family. He and Chang boss us all. But I'll tell him you
could use some help tomorrow, shall I? Oh—and Abby,
welcome to Trueheart!"

"Well, it's only for a week or—" But Kaley had already dashed back to her own double serving of trouble.

Abby heaved a sigh and put the phone away.

"TOLD YOU Hutchins would never grant a restraining order," said Alec Fielding. "Simply because the creep sits
in his car in front of her house every night till 2:00 a.m.?
Now, how could a woman object to that? She ought to be
flattered, bless her hysterical little soul."

"Maybe if I'd told the judge he cleans his gun while he
sits out there?" Jack growled, suppressing an urge to kick
the trash can they were passing on their way back from
the courthouse.

"Hutchins'd say the defendant's devotion to tidiness
demonstrates that he's an upstanding, commendable citi-
zen—give him *full* custody. As for me, I want a pastrami
on whole wheat next time, with extra pickles."

"So noted." Jack had known it was a stretch, asking

Hutchins for a restraining order. Still he'd had to try. And honor demanded that anything he took to court, he had to back with a bet.

Meanwhile, since the legal system had failed her, Susie Murphy and her two children would probably move in with her parents. Her father was a retired marine drill sergeant from Texas, who'd been threatening to get out his gun and settle the problem of Susie's ex-husband if the judge wouldn't. Which would make more problems for everyone. "I hate it when the law is an ass."

"Don't we all," agreed Alec. "But it's Friday thank God, and how's your hot neighbor? Asked her for a date yet?"

"Dream on. Abby needs a date like a trout needs a go-cart. She's too busy *finding herself.* She's going to write children's books when she grows up." Jack's mood shaded from cobalt blue to black as he heard himself speak. She'd told him her dream last night—a preposterous, impractical dream to be sure—but still, she'd spoken from the heart and here he was blurting it out on a street corner.

Alec nodded. "Sounds like a clear and flourishing case of the Divorce Crazies, all right. But is it divorce itself that causes the syndrome? Or sexual deprivation? Maybe you'd be doing her a kindness, if you—"

And maybe sometimes you run off at the mouth. Jack clamped his teeth on the words as he stopped short. "I forgot. Left an order for some prints at the copy shop. See you Monday?"

"I've got an alternative?" Alec flashed a too shrewd grin over his shoulder and kept on walking.

FROM HANSEN'S, they'd searched along Main Street, checking the trash cans behind a half-dozen small shops and stores. They'd seen a black cat who ran away and a gray who wanted his stomach tickled, but not a sign of the one cat that mattered.

"He's walking back to New Jersey," Sky muttered, fighting back his tears. "Cats always go home." Or try to. But how many rivers and highways lay between here and home? DC couldn't swim the Mississippi. And what about all the dangers along the way, the whizzing cars, the mean dogs and hungry coyotes?

"Maybe not. Maybe he's in the park." Kat led him down Quail Street to where the shallow valley in which the town was built bottomed out. Splitting Trueheart in two, a narrow creek meandered along, bordered by a strip of park on each bank.

There they peered under each of the three footbridges that spanned the creek. Looked into and under the bandshell where Kat told him the school orchestra performed every other Saturday in the summer. Asked the little kids playing on the swing set and the seesaw if they'd seen a white cat, but to no avail.

Hot and disheartened, they ended up lying on two big smooth stepping stones, just above a tiny, burbling waterfall, while Kat showed him how to catch fish without a pole.

"Don't move, don't breathe," she chanted, her head almost touching his own as she leaned from her rock, peering down into the creek. She'd insisted that Sky hold the dented soup pot she'd taken from a hiding place under the bridge while she sprinkled bits of her ice-cream cone that she'd saved for fish bait. "Let him eat that crumb for free, then go tell his friends how good it tasted."

A three-inch perch hovered just beyond the submerged rim of the pot, eyeing the floating crumbs within. Sky's hands ached with the cold. The water was clear as ice. It must come down from the mountains to flow through this lousy little park. "He's not going to come in and eat it. And even if he did, who needs a fish?"

"He will so. You just have to be patient. And everybody ought to know how to fish. When I'm a navy SEAL and I go on missions, I'll need to know how to live off the land. Eat grubs and worse things to survive."

"What's worse than a grub?"

Kat giggled. "Two grubs?"

"Chicken feet and pig ears."

"Horse pats! You pick out the oats they ate and then you—"

"*Ee-euw*—oh, *hey!*" The perch darted over the rim, seized the bit of cone and was gone with the flick of a tail. "Did you see that?"

"Yup." Kat sprinkled another bit of cone into the pot. The perch cruised back out of the green weeds that waved in the current, then a second, smaller fish joined him. They floated, fins barely fanning, gazing solemnly at the treats within the trap. "Let 'em eat this one for free, too."

If his hands didn't fall off first. To distract himself from their growing numbness, Sky sent his mind back to last night, when he'd been almost happy, thinking DC was still up his tree, the four of them eating together almost like a— He closed his eyes and shook his head. Not like a family, not in the least! Like a…a party, a nice birthday party.

"Oops, you spooked them. You can't move like that."

Who cares? Stupid fish. "That picture on your dad's desk." In her living room. Sky had noticed it when they'd run to get the lantern last night. "Who's that guy in the uniform?" Navy whites, like his dad used to wear.

"Him? Oh, that's Todd." Her tone was coolly indifferent but with a funny edge.

"Who's Todd?"

"My half brother, I guess. Though it doesn't feel like he is. We didn't grow up together. My mom kept him."

"He's a sailor?"

"Uh-huh. Just joined, after he got out of high school. He's going to be stationed on an aircraft carrier, but I don't care what everybody thinks. That's nothing special. It isn't dangerous, not really, not like being a SEAL."

Who cared about SEALs? "Where's your mom?"

"San Francisco. She and Dad're divorced. *Ha,* here they are again!" She nodded at the fish, two of them—no three, now—contemplating the bait.

So Kat had to be hurting as much as he was. "That stinks. Divorce, I mean. It's stupid."

Kat shrugged. "People do it all the time, my dad says. I can't remember it. Remember my mom, I mean. I was only a year old when they broke up."

"And she didn't take you?" He could have kicked himself the minute he said that.

"No-o." Poised in the clear mountain air, Kat sat as still as the perch, refusing to meet his raised eyes. "Anyway, it's good, the way things worked out. My dad needs me. He'd be awful lonesome without me for company, and he'd never remember to wash his socks if I didn't remind him. And if he didn't have to set me an example, he'd never eat his vegetables. He'd live on frozen pizza and Whopper burgers. If he didn't need me, I'd have run off and stowed away on a tall ship by now. Be a second mate, probably."

Sky opened his mouth to tell her she was crazy, then shut it again. The largest perch shot into the pot—and he tipped up the rim. "Gotcha!" The fish darted in frantic circles.

Kat shared his triumphant grin. "But now...you've gotta eat him."

CHAPTER EIGHT

JACK NEVER SCHEDULED an afternoon appointment on Friday if he could help it.

Today being one of those days when he could, he rolled into Trueheart around four. Plenty of daylight left if cat-hunting was still on the agenda. Not that he couldn't think of half a dozen better ways to start the weekend. Fielding's comment about a hot date skittered across his mind as he pulled into his driveway.

Forget it, Kelton. Never hit on a brand-new divorcée who drives a—what color did Abby call it?—crimson bus. That way madness lies.

The same madness that inspired Rocky Mountain rams to butt heads and bull elks to bugle at the moon. Mourning doves to sit on the branches, shoulder to soft gray shoulder. Stealing a glance at the house next door, Jack felt a dangerous quickening in his blood.

Okay, he could think about it; it was springtime in the Rockies, after all. But he'd never act. He'd learned his lesson very well, thank you, at sweet Maura's hands. Might as well court a buzz saw as a woman who was still making up her mind about Life, Men and Love. You ended up losing parts of yourself you'd rather keep.

And if this sudden sweet ache in his chest meant it was time he looked for company, well, Durango was full of safer prospects. Single women who'd yet to have their romantic illusions shattered. Longtime divorcées who'd swept up the marital breakage, then returned to the game with no hard feelings. Women who knew what they wanted.

But for no reason he could put his finger on, none of those women called him like the woman next door.

Entering his own house, he found the air warm and stale, smelling faintly of this morning's burned toast. Kat must have been out and about all day, searching the town. But by now she was probably over at Abby's; at least that was the first place to look. He changed to a pair of well-worn jeans and a T-shirt with a sigh of relief, exchanged his office boots for sneakers, and sauntered next door.

"'Lo the house! Anybody home?" He rapped on the back screen door.

"J-Jack?" Abby's voice came faintly from a distance. "Is that— C-could you—?"

The quaver in her call sent him bounding through the kitchen. He halted in the door to the living room with a grunt of astonishment.

Hugging the wagon wheel chandelier for dear life, Abby teetered on a tilted chair, which she'd stacked on top of the couch, which she'd somehow pushed into the center of the room. She turned her head as far around as she could, showing him a flash of wild green eye through a storm of disheveled hair. "C-could you…"

"Jumping *Jehosaphat*, woman!" The chair must have tipped while she was changing the light bulbs. He gripped her waist with both hands—and an electric thrill sizzled up his arms. Slenderness and warmth, his for the taking.

Her hands were frozen tight to the wagon wheel. "I c-couldn't jump after the chair moved. I was afraid if I landed wrong on my ankle…"

He laughed with the absurdity of it all, with the sheer

pleasure of holding her. "How long have you been hanging around?" *Waiting for me?*

"Oh-hh, five years or so. I didn't notice the time till I slipped, and after that..."

Long enough to leave her with every muscle shaking. Sewing-machine leg was what rock climbers called it. "You could let go now," he coaxed her. "I've got you."

"Mmm," she agreed earnestly—and managed to pry one forefinger loose. "I guess it's been half an hour, maybe?"

The best way to override her fear of falling was to lift her straight up, five inches or so. "Then we're outta here." She weighed just enough to make his muscles swell and flex, to set his heart slamming in his chest.

She squeaked as she rose toward the ceiling, but at last she released the chandelier. A bulb came loose, bounced off his shoulder and smashed on the floor. "Oh, I'm sorry!"

"No problem." The only problem was his self-control. He wanted to pull her in, lower her inch by inch along his own body, suddenly achingly alive. Bruise her mouth with his own when they came level, till she moaned and wrapped those long legs around his waist.

Hell. One touch and he'd advanced from arm's length attraction to urgent lust.

Still, let him succumb to that fantasy and Abby'd grow more claws than her tomcat, something told him. Her eyes had widened with alarm and she'd caught her bottom lip between her teeth.

He brought her to the ground with a chaste six-inch margin between them. "There you go, safe and sound." *But only just.* To damp down his own rioting instincts, he scowled. "And just what the hell did you think you were doing?"

Though he should have foreseen this when she'd asked him last night to bring her twelve sixty-watt light bulbs along with her gallon of milk...

"I can't bear fluorescent lights," she said, on her dignity as she retreated a step...and her knees gave out.

"Easy!" He caught her halfway to the floor and swung her over onto the couch. "Sit still for a minute, will you?"

At least for now, she had to obey him. While she sat, kneading the cramps out of her legs, he brought her chair down to the floor and stood on it to change the remaining bulbs. "Seen the kids?" he asked, trying to keep his eyes off those graceful hands sliding along slender thighs.

"Not since this morning, although they've been terrific about checking in. In fact—" She glanced toward the kitchen. "That must've been them a while back. My phone rang, but I couldn't..."

"They'll call again." That was the one bit of training he'd successfully drilled into Kat's stubborn skull—stay in touch. "I take it the cat hasn't shown up?"

Mournfully she shook her head and he wished he could hug her. If she'd been divorced even a year he might have risked it. But raw as she was? *Forget it.* He walked into the kitchen and found a broom and dustpan in the pantry. "I see you've been busy," he said as he swept the shards of broken bulb into a pile. She'd mopped the floor, scrubbed the kitchen walls and grubby cabinets. "But how could you bring yourself to lose that poster?"

She'd replaced the snow-boarding babe on the fridge door with another sketch of her tomcat. This one was as wonderful as the first, a dizzying perspective looking straight up the tree trunk, with DC-3 staring dolefully down at the viewer.

Abby made a face as wry and comical as her cat's. "The snow bimbo? It finally hit me why I hated her so much.

She reminds me of my ex's new wife.'' Her cheeks turned a delicate shade of pink as their eyes met. Then she looked abruptly away, swallowing hard.

He cocked his head and waited for her gaze to come back to him. Gave her a quizzical smile when it did. ''He's remarried already? That was fast work. How long had you two been divorced?''

Her eyes dropped to her fingers, twining around each other. ''It's been final since March. But he'd already found her, months, maybe a year before... That's why I...when I realized...''

A rat *and* a fool. Abby deserved so much better than that.

''And she's...pregnant!'' she said in a tragic whisper.

''With his child?'' Jack prodded, just to be sure.

She nodded too many times, then added, ''Children. She's expecting...triplets.''

''Triplets!'' He couldn't help grinning. ''Well, there's *some* justice in the world, after all!''

She flashed him a look of wounded astonishment. ''What do you mean?''

He dropped on his heels before her and collected her hands. ''You really think your wandering boy, when he asked her out for that first friendly drink, was hoping to quadruple his offspring? Picturing potty-training times three? Wanting an extra three kids to put through college—all at once?''

''Well, no, but—''

''Believe me, your ex's looking back on the good old days and wondering what hit him.'' *Having second thoughts.* All the regrets in the world.

But suddenly Jack didn't want Abby following his line of thought. She was well rid of that relationship. No use encouraging her to wonder if the jerk might still change his mind—which he might. Jack had seen plenty of boomerang spouses in his practice. It was just another kind of divorce craziness. Men and women driving each other to distraction, clueless about what they really wanted or needed.

"All right, then." He squeezed her hands and let her go. "That chandelier took eight bulbs, so what death-defying plans did you have for the other four?"

AFTER THE PARK, Kat led Sky up the opposite slope from the creek, zigzagging along bird streets toward the north side of town. A gray pickup stopped to let them cross Blue Heron, and the cowboy behind the wheel tipped his hat at them and smiled.

Kat gave him a narrow-eyed, vicious glare and stalked on, chin high, shoulders stiff.

"Who was that?" Sky asked, staring after the pickup as it drove away. A big black and tan Airedale rode in back, leaning wistfully over the tailgate with his stump tail wagging.

"That's Anse Kirby from Suntop Ranch. He burns calves."

"Burns them!" Sky pictured a flaming pile of cows.

"Brands them with red-hot metal. It isn't right and I told him so, but he just laughed at me and kept on doing it."

Maybe that's his job? But Sky only said, "So where are we headed?" Kat always seemed to have a plan.

"To the house Dad and I are building. The cottage next door to yours? We're only renting that till we finish our real place. Dad wanted a view of the mountains."

And he'd gotten it. On an unpaved lane, a big lot sloped up to the top of the ridge that sheltered the town from north winds. Miles beyond it loomed the mountains, a wilderness of red and purple fangs in the late-afternoon light. If DC had wandered in that direction, he was gone forever.

Low, gnarled trees dotted the property and a house foundation had been poured. "It used to be part of an apple orchard," Kat told him. "We picked half a bushel last fall when we bought the place."

"Cool." Sky scanned the unmown meadow for a scrap of moving white. He turned on his heel to stare back down the valley toward town. He'd felt good for a while there, catching and then releasing the fish, but now... *DC. Kitty, kitty...oh, kitty.* Last night was the first night he'd slept without the tomcat since he chose him at the pound as a tiny kitten two years ago. Twice he'd woken with nightmares of DC in trouble, lost and needing him. *Please, please let him be back, purring on my pillow tonight!*

"And that's my dad's toolshed where I was weld—" Kat paused, and Sky turned to see where she was staring. "Somebody's up there!"

"A cat?" he demanded as she caught his sleeve and pulled him along.

"Uh-uh. Somebody peeking at us..." Kat gasped in outrage. "It's Sam Jarrett!"

A boy a few years older had come out from behind the metal shed. Out swaggered a second kid, even larger than the first, or maybe it was only his cowboy boots and hat that made him seem so. Pretending to ignore Kat and Sky, they wandered over to the house foundation and vaulted up onto its plywood decking to sit, swinging their legs, facing the mountains.

"They shouldn't be here on our property," Kat fumed, stalking up the rutted driveway.

"Um, maybe we should..." But she wasn't listening. Sky shrugged and followed.

"Sam Jarrett, what d'you think you're doing here?" Kat marched straight up to the pair.

The blond one grinned at her, struck a match on the zipper of his jeans and lit the cigarette he held between his lips.

Kat planted her hands on her skinny hips. *"Well?"*

Sam blew out a plume of smoke. "Me and Pete just stopped by to see if you'd really burned the place down like we heard."

"Huh! You're the one who's going to start a fire, smoking on our property. You're trespassing, you know."

"Gonna arrest us, Kat?" Sam grinned at his companion.

She gave him a snooty shrug. "Maybe not. Maybe I'll just tackle you myself and throw you off my land."

The boy in the hat let out a hoot of delight. "Yeah, Jarrett, and she can do it, too!"

Sam turned red as a brick. "The hell she can! That last time was nothing but dumb-ass luck."

Sky had no idea what they were talking about, but clearly it was time to change the subject. "Hey, have either of you seen a white cat?"

Cowboy Hat smirked. "I hear there's a reward out on him. A hundred dollars?"

Sky nodded warily. It was too much money, he'd thought, when his mom decided on that amount. He'd cost her too much already, wrecking the bus. "Yeah."

"That's good." The kid grinned from one stick-out ear to the other. "But can I collect dead or alive? 'Cause I caught the critter this morning and skinned him."

"You're a *liar!*" He had to be lying! Sky lunged at him and bounced off his outthrust palm. "Liar! *Jerk!*"

Kat caught his arm and tugged him back. "Of course the creep is lying! What would you expect from a guy who'd stick his tongue in ol' Marylou's mushy mouth?"

"His *tongue!*" Sam Jarrett whooped and fell blissfully backward on the flooring. "You tongued ol' *Marylou?*"

"Shuddup, Jarrett!" Cowboy Hat stuck his finger in Kat's face. "And you, midget, what were you doing— spying on us the other night?"

Kat crossed her arms and tipped up her chin. "Yup, till I got bored—and that sure didn't take long."

"You're the guy Mr. Kelton threw out of his house," Sky realized.

"Who's this four-eyed runt?" the cowboy demanded.

Four Eyes. Oh, Sky had had enough of that back in Jersey—too much! And what if Kat was wrong? What if this creep really had caught DC and—

"His name's Sky," Kat declared. "And his dad's a pilot with American Airlines."

Didn't she know *anything* about when to keep her mouth shut?

But it was too late now. The cowboy smirked and came in for the kill. "Oh, yeah? So what if he is? Ol' *Four Eyes* here'll never get off the ground. It takes twenty-twenty vision to fly a plane."

A blow straight to the heart. Sky staggered—then came in swinging. It was either cry or attack. His first wild punch clipped the jerk's nose. The second knocked off his stupid hat.

JACK HAD INSISTED on changing the fluorescent bulbs in the kitchen, even though Abby tried to tell him she could do it herself.

"Now what else?" he asked, stepping down from a chair.

"That's plenty. Truly all I need." She'd always been shy about asking for help, and her years with Steve had made her more so. She'd rather fend for herself a thousand times over than nag, and he'd never remembered her requests if she didn't repeat them again and again and again.

"What about that couch? Shall I put it back where it was?"

"Well, actually I was going to…" The living room was her next project, now that the kitchen was minimally habitable, but she'd do it later, in blessed privacy. She was still feeling flustered from Jack's rescue, still feeling the warmth and strength of his hands on her body. He'd looked so odd and fierce there for a moment as he'd held her above his head, and she'd felt so…totally out of control, with her feet dangling.

Getting her life back under control was what this trip west was all about. Standing on her own two feet. Depending on no man, not even one as kind as Jack seemed to be.

"You were going to start rearranging," he guessed with a grimace. "Ooo-kay." He preceded her into the living room. "What first?"

"Jack, you don't need to do this."

"Of course I don't. But since I'm killing time till the kids show up…"

As easy to stop a train with a flyswatter. Abby sighed and gave in. "All right, then, this carpet's a disaster. If we rolled it up, could you carry it out to the toolshed?"

Half an hour later he'd patiently moved the couch to four different positions. Finally she'd realized the pleasing place wasn't parallel to any wall but in one corner on a diagonal, with the shabby little pine coffee table in front of it. Then the La-Z-Boy went near the fireplace with the antique brass floorlamp beside it.

"Feels much more roomy," Jack observed, surveying their results. "So now what? Upstairs?"

"No! I…" She didn't want him up in her bedroom. This

room was twice the size of that and yet he made it seem small. Her eyes lit on the stuffed elk head. "That monstrosity, it's got to go."

"You'll break your poor landlady's heart. Maudie's father shot him back in '52. Nobody in Trueheart's taken a rack like that, before or since."

"If you want a dead animal in *your* house, you're welcome to him."

Jack smiled and shook his head. "She offered him to me last fall, and it took all my considerable tact to turn him down. But maybe I should put on a flea collar before I touch the mangy brute."

Abby limped along purely out of sympathy while he lugged the dusty horror to the shed. They were walking back up the drive when their missing offspring turned in from the street.

"And high time," Jack noted. "My cardinal rule is that Kat's always home by dark. I was going to suggest that I take you guys out to Michelle's Place for—" He cocked his head. His brows pulled together. He left her side at a purposeful walk, then broke into a jog.

What now? Abby wondered, hurrying in his wake. Then she gasped as the children's rueful faces grew clear through the gathering twilight.

CHAPTER NINE

ABBY WAS CURLED UP asleep in the La-Z-Boy when a light tapping roused her. "Jack?" She stretched, started to rise, then paused as he cracked open the front door.

"Blast. Sorry to wake you."

"Not at all." She rubbed her fists through her lashes and leaned back to study his face. "I must've just dozed off." Unlike Kat and Skyler, he hadn't come home battered and bruised, as she'd half expected. "Did you find Sam Jarrett's father?"

At the sight of his daughter's black eye and skinned knee, Jack had gone on full-testosterone, outraged-father overdrive.

He'd sent Kat straight to bed, ordered—not asked—Abby to watch her for him, then roared off into the night, declaring, "Nobody—but *nobody*—punches a kid of mine!"

That had been hours ago Abby saw now, glancing at her alarm clock, which she'd placed on the mantel. It was after ten. All evening she'd been listening for the sounds of sirens or gunshots. Who'd have thought that such a temper lurked beneath Jack's easygoing smiles? "So you two didn't come to blows? The way you left here, I was worried that…"

Jack dropped onto the couch across from her. "The Jarrett ranch is twenty-five miles northwest of Trueheart by gravel road. By the time I'd bounced out there—and changed a flat along the way—I'd had a chance to cool down.''

''I'm glad. I was afraid you'd slug Sam Jarrett's father, and next thing I knew, we'd be smack in the middle of a range war.''

''Mmm.'' Jack rubbed a hand across his jaw, which was showing a faint sexy shadow of beard. ''Kat's not in her bedroom, so I take it she's here?''

''Upstairs on my bed. I didn't want to leave either of them alone, so after I fed them…'' And washed their various scrapes, then applied a bag of frozen blueberries to Kat's black eye and a bag of green peas to Sky's fat lip and bruised cheek. And heard their side of the story. She slid to the edge of her seat, bringing the footrest down. ''Have you eaten yet? No? Then come have leftovers. I scrounged your beans to make vegetarian chili.''

His stomach growled at the invitation. With a rueful laugh, he rose quickly enough to haul her up from the recliner's depths. ''Sounds wonderful. I was ready to settle for Raisin Bran this time of night.''

She promptly reclaimed her hand. ''So you talked with the Jarretts?''

While she moved around the kitchen, turning on the heat under the pot of chili, laying bread and butter out on the table, then pouring two glasses of orange juice, he sat down and told her. ''I also spoke with Joe Sikorsky, Pete's father, who's one of Jarrett's hands. They were just headed into Trueheart to find us when I arrived.

''Ben had already pried the story out of his kid, that he'd been fighting with a girl, and he was pretty well mortified, as was Joe. Wanted me to know he'd already taken the matter in hand. The boys are going to write letters of apology to Kat and Sky tomorrow, then that's the last we'll hear of 'em till September. They're confined to the ranch for the rest of the summer.

"But the real punishment is that they won't be riding on roundup this fall, when the herds are moved down out of the high country. For a junior cowboy, that's a fate worse than being staked out for the ants."

"Surely that's too harsh." Abby set a bowl of chili in front of Jack, then settled across from him. "Because I'm afraid Sky started the fight—or at least escalated it from words to violence."

"Mmm." He nodded, digging into the chili. "Sounded that way to me, too. But Sam's fourteen and Pete's sixteen and they're both sizable kids. They should've been mature enough to back down—and somebody did break Sky's glasses. And once Jarrett heard that Kat had a black eye, he was adamant. Code of the West says boys don't sock girls, no matter how provoking they are."

"Well…it sounds as if they were trying not to. Kat apparently waded right in to help Skyler, and the punch she took was probably aimed at him, not her."

Jack groaned and shook his head. "Hardly matters at this point. The damage is done and Jarrett doesn't strike me as one to back down once he's laid down the law." Jack spooned up another bite of chili—fiery and flavorful—and sat, musing as he swallowed.

"Now it's my turn to be judge and jury. What do I do with my little prizefighter? It's not fair for girls to smack boys when they're not supposed to hit back, and if Kat tries that again with some kid who's got less restraint, she'll come home with more than a shiner.

"Meantime she's supposed to be grounded already because of the welding fiasco. I'm running out of options here. I cut off her allowance three weeks ago when she broke Jodi O'Malley's window with her slingshot. So what do I do this time? Can't give her away. Can't shoot her.''

"Sleep on it," Abby advised. "At least that's what I plan to do."

"Yeah," he agreed wearily. "This was a long day." He finished the chili and stood. "Thanks for feeding me, Abby. That hit the spot. And thanks for taking care of Kat while I vented."

"My pleasure." She frowned and looked down at her hands clasped around her glass. "But, Jack, there's one thing. You don't think those kids really found DC and…hurt him? That's what started this fight, you know, their saying—"

"Oh, Abby, no!" He placed a hand on her shoulder. "That was just teasing. Rough, mean teasing, I'll grant you, but only that. Just boys being boys."

"You're sure?" She blinked, then blinked again as tears gathered along her lashes. "He's such a big timid softy, and Sky really loves him. If anything happens to him…"

"Nothing will." Reaching down, Jack traced a big knuckle along her cheek, brushing tears away—a gesture that pierced her with its unexpected gentleness. "We're going to find him safe and sound tomorrow, I promise you."

"I guess…" She yearned to lean her head against that comforting warmth, but turned aside, breaking the contact. "No, I'm sure you're right." She managed a shaky smile, although she couldn't meet his gaze. "Thanks. As you said, it's been…a long day."

A long, long painful year.

"Yeah." Jack stood beside her for a moment, then moved on. "Guess I'll collect my slugger so you can get some rest."

AT DAWN Jack woke up as refreshed as an eighteen-year-old, with a hard-on to match. He contemplated himself with wry bemusement—the outer man might have no problems with celibacy, but the inner one had his own ideas. *The least you could do is let me in on our dreams, buddy.*

Donning a terry-cloth robe, he shuffled down the hall, cautiously turning all corners till he'd deflated to workaday size. Luckily, Kat, usually an early riser, was sleeping in.

Safe at last behind the bathroom door, he used the facilities, then set out his razor and shaving cream. Some Saturdays he didn't bother, but today, considering…

Abby. Abby next door. A wave of tactile, not visual, memory washed over him, raising goose bumps, hardening him all over again. *I was dreaming about Abby?* He shifted a step to peer through the window beside the sink, which would have overlooked her backyard but for the tree in the way.

Drifting out of focus, his eyes wandered through the intervening greenery, but still his dream stayed locked up tight. A sense of happiness…an impression of luxurious warmth and exuberant motion lingered. With no accompanying pictures.

Something moved beyond the branches and his gaze sharpened. He sucked in his breath.

Through a gap in the leaves, he could see a ragged patch of Abby's backyard—and a woman standing on her head. "You gotta be kidding me!" He closed his eyes, then looked again, but the hallucination persisted.

Abby still balanced there, upside-down—a column of pointed toes and slender bare legs, banded by a pair of silky blue jogging shorts, then a body-clinging black tank top, with a pile of pale hair puddled around her braced forearms and the blanket she rested on. Jack reminded himself to breathe. *Holy smoke, woman!*

If he wasn't still dreaming, he should march straight over there. Grasp those slender ankles and nibble her toes. After which he'd lick his way slowly down those luscious calves toward—

He blinked as she broke the stand, one leg descending gracefully, followed by the other. She folded into a kneeling position, then sat upright, her smile in profile like a dolphin's serenely mysterious curve. She braced her hands and rolled backward, vanishing from view beyond the foliage.

Jack groaned and gripped the window frame. *Come back here!*

She didn't. He stared hungrily at the patch of vacant blanket for a minute more, then refocused on his own hands clutching the sill. Jack Kelton, officer of the court— and voyeur. *Was* he technically a voyeur if he was peeking out through his own window rather than in through a neighbor's? That was more Fielding's area of expertise, not that he'd ever ask. This was one of those moments a man hugged to himself.

He wanted another.

Two minutes in which his eyes watered with the need to blink, then he was rewarded by a hand, palm-up, fingers relaxed, beckoning gracefully, horizontally beyond the leaves, then gone. A teaser.

Jack scowled to himself and shifted back to the mirror. Slapped on shaving cream, made two careful swipes of the razor and then was drawn irresistibly sideways to check the gap in the tree.

Zip. Maybe she was done with whatever she was doing?

No, the blanket was still in place.

He went back to his shaving. None of his business if his next-door neighbor cavorted in her own backyard, clothed or mother-naked.

"Divorce Crazies," he muttered, scraping carefully under his nose. She'd fit right in when she reached Sedona.

Being a man of iron will, Jack managed not to peek again till he was ready to step into the shower. This time Abby stood squarely in his leafy spy hole, pushing air. Her hands flowed, her body revolved slowly from right to left; she pushed again. Tai Chi? Or possibly another of those Oriental forms of self-defense. He'd known several divorce clients who took up martial arts, come to think of it—and come to think of it, all of them female.

Jack grimaced. *That's right.* He'd forgotten. Maura had done a stint of kung fu, hadn't she, that first month when he'd taken on her case? Once they'd started seeing each other, she'd dropped it in favor of more intimate acrobatics.

Why do you all do it? he wondered, watching Abby sweep her hands slowly skyward in a graceful arc. Was it just a hobby to fill in the gap where there used to be a husband? Or was it a way to feel secure?

Any guy could have told them a more effective way to fill that empty feeling: buy a motorcycle.

But do they ever listen? Jack turned the water on, adjusted it to a cooler temperature than he normally used, and stepped under the spray.

"ANYBODY HOME?" Abby called, although she could hear Kat chattering in the kitchen. So she wasn't too early; the Keltons were awake and about.

"Yep! We are." Kat darted to the screen door. She glanced over her shoulder, to where Jack sat at the table with a folded newspaper beside his plate. "See, Dad? I told you they'd be up. Come on in, Abby." She shoved the door wide.

"Oh, Kat!" Abby exclaimed in dismay. "You're half a

raccoon.'' Her delicate little face was marred by a bruised-bandit mask, out of which gleamed a bloodshot, swollen eye.

"Like Sylvester Stallone in *Rocky*," Kat agreed proudly. "After he won the fight."

"We watch only the classics," Jack confided with a grimace, rising and setting his plate in the sink.

"*Now* can I go see Sky?" Kat added her plate to the stack and jittered around her father.

"Teeth, jam off the chin, hair brushed, and then you can. And don't forget shoes."

"Huh! Like I would." She danced out of the room, followed by the sound of bare feet thumping double-time upstairs.

The adults exchanged rueful grins. "Don't know why they keep searching for the secret to nuclear fusion," Jack said. "If they could harness kid power instead..." He tapped the half-full pot resting in the coffeemaker. "Care for a cup?"

"Thanks, I'm all set. But I was wondering if you'd had a chance to take my poster by the copy shop yesterday? I know you were probably rushed off your feet, yesterday being Friday and all, but I thought I'd..."

Ignoring her apologetic babble, Jack strolled across to another counter, where he picked up a typing-paper box. "Fifty copies, as ordered. Let me get the jam off *my* face, and I'll be ready to help you hang 'em."

"Oh, Jack, you don't have to—"

"Nope, but it won't take any time at all. And you owe it to your cat to take advantage of our hard-won local knowledge. I know where the biddies gather and the geezers stop for coffee. Kat knows where the kids roam."

"Sure do!" Kat shot between them and banged out the back door.

Abby was hopelessly obligated to him already. He'd even saved her neck last night. Better not to go any deeper in his debt. "I don't like to bother you."

"Bother?" Something about his smile seemed the tiniest bit strained. "Ms. Lake, when you're a bother...I'll let you know." Jack placed the box in her hands. "I'll be over in a few."

CHAPTER TEN

ABBY RETURNED TO HER YARD to find Kat and Sky rummaging through the bus in search of Sky's bike, which naturally was at the bottom of their jumble of household goods. "Oh, Skyler!"

Call her superstitious, but Abby felt it was bad luck to unload the vehicle. Packed, her whimsical crimson bus was a symbol, a promise that this was only a short detour on the road of her life. As soon as Whitey fixed it, she could start it up and they'd drive away.

But let Sky drag out half their treasures and strew them around, and maybe they'd stick, here in Trueheart. A space rocket took a certain thrust to escape the earth's gravitational pull; Abby didn't need her unpacked possessions exerting their own inertia, holding her to this place.

It was too late now. Here came the bike, tipsy-turvy down the front steps of the bus, preceded by Sky and followed by Kat, then the girl dashed away to collect her own. "Helmet," Abby said sternly, and Sky ducked into the bus again to the sound of more tumbling boxes.

When Jack joined her a short while later, he was just in time to see Whitey's truck backing away down the drive.

"There goes five-hundred dollars," Abby murmured grimly as she waved. "He and Chang wanted a check to begin their hunt for used parts."

"Whitey's good for it, Abby—rock-solid—if that's what you're worrying about."

"Oh, I never doubted that for a minute. He's a sweetheart. I'm just...worried." Five hundred for parts and that was only for starters. Add to that Whitey's labor, plus Maudie Harris's rent for the house. She'd spent a twentieth of her year's allowance in less than a week! "Mathematics and I never did get along."

"I had some thoughts on that," Jack said easily. "But first, why don't we get this cat-finding show on the road?"

In the end it was decided that Kat and Skyler would cover the near end of Trueheart, including all three school buildings, while the adults would take the northern half of the valley, plus all outlying landmarks. Equipped with tape, tacks, posters and peanut butter and jelly sandwiches, the bicycle corps pedaled away, while Jack and Abby climbed into his Jeep.

As they drove across town Jack said, "Thanks for lending her those glasses."

Abby had set aside her own misgivings about unpacking to dig out her favorite pair of sunglasses, the ones with wacky daisy-yellow-and-red-polka-dot frames that any child could love. "I thought she might wear them rather than explain where she got the shiner to everyone she meets."

He gave her a warm smile. "Well, I damn sure prefer she hides that eye, even if she doesn't. I feel like a failed dad, letting my kid get socked."

"Don't be silly! You weren't there."

"Doesn't matter. It happened on my watch. Till she's twenty-one, it's all my watch, and I wonder if it even stops there."

"I know what you mean," Abby said softly. "I remember hearing once that having a child is like having your heart wandering around outside your body."

"*Brrr.* Too true to contemplate. Why don't we hang a

poster…here.'' Jack braked the Jeep beside an oak tree at the corner of Main Street and Golden Eagle.

After that they worked their way west along Main, tacking a poster to the door of the sheriff's office, which was closed. ''When Joel returns, he'll move it inside to the board where he keeps his Most Wanted posters,'' Jack assured her.

They posted another portrait of DC on the community bulletin board outside the volunteer fire department shed, then stopped in at the town's lovely little stone library to put one on the bulletin board in its foyer. Abby was introduced to the librarian, old Mrs. Wimbly, who promptly issued her a library card, in spite of Abby's protests that she'd only be in Trueheart for a week. ''You never know, dear, do you, and of course I'm sure you'd never *abuse* the privilege?'' Her plucked eyebrows climbed toward her fluffy blue hairline.

Trapped into admitting that she certainly would not, Abby meekly accepted the card—saving her glower for Jack after they escaped.

''Open only on Tuesdays, Thursdays, Saturdays and Sundays-after-twelve,'' he reminded her with a grin. ''And don't believe that sugar-coating for a minute. If you ever forget to return a book, she'll track you to the ends of the earth.''

The vet's office was closed with a sign hanging on the door that announced that Dr. Kerner was out at Kristopherson's ranch, if anyone had an emergency. So they taped a poster of DC to its frosted glass. ''Big animal vet,'' Jack told her, ''though in a pinch he'll treat a dog or a baby or a run-over skunk. And he has three cats himself, so he'll keep an eye out for yours.''

Next down the line was Hansen's General Store, where Josie Hansen gave DC's poster pride of place on the front of her counter—but only after Abby submitted to an extended inquisition concerning her origins, intentions, vocation and views about snowmobiles and the N.R.A. "I was waiting for her to pull out her fingerprint pad," Abby fumed as the screen door banged behind them.

"Your father painted portraits?" Jack repeated, licking his ice-cream cone.

"How*ever* did she pry that out of me? I don't talk about myself to strangers."

"Like it or not, within five minutes nobody's a stranger to Josie," Jack consoled her. "The world lost one of its great investigative reporters when she married a storekeeper in Trueheart. But Josie also saves time. Now you won't have to explain yourself to anybody in town."

"Not that I was planning on explaining myself." But her own scoop was melting, so Abby licked a drop of garish yellow as it slid down the cone. "Oh... What flavor is this?"

"Haven't a clue, but you'd better eat your share. Josie features only one special flavor at a time, and her customers have to finish the batch before she'll make another." He tasted his own scoop. "Hmm, lemon?"

"And banana," Abby decided, licking again.

"With—*aha*—peppermint candy, which probably means she had a shipment of hard candy that wasn't selling, so she threw it in. You'll find the special tends to evolve later in the week, after she inventories her shelves."

He led her down to a park below Main Street, where Abby settled on a swing to finish her cone while Jack stood beside her. "This is charming!" A pack of children even younger than Sky were shrieking and splashing in the shallow, meandering little creek. And the park was graced by a Victorian-era bandshell, pretty as the topping on a wedding cake, trimmed with latticework and lacy white gingerbread. A banner draped from its eaves promised a brass band concert next Saturday.

"Mmm," Jack agreed. "It's all on a human scale. Seemed a pretty good place to raise a kid, which is why we moved here last year. Kat was getting old enough to want to roam. But Durango's too big a city to let her run free without me worrying. Whereas up here, people may mind your business, but they also look out for each other. So Kat's safe on her own, but..."

"But?" Abby prompted, studying his frown.

"But she's *on* her own—not fitting in. Not that she was doing all that well in Durango, I suppose, but at least her playmates were used to her. She'd carved a niche from long association. But here in Trueheart where Kat's the new kid on the block..." Jack finished his cone with a crunch, then wiped his big hands on his napkin. "Or maybe it's just her age that's the problem. It was okay for her to be a tomboy in fourth grade, but then this past year... And now here she's headed into sixth.

"You look at her little schoolmates—they're all teetering on the verge of puberty, doing their nails and their hair, practicing their girlie moves, dressing in ways that must scare the dickens out of their poor old dads. Gearing up to drive the boys wild.

"But Kat? She's trying to join the football team. Except she's not a guy, so she doesn't fit in there, either. And the harder she tries for acceptance, the worse it gets. She tackled Sam Jarrett last fall—made a fool of him in front of his teammates and quite likely that was the root of this last fight. But sacking the quarterback doesn't make her a hero. It makes her a freak, a misfit.

"She's falling between two chairs, Abby, and it's my fault." Jack fingered one of the chains that supported her swing.

"Oh, come on, she's not eleven yet. Kat's got plenty of time to work it out."

He scowled and shook his shaggy head. "She's off on the wrong foot, and I'm not sure she'll ever get it right again, at least not in Trueheart. Small towns are conservative and first impressions stick. I'm not much of a conformist myself but, dammit, I want my kid to fit in, at least to the extent that she has friends. She shouldn't have to run off to sea or to the SEALs to find her own kind."

"Of course not," Abby agreed, trying not to smile.

"If a lion or a tiger were after her, I'd take him apart with my bare hands. But how do I protect my daughter from the snubs of a pack of sixth-grade girls? I can't offer to deck them if they won't invite Kat to their pajama parties."

He was worrying too much, surely, but his love for his daughter and his desperation were…quite adorable.

"So…" Jack moved to stand in front of her and gripped both chains, looking down at her fiercely. "That's where you come in."

"Me?" Their knees were almost bumping and all of a sudden Abby felt…edgy. Trapped.

"I have a proposition for you." Jack pushed absently on one chain as he pulled on the other, setting her swing oscillating gently back and forth.

Not that kind of proposition, Abby assured herself, but still, heat shimmered in her stomach. Or maybe that was heat coming off his big body, so close to hers. Their knees did brush, ever so slightly. "Y-you do?"

"Uh-huh." He moved the chains again. "You need money, it seems like, and Kat needs girlie lessons. I want to hire you to teach her."

"Jack!" Abby couldn't help but smile. "Don't be ridiculous."

"I'm not. This fight was the last straw. I've been thinking it through all morning, and this is just what Kat needs. I've botched the job, Abby, hard as I've been trying. But I haven't a clue how to dress her, how to help with her hair—never did, and it shows. She knows how to change the oil in a car or change a tire, yet she can't cook anything but frozen pizza and scrambled eggs."

"I'm hardly Betty Crocker myself."

"But you know how to wiggle."

"I don't *wiggle!*"

"Well, whatever you call those moves. Look at your fingernails."

Abby took a hand off the chain to frown at her nails. "What about them? No polish and I keep 'em filed short."

Jack grinned. "But look at *how* you're looking at 'em. No man would arch his fingers back like that. If he did, he'd have his guy epaulets ripped off his shoulders. I rest my case. You're as girl as it gets." *And I like it,* was the message his crinkled gray eyes were sending her.

She felt her cheeks go pink under his unwavering gaze. But she didn't *need* to feel like this—didn't want to feel burdened with his awareness. The swing turned, their knees brushed, and a jolt of electricity shot up her thighs. "Whatever, Jack, but the point is, I'm—Sky and I—are leaving next week. I couldn't turn Kat around in seven days if I wanted to. Which I don't. She's a sweetheart just the way she is."

"She's a sweetheart who wants to be a navy SEAL instead of a ballerina. But before she joins the SEALs to kick butt, she'll need a bra. Should she be wearing one yet?"

"She's flat as a board!"

"Yep, but I'm asking what the culture demands. Will the other girls make fun of her in gym class this fall, if she doesn't have one of those what-d'you-call-'em, trainer bras, and if so, should it be white cotton or pink satin or what? Abby, you've gotta help me here! I'm drowning— my SEAL's going down for the third time, whether she knows it or not. Look, I'll double my offer.''

She couldn't help laughing. ''You haven't offered anything yet!''

''A*ha*, now we're talking. So…let's discuss this.'' Jack moved around behind her and caught the chains again. ''What would it take?'' He gave the swing a gentle push.

''We're *not* negotiating, here. I'm leaving next week,'' she insisted, glancing up and over her shoulder.

''If Whitey can work that fast. But even a week would be something.'' He pushed her again.

''Jack…'' He was just about irresistible, his smiling determination like a big wave, bumping her back toward a shore she was trying to escape.

Still, there was something tempting about being lifted off her feet, carried toward the beach in a tumbling rush. As a child she'd always loved the ocean, even when it had scared her. Abby pointed her toes as the swing carried her higher. She leaned back, holding on to the chains. ''Tell me this, Jack. Say Kat did need a role model—not that I'm agreeing she needs to change for a minute… But could I ask, where's her mother?'' There was the logical solution, if a solution was needed.

''Ah…'' He pushed her higher, once, twice. ''Maura's in San Francisco.''

''If Kat needs a role model, then couldn't you—''

''I couldn't.'' He pushed her higher. ''We couldn't. Maura doesn't want any part of her daughter, and hasn't from the start. She left us when Kat was eleven months old and she never looked back. Kat and I were just a whim, an oops, something she tried in the midst of the Divorce

Crazies. When the dust finally settled and her head cleared, there she was, looking at a couple of strangers, one of whom needed diapering.

"'Like a bargain a woman grabs at a close-out sale,' that's how Maura put it to me once. Then she gets the dress home, tries it on again and wonders what in heaven's name was she thinking when she bought it. Color's all wrong and a silly style and it's too tight in the hips.''

"She said that?''

"Sweet Maura had—has—a way with words. She's in advertising, a copywriter. She could sell a car, or flay a man, in one sentence.''

Even so, to walk away from her own child? Abby could no more have left Skyler at eleven months than she could've flown to the moon. "I see…'' she said slowly, although she didn't. "But have you asked her *lately* if she—''

"Nope, and I don't plan to. We're on our own, which means it's up to me to do right by my kid, which brings me back to you. A week's worth of girlie lessons, Abby. How much?''

"Stop pushing, okay?''

"Sure.'' He caught the chains as she swung down, took a few running steps backward, brought her gently to a halt.

"That's not what I meant.''

"Oh. Well, I'm not pushing—I'm pleading. Just name a price and I'll meet it.''

Still grasping the chains, he leaned directly over her, looking down so that she had to tip back her head to meet his gaze. Abby sighed. *Yeah, you're not pushing.* "Well, first, I don't agree that Kat needs anything. She'll discover boys in her own time. You don't need to push *her,* either. Second,'' she emphasized as he scowled and started to object, "don't you *dare* offer me money, when you saved Skyler's life."

"Don't exaggerate."

"I'm not and you know it. Plus you've helped us in dozens of ways this past week. I'm so deeply in your debt, I'll never get out, but still—*mmmph!*"

He'd dropped a big hand over her mouth. "Hush."

Gazing helplessly up at him, she was suddenly dizzy, the world a kaleidoscope of green leaves, blue sky, with Jack's face at the center, like the sun blazing down upon her. The heat of his fingers was hot and seductive as sunshine.

"You don't owe me a thing, Abby." His voice had dropped to a husky growl. "I was happy to help, glad to be of service. That's all."

"But—" she tried to say, her lips moving against rough, warm skin. She frowned and caught his wrist.

"No buts. You were doing me a favor, letting me play white knight. How often does a guy get to rescue somebody?" He allowed her to lift his hand away. "But now *I* need a favor. I need you to let me buy some lessons for my daughter."

The second his hand moved aside, Abby shot out of the swing. She crossed her arms hard over her middle and stood, giving him nothing but the back of her head.

"Abby?" he said after a minute. "What's wrong?"

Nothing. Everything! The warmth of his fingers on her face; the shape and strength of his wrist on her hand… A pulse strobing deep in her body. To hunger for a man's touch again—this was something she'd never dreamed would happen, at least not for years and years and years! "N-not a thing. I'm just…thinking." She stared down at the dust, clutching after her stampeding thoughts, and finally managed to say, "She doesn't need femininity lessons. And I couldn't possibly take your money."

He came around the swing and loomed large beside her. "Then how about this? Could you teach her to cook a few dishes this week? Take her shopping a time or two for clothes?"

"Of course I could. I'd be happy to."

"And if you won't take my money, then why don't I pay Whitey for your bus?"

Oh, he was good! She could just see him wheedling a jury. Cutting deals at the courtroom door. A lawyer who overpowered the opposition by charm or logic or guile— or sheer pigheaded refusal to take no for an answer. "You don't need to do that."

"All right, then look at it this way. We've known each other—what, four days? So maybe I've helped you out a tad, here and there, since you've been in town, though I'd call that a gross exaggeration. But if it makes you feel better, say you allow Kat to hang around with you for four days for free, then we're square. After that, I start paying Whitey."

"Do you ever *quit?*" She laughed, looking back at him.

"Sure…once I win."

She threw up her hands at the sky. "Okay, okay, *okay,* I give! You can pay for three days of girlie lessons, after four days for free. *Now* can we go look for my cat?"

CHAPTER ELEVEN

HALF A DAY'S WORTH of hunting and postering the town failed to find the varmint. "But don't worry," Jack tried to console Abby as they headed home, "somebody's bound to spot him."

She sat chewing on her knuckle as she stared intently into the yards of the houses they passed. "Oh, God, I hope so. Skyler blames me enough already. He'll never forgive me if we lose DC."

"Blames you for what?"

She said over her shoulder, so low he could barely hear, "What *doesn't* he blame me for? Divorcing his father. Dragging him west. The fact that Steven insisted I take full custody instead of half, at least for the next few years, since he'll have his hands full with Chelsea and three babies."

"Hardly seems fair."

"Yep, but there it is." She shrugged and turned forward and flashed him a brisk smile, visibly setting her sadness aside. "Anyway, I've been thinking. About Kat's cooking lessons and how to set them up—without being obvious about their real purpose."

"That's the problem, yes."

"Last night you were wondering how to punish her for the fight?"

He grimaced. "Right. I told her this morning that the

verdict was 'guilty,' but she could help Sky hang his posters before I passed sentence.''

"Excellent. Well, considering that she cost you several hours, driving out to the Jarrett ranch, what if you sentenced her to make up your lost time? By cooking all your suppers for the week.''

"Frozen pizza seven nights in a row? Kat wouldn't call that a punishment.''

"No, you stipulate real, made-from-scratch meals. And meantime, since I now have to pay for Skyler's new glasses—he's still broke from the last pair he lost—he gets the same sentence. He's costing me money, which sooner or later I'll have to replace by working. So he cooks for me.''

"The road to justice is sounding rougher and rougher. Can he cook?''

"A few dishes, but it's time he widened his repertoire. I'll do the menu planning, then they can help me shop. That is…if you've got time to drive us into Durango at some point this weekend?''

She finished her last sentence in a lurch and a breathless rush and Jack cocked his head, pretending to consider. She really hated to ask favors, didn't she? Made him wonder what kind of selfish rat her ex had been.

On the other hand, he'd lost half a day already. *I want to spend time with you, Abby, but my fantasy doesn't take place in a grocery store.* "I'd be happy to, but the problem is, I have to get this house I'm building skinned in and roofed before the snow flies, and weekends are prime building time.''

"Oh, Jack, I'm sorry! I never should've let you waste this—''

"You didn't and it wasn't wasted.'' This morning had been productive—and how. He'd finally realized, somewhere around the swing set, that Divorce Crazies or no, Abby and he were meant to be. *No ifs, buts or maybes about it.*

Not that he'd forgotten Kelton's Rule One and Rule Two—far from it! He hadn't the slightest wish to remarry and even if he had, the last woman he'd choose would be Abby, still trapped in the spin cycle of a painful divorce. *I may be crazed, but I'm not crazy.*

But if Jack refused to break his own commandments, still the second clause of Rule Two allowed for some judicious bending in extreme circumstances. Like this one: have a hot, short, sexy affair with her if you must. Be her Transition Man between her last cad and her next husband. Teach her how to smile again—then *Run for your life!*

And in this case, he wouldn't even have to run. Abby would be hitting the road as soon as her bus was drivable.

But in the meantime. *Oh, sweet Abby, in the meantime…*

But Abby wasn't ready to hear his plans yet. "So now I've got to get to work," he told her. On both fronts. "If I lent you my winter car, the Subaru, do you think you and the kids could handle the shopping? Your ankle's not bothering you too much?"

"No, it's much better, thanks, but I can't take your car."

"Why not? Just don't let Sky behind the wheel. Which reminds me, speaking of meting out justice, what did you do to him for wrecking your bus?"

"Nothing," Abby admitted. "We're on such shaky ground already, I thought—"

"Big mistake. Actions ought to have consequences, at least that's what my old man always said." He smiled to himself, remembering some of his and his older brother's escapades in their teen years, and the consequences they'd reaped.

"I suppose," Abby murmured, although she didn't sound convinced.

Jack opened his mouth to argue, then shut it again. He wanted to kiss her dizzy, not tell her how to parent. He swung the Jeep into her drive and spotted Kat and Sky slumped on the front steps. "And there's the posse." Looking glum and catless.

AFTER HE'D GIVEN his daughter her sentence—received with thunderous indignation and a pout that didn't do much for her prizefighter mug—Jack presented Abby with the keys to the Subaru, then drove off to the building site.

As always, he stopped the Jeep at the foot of the drive to gaze up the slope, picturing his completed work rising from its foundation. A passive solar house built to his brother's design—simple, roomy, full of character. It would have a nice deep porch on this side to overlook the valley, three bedrooms, one of which he'd use for his office, and a two-car garage. Absently, Jack patted the Jeep's wheel.

Basement with full headroom for his workshop. A story and a half in height, with the master bedroom above, where it would have a view of the mountains to the north that he'd insisted upon, no matter how Drew had protested that a sensible house ought to crouch below the ridge, sheltered from the winter winds.

Jack would rather install an extra six inches of insulation on the windward side and pay for triple-pane windows for his bedroom, whatever their cost, than live without that panorama. He meant to place his bed facing north, so the first thing he saw when he woke…

A vision of Abby intruded, all smiling and drowsy, rosy as the mountains with the sunrise touching their peaks... *Get a grip, Kelton! You've got a house to build.* He stepped on the gas.

JACK SPENT THE AFTERNOON in blissful preparation for Sunday, when he'd frame the first wall. This stage of construction was always exciting, as the actual outline of the structure started to rise, providing bones for his imagination to fill in. *Don't get too excited,* he warned himself. Today was the day to measure twice—then twice again—so that tomorrow he could cut once with speed and precision.

It was just as well that poor Kat wasn't here, helping him as she usually did on weekends. He welcomed her chatter when he didn't need to concentrate, but today, it was just him and his tape measure and his architectural plans—and that was perfect.

Absorbed in his task of marking the plate and cap for wall stud and window positions, Jack worked steadily till he realized he was squinting to make out his pencil lines. He glanced up and was startled to see the sun poised on the mountains to the west. He hurried to put his tools away before it set.

By the time he came through the garden gate, it was full dark. Heading for the back door of Abby's cottage, he paused when he noticed the small shape crouched on the front steps. "Abby?"

She didn't reply, but lifted a mug and sipped as she regarded him over its rim.

Something wrong here. "Where are the kids?"

"Making salad." Her voice held none of its usual warmth, no inflection at all.

She'd wrecked the car and didn't want to tell him? Or he was late for the meal he hoped she planned to feed him? Or... "How did the shopping go?"

"Oh-hh, just fine. And we met an old friend of yours at the market—Alec Fielding? He recognized Kat and stopped to introduce himself."

Uh-oh. "Did he." *You hound, Fielding.* Unable to see her face clearly in the gloom, Jack sat beside her.

She slid over a couple of feet and twisted around to bend her leg, clasping her shin as she leaned back against a porch post. The body language was clear. *Keep off.*

"So how's Alec?" he asked, carefully indifferent.

"Seemed to be doing well, but I was wondering…is there a…woman shortage in these parts?"

"Not so's I've noticed," Jack allowed, treading warily. Where was this going?

"I see." She drank again, eyes narrowed beyond the rising steam. "Then…by any chance did you tell him I'm…divorced?"

You're hamburger, Fielding! Dog food deluxe. "Um…" Jack scowled thoughtfully at the porch rafters overhead. "Can't remember. I s'pose it…might have come up—or maybe not. Why?"

She smacked her mug down on the deck and the liquid inside sloshed over. "*Because,* after we'd passed for the third time—right there in the frozen food aisle—he asked me out for a drink!

"What *is* it with men and divorcées? Do you all think we can't live a minute without you? I wasn't divorced *a week* before Steven's best friend, another pilot with a wife and two children, stopped over to see if I needed anything—and what he assumed I needed was my bones jumped! And my plumber, fat and balding and fifty. When the sink disposal jammed, I swear he thought I'd stopped it up on purpose, just to lure him in my door. Even my lawyer—my own lawyer—hit on me!"

"Grossly unprofessional," Jack agreed, though considering he'd met his own wife that way... "But maybe he meant it as a compliment?"

"Who, your friend?"

"No—your lawyer. The plumber. Those, er, other guys." And Fielding, too, of course. *Never should've let her shop alone, but who'd have thought...*

"I should be *complimented* that men think I'm easy? Available? Starving for sex?"

"Well, in your place they would be, so..."

"Well, newsflash! Men and women are different!" Abby snatched up her mug and bounced to her feet. "And if anybody else should happen to ask you, going on a date is the *last* thing on this woman's mind!" She stomped over to the door, opened it, then paused and glanced back. "You'd better come in and collect your vegetable lasagna. It's out of the oven, but it's too hot for Kat to carry."

"I thought we'd—" *Shut up, Kelton. Shut up.*

She shook her head. "I'm awfully tired tonight, I'm afraid, so I had the kids make two pans. And separate salads."

And that just about said it all. Driving home, he'd felt as if he were headed to a party. Now Saturday night looked flat as a blown-out tire. Just him and Kat at the supper table, and no doubt she'd want to watch her *G.I. Jane* video for dessert.

For his own after-dinner treat, maybe he'd call Fielding.

THIS PAST YEAR, Abby had taken up yoga, then Tai Chi, first as a way to shut out her pain and confusion, then more lately for the pure pleasure of the exercises.

She'd let her early morning routine lapse during the drive across country, but as of yesterday, Saturday, she'd started again.

Before Skyler rose she took this time for herself, using

the ancient, ritualized movements as a form of meditation, the path on which she sought her still center. A way to set all worries aside, all regrets of the past or plans for the future, simply to *be* in the present moment.

At least that was the theory.

Today she was having trouble focusing, Abby admitted as she stared out at her upside-down world. *It's not my time of the month, so why did I flip out like that last night?*

Hush, she told herself, then repeated her mantra. *All will be well.* At least it would someday; she had to believe that.

Don't think about someday, think about now. This green, dew-spangled world. Green, everywhere she looked; she'd purposely faced away from her house and from Jack's house, so that she gazed west across her yard. *Grass getting rather high.* Or so it appeared from this angle.

Not her problem. In a week she'd be gone and somebody else could cut it. "Hush." She spoke out loud this time, sternly.

But her thoughts rambled on, flowing out from her still center to embrace the world, instead of spiraling inward as they ought. Alec Fielding. He'd been perfectly polite in his smiling invitation—and she'd wanted to smack him with the bag of frozen shrimp she'd just pulled from the cooler. *Either he knows I'm divorced, which means somebody—Jack Somebody—told him. Or he thought I was married, since he met Sky, but he just didn't care.*

No, Fielding had been too sure of himself, too sure she was datable, which meant—

"Hush!"

So maybe Jack had gossiped about her, so what? It might have been—no, doubtless *had* been—entirely innocent, something along the lines of "Guess who moved in next to me? A woman with a kid Kat's age."

Then Fielding could have said, "Oh, where's her husband?"

So how could she blame Jack if he then said—

"Oh, be quiet!" she snapped, and brought first one leg down, then the other. Sitting in a kneeling position, she faced Jack's house, though a tree's low-hanging branches blocked the view.

Or most of the view. Her gaze zeroed in on a window up on the second floor, as something moved beyond its glass. Or maybe a bird had flown by and been reflected there for a second? Because now the glazed rectangle was a motionless mirror to leaves and sky.

Abby planted her palms by her thighs, lifted her weight off her legs and pushed off into a backward somersault— her own embellishment to the exercises, included simply for the childish joyfulness of the move—then ended as she'd started, on her knees. Planting her palms again, she extended her legs behind her and arched her spine into the sun stretch. Held it, staring upward.

So if it's not fair to blame Jack for speaking to Fielding, why'd it bother me so much?

Or perhaps more to the point, why did Fielding's flirtation bother her, when Jack's, these past few days, had…made her feel good?

Her muscles were warming. This move stretched her from throat to thigh. A hot current of awareness rippled out from her pelvic muscles, swirled up into her stomach, eddied around her tightened hips…a delicious sensation stirring, awakening…

Fielding was a wake-up call, that was why he'd bothered her. He'd made her realize on some subconscious level that she felt…taken. As if he sought to intrude on a relationship she valued.

These past few days since the bus disaster, she'd been

so needy, and Jack had made himself so easy to be with, so easy to lean on. She'd let herself be lulled into forgetting her resolutions. Into almost pretending that he and she were—

No, I didn't!

Well, yes, to be honest, she had felt a little yearning.

But no, she'd never thought, never dreamed, never wished that they were a couple—nothing like that! There'd simply been a warm and comforting feeling of...of comradeship, that was it. Two single parents coping with the ups and downs of preteen children, nothing more than that.

Still, Fielding was a good and timely reminder that she'd been backsliding into old bad habits, starting to think like one half of a pair again. For a day or two she'd almost forgotten: she was on her own now.

And so must stand alone.

Depending on a man had been disastrous last time. It wasn't a mistake she intended to repeat.

With that reaffirmation, Abby was able to focus again on her routine, till halfway through the Tai Chi form called Part the Wild Horse's Mane, Whitey's truck came rolling into the backyard. "Drat!" she muttered as he grinned broadly and waved. Snatching up her exercise blanket, she whipped it around her skimpy nylon shorts, called, "Morning!" and retreated into the house.

After she'd showered, dressed, nudged Skyler awake, Abby fixed a couple of mugs of coffee and returned to the yard to give her mechanic a proper welcome.

But he already had company. Elbow to elbow with the old man, Jack leaned into the engine compartment, nodding judiciously while Whitey expounded on this part or that. Surly as a moulting buzzard, Chang sat on Whitey's left boot, his muzzle wrinkled in a toothless snarl as he studied Jack's nearest ankle.

"Gentlemen." Abby handed each of them a mug, then gestured at her bus. "Any luck with parts yesterday?"

Whitey had found a radiator that would do, apparently, and a new muffler that with some creative rerouting of exhaust pipes could replace the old, but as for the transmission... "Nothing useful at the three yards I tried. But Johnnie Tso seems t'recall his cousin told him there's a bus like yours, a wrecker, over past Flagstaff. He's gotta drive his grandma there to help with his niece's comin' young 'un next week, and he said he'd try to track it down. See if the transmission'd fit, and if nobody else has got to it first."

"Oh," Abby said blankly, uncertain if this was good news or not. But a week's delay, before they even knew if there was a transmission? "There's no way to, um, expedite finding out?"

Not unless she knew some way to expedite when Johnnie's niece was going to drop her baby, there wasn't, Whitey assured her with patient good humor. "Meantime, me and Chang are gonna whip out this hunk of rust." He patted the leaky radiator. "Then we'll look at your pipes."

"Er...great," she said, ignoring Jack's wide grin past Whitey's shoulder. "If there's anything you need..."

"I'll holler," he assured her. "But a job like this's mainly elbow grease and cussin'."

"And don't forget prayer," Abby muttered as she left Whitey to it.

"Never hurts," Jack agreed, sauntering along beside her.

He handed her his empty mug as she turned to face him at the kitchen stairs. If she was going to stand alone, one way to do so was to prevent him from wandering in and out of her cottage four times a day at his slightest whim. "So I suppose you're building today?" she asked briskly.

Jack had cocked his head and was staring at her chest. She crossed her arms.

"Yes," he agreed—and reached out to finger the short sleeve of her T-shirt. "I'd forgotten this."

"This" was the T-shirt she'd been wearing the day they'd met. She'd done a load of hand-washing yesterday. Feeling the need to reassert her independence this morning, she'd chosen this one. "Yes, it was a graduation present," she said coolly. "A friend of mine gave it to me the day I went to court for my divorce."

"Ah." He cocked his head the other way. "Always wondered what kind of fish that's supposed to be."

She glanced down at herself and shrugged. "Any fish. Figurative fishes."

"I always thought the *real* question was, not does a fish need a bicycle, but does he *enjoy* it once he's got his hands—his fins—on one? How do you keep him down on the fish farm, after he's popped his first wheelie?"

She'd have teased back if the topic of debate hadn't been plastered to her chest. And folding her arms had only made matters worse. "Beats me." She jammed her hands into the pockets of her shorts. "Well, I suppose I'll see you lat—"

He tore his eyes away from her fish. "Actually, I came over to ask a favor."

"Oh?" Far be it from her to point out that she was already working off half a week of his favors.

"Could I borrow Sky for most of the day? I'm framing my first wall, and Kat and I could use another set of hands."

"Take him. I'd love some time alone." She was dying to pick up her sketchbook. Whitey and Chang presented a wealth of comic possibilities and she'd had another idea she wanted to explore.

"Great. I'll send Kat to fetch him in, say, half an hour."
Jack started to swing away, then turned back. "About tonight, were you planning a cooking lesson or anything?"

"Only the lesson that leftovers are a woman's best
friend. If you could possibly deliver her half an hour before
you want to eat?"

"Will do." He opened his mouth, then shut it again to
give her a quizzical smile. "Later, Abby."

He'd been about to propose something about their eating
together tonight and then he'd changed his mind. *Message
received,* she told herself bleakly. Jack Kelton was hardly
stupid.

Funny how she wanted to take that message back.

Instead she clenched her fists in her pockets and chanted
inwardly, *I'm strong, I'm whole. I don't need a man in my
life.*

Or any more sorrow, thank you very much.

Even so, as an artist and a woman, she couldn't help
but admire the view as he strode purposefully away. Body
by Michelangelo on one of his best days—long of leg, with
broad, brawny shoulders that made her palms itch.

Pity she wasn't in the market.

CHAPTER TWELVE

"YOU'RE *SURE* he's not your cat?" demanded the older of the two cat rustlers.

"Joey, I want you to listen to me ve-ery carefully," Abby said as she closed the lid of a box containing a highly indignant black-and-white tomcat. "The cat I want is white, all white—no other color on him. And he's *very* big. Even bigger than this guy, okay? Now you've got to take this kitty back *precisely* where you found him. And don't bring me *any* more cats unless they're all white."

This was Joey and Al Cooperman's third presentation of the morning. The last one had been orange and white, and female.

"Okay." Eight-year-old Joey wasn't one to hold a grudge. He had the dreamy look of someone already calculating where to find his next candidate.

"Do we get another ice-cream cone?" his younger, more practical brother wanted to know.

Seeing their disappointment after their first cat hadn't won her hundred-dollar reward, Abby had given them a compensation prize—money for ice cream at Hansen's. Big mistake. "No more ice cream till you bring me an all-white cat," she said sternly. "And if you bring me another cat that isn't white, Al, you have to buy *me* an ice-cream cone!"

"That's tellin' 'em," Whitey chuckled as the dejected entrepreneurs trudged down the drive.

''But are they listening? And where are they finding their cats? I haven't seen many strays around town.''

''Well, that last one there generally lives 'cross the street from my sister Emma. Sits like a broody hen up on the Hendricks's porch rail all day.''

''Great! I'm inciting a couple of cat-nappers. At this rate I'm going to be popular around town.''

''Leastways, pretty well known,'' Whitey agreed, returning to his task of stringing extension cord from the house to the bus.

The blissful Sunday morning of artistic endeavor that Abby had envisioned had been fractured roughly every half hour so far. She'd received two phone calls from perfect strangers—both of them elderly ladies by their voices—who'd been anxious to know if she'd found her kitty yet, and then welcomed her to Trueheart. Another caller had offered Abby her choice of a newborn litter of kittens he'd found in his barn if her own cat didn't turn up.

Still another wanted to know if the famous DC-3 had one black ear and a black spot on his chest? But thanks to the Cooperman brothers, Abby could reject that cat with assurance; she'd seen him already.

When she wasn't fielding phone calls, Abby had spent most of the morning viewing the latest offering of the Relentless Duo, who'd confided that they meant to buy a twenty-two rifle with the hundred-dollar reward.

Well, if wishes were kitties, she'd have DC by nightfall and the Coopermans would be gunslingers.

Between interruptions she'd sat in the backyard, sketching Whitey and Chang as they went about their business. And really she shouldn't complain; working in snatches, she hadn't had a chance to dawdle over her drawings or overwork them. They reminded her of her father's style, fluid lines abstracting the very essence of a shape or a movement or the emotional relationship between man and dog. Several were good enough to serve as studies for more finished works.

Tomorrow she'd find the box that held her watercolors and oil pastels and she'd drag her easel out of the bus. Perhaps she should also set up her drawing table? Because if Whitey didn't locate a transmission before next Saturday, they were stuck here for the week after that, he'd explained. Replacing that part was apparently no easy job, and for good or ill, Whitey was a pains-taker.

Abby gnawed on her lip. *Which means another week's rent for Maudie Harris. I'd better go see her.*

When the phone rang again, she lifted it to her ear with more resignation than hope. "Hello?"

"Is this the mother of DC-3, world famous in Trueheart?" inquired a female voice on a note of wry humor.

"The very same."

"Well, this is Michelle of Michelle's Place. I may have seen your cat."

"So WHAT ABOUT this one?" Jack lifted another ten-foot stud off the pile, sighted along its edge, then passed it to Skyler.

"Um…" The boy propped one end on the ground and squinted down its length exactly as Jack had demonstrated. "It's got a hook at that end?"

"Yup. You've got a good eye."

"Yeah, right, all four of 'em," Sky muttered under his breath.

"It's not how far you see, I always figured, but what you see along the way," Jack observed, keeping the sermon casual.

So the kid's glasses bothered him; Jack wasn't surprised.

At Sky's age, boys were jostling for their place in the pecking order. Any sign of weakness could be brutally exploited. "So we'll cut that one for cripple studs." He set the crooked stud aside. "While I do that, choose me another ten. And they've gotta be perfect. We'll be using 'em to frame windows and doors."

The boy stood frozen, panic written plain on his face.

But how else would a kid learn to make his own decisions if you didn't entrust him with real ones? Jack busied himself setting the proper measurement on his radial arm saw, so that he could cut the dozens of shorter studs he'd need to support the windowsills. When he looked again, Sky had chosen two studs and was scowling anxiously down the length of a third.

He discarded it as Jack called, "Where's Kat?"

"She saw a hawk." Sky nodded over the ridge, then stooped for another two-by-six.

That was his Kat. Jack grinned. Thanks to his teaching, she was as handy with tools as a ten-year-old could be, but her attention span for mechanical phenomena was about as long as she was tall. On the other hand, anything that grew or flew or crawled held her like a magnet. *Might make a biologist or a botanist someday, but she won't be an engineer or a physicist,* Jack suspected. Which was fine by him. He positioned the stud on the table, switched on the saw, and pulled the whirling blade toward him. The saw's hum turned to a wood-chewing snarl, then back to a contented purr as the board parted. Sawdust rose and the aroma of resin sweetened the air.

By the time he'd cut all the cripples and double-checked Sky's choices—every one of them satisfactory—Kat had returned.

She scrambled up onto the foundation floor and found

her discarded hammer. "Dad, where could I get a net? A big net."

He positioned his first nail for the next stud in the frame before he paused to consider. "For?" Last year she'd been into bug collecting; he'd hoped they were done with dried beetles.

"To trap a hawk—a falcon. I wanna train him to ride on my shoulder."

He managed to keep a solemn face. "That would be something." *My daughter the falconer.* He could picture Abby's smile when he told her. *"Maybe the army-navy store in Durango?"*

"Yeah, mosquito netting!" Sky chimed in.

They passed the next hour as they framed the wall tossing off ideas and designs for a falcon trap. Bait would be road-killed jackrabbits, of course, since Kat couldn't imagine using a live bunny. Jack didn't spoil her fantasy by asking what she planned to feed her hawk on days when the bunnies dodged the cars; he trusted the birds to stay out of her net. Meantime, it made a pleasant daydream.

With the trap design finalized, next came the matter of perches, cages and falcon attire. Jack had an old pair of leather gloves, one of which Kat could adapt as a hood for the raptor, though he specified that she catch her bird before she sacrificed his glove. He cut another batch of cripples, the saw drowning out all conversation—and when he looked again, only Sky remained, still hammering away. *Good kid,* he silently congratulated Abby. A man who could stick to his purpose would go far.

He stopped to inspect the window studs that Sky had positioned and nailed. "Very good." The kid placed his fastenings precisely as instructed and he could hammer a nail without bending it. "Ready to try a full-length stud?"

Sky glowed with pleasure and Jack had to smile. He

was a tryer, all right. Leaving him to the more challenging task, he strolled to the cooler in the Jeep for a couple of sodas, then returned to inspect the results. Sky stood, nervously clutching his hammer. "That'll do," Jack assured him. "Want a job?"

"Do you mean it?"

He'd meant it only as a compliment, but Jack cocked his head at the boy's tone. "Short of cash?"

Sky had his mother's clear, give-away complexion and now it reddened. "Yeah. I've gotta pay for my glasses." He touched the tape that joined the two broken halves across his battered nose.

Jack nodded. "And then there's always the bus." Consequences, as his dad would have said. *Let's see what you're made of, kid.*

"The bus?"

"It's going to cost over a thousand dollars to have it repaired. You were sitting at the wheel. I expect you released the emergency brake?" That had been Whitey's guess.

"I, uh...I might of..." Sky studied the plywood at his feet. "But it was an accident."

"Which somebody's got to pay for," Jack noted, voice utterly neutral. *No excuses, kid. Are you a buck-stopper? Or do you duck and run?*

"Oh..." Sky's shoulders sagged under the concept. "Yeah. I s'pose..." He gulped, then met Jack's eyes squarely. "You'd...you'd really hire me?"

"Five bucks an hour, every weekend while you're here." He was worth that much, and even if he hadn't been, responsibility was always worth subsidizing.

The idea was starting to take root. A timid smile came and went. "Do you pay Kat?"

"Nope. This'll be her home when we're done, so Kat

works for free.'' Before they'd turned eighteen, Jack and his brother had helped their contractor father build three family houses, a more useful education than either had acquired at school. Nice to be able to pass the skill on. ''So what do you say, Sky? Deal?'' Jack held out his hand.

''I'M SO SORRY I didn't nab him,'' Michelle apologized after Abby had returned from inspecting the garbage cans that stood behind the kitchen at Michelle's Place. ''But my waiter called in sick this morning. I was cooking and serving brunch for six tables when I looked out the window and saw him—at least, saw his hind end sticking out of a can. At the rate he seemed to be chowing down, I assumed he'd stay put till I had a moment.'' The tall, attractive blonde had set two mugs of coffee on a table in Abby's absence, plus a plate with thin golden cookies. ''Sit down and let's figure this out. He's bound to come back. Four-legged or two, I never met a guy who didn't like a free meal.''

''You didn't see which way he went?'' Abby asked, trying to hide her disappointment. *So close.*

''Afraid not. I had fourteen eggs sunny-side up on the grill and by the time I'd plated them…'' Michelle brushed a honey-colored wisp of hair off her brow and shrugged.

''And you're not even sure he was all white?''

''No-o. But by the size of that tail, he was a bruiser. And he's definitely a new boy in town. I have a dainty gray that stops by for the spoiled milk every evening, and a marmalade tom with shredded ears and an attitude, but nobody with a white rear end.''

Abby heaved a sigh. ''Then it was probably DC.'' She managed a smile. ''Only sighting we've had so far, so I can't tell you how grateful I am. It's just…''

''That you need him back,'' Michelle agreed. ''I hear he's your son's?''

''The first pet Sky's ever owned. He's very attached to him.''

''Then we'll just have to find him.'' Michelle lifted the plate and waggled it in front of her. ''Now fortify yourself with some serious sugar and let's think. Is there any particular time of day he eats?''

A few minutes of munching and strategizing suggested that Abby or Sky should stake out the restaurant garbage cans at dusk and dawn, when DC was usually most active. Michelle and her staff would keep an eye out as best they could in the hours between. ''And if all else fails, we'll borrow Doc Kerner's Havahart trap in a day or two,'' Michelle said, ''and set it out by the cans. We'll find the beast. Hey, excuse me a minute.''

She took coffee to two grizzled old cowhands who had settled across the room, then stood, laughing at the yarn one of the men was spinning for her at wistful length.

Abby took another delectable bite of cookie and glanced around the room. The space was simple, sunny, assured as its proprietor. Subtly sophisticated. All choices had been made by someone with a sense of style, from the extra-heavy stainless flatware and the simple honey-colored ceramics, to the blue-checked cloth napkins on the rugged old tables of mellow pine. The walls were rough plaster, glazed and ragged in two tones of cream and ochre, then hung with a wonderful display of photographs—blowups of cowboys in action. The flower boxes outside the windows blazed with red geraniums. This place might once have been a small-town café, but clearly it had evolved; the aura was more French bistro than fern bar, but it was Bistro West.

"Kaley tells me you're living next door to Jack Kelton," ventured Michelle as she swooped back into her seat.

Kaley? Oh, yes—Whitey's boss, the one with twins. "That's right."

"Gotta be exciting. Or at least scenic," Michelle teased gently.

"You mean—"

"Who else but Harrison Ford's younger, sexier brother? Don't tell me you don't think he's gorgeous."

"I guess so," Abby admitted. "But I'm recently divorced, so I'm not in the market. Not even window-shopping."

"But surely that's the beauty of the situation? Because neither is Jack. A divorced divorce lawyer? We call him the King of Can't Commit."

"That bad?" Abby said mildly.

"A girlfriend down in Durango tells me he's dated every available woman in the city. But let one of 'em try to stake a claim and he's gone yesterday—just watch that bachelor bolt."

Refusing to commit was the flip side to Jack's flirtatiousness, Abby supposed. How else to explain why such a good-looking guy could have stayed unmarried for the past ten years? Anyway, Jack Kelton's marital status had nothing to do with her. So why this twinge of…melancholy?

"You've never dated him yourself?" she asked. Maybe the blonde was subtly staking a claim of her own. Hoping to discourage the competition.

But Michelle's grin was wide and unabashed. "Sure, we dated once or twice when he first came to town, and I'm here to attest that he kisses like a girls' boarding school dream. But we didn't click. I've got no patience for that type. I worked as chef on a charter boat in the Med for several years. And once you've lost your heart to a professional yacht skipper or three..."

If there was the tiniest trace of bitterness in the woman's voice, it was aimed backward in time, not at her present listener. "You haven't seen love-'em-and-leave-'em in action till you've met the over-the-blue-horizon boys. They think serious is a navigable star, not a stage in a relationship."

Gradually, Michelle's gray eyes returned to the present. "On the other hand...if you're in the mood to *play,* Jack's perfect."

"I'm not in the mood." And even if she had been, she wasn't a "player" when it came to love. "Besides which, I'm just passing through. As soon as Whitey fixes my bus..."

"Sure. In the meantime, Abby, while I've got you here, I need an opinion. And as you're an artist—"

"I'm not. Not really." Till she sold her work, she was merely a wannabe.

"Could've fooled me. I'm planning to frame your lost cat poster, once it's done its job." Michelle nodded at the portrait of DC pinned up behind her cash register. "But really, tell me. What do you think of these cookies?"

"Seriously dangerous," Abby reported truthfully.

"Yeah, but aren't they sort of...plain?"

"Elegantly understated."

"In other words, blah. I'm thinking of starting a bakery on the side, and all my customers keep whining for these cookies. But I can't help feeling they need...something."

"Make 'em taste any better and they'll be reclassified as a controlled substance, available only with a prescription."

Michelle shook her head. "Steak without sizzle. They need sizzle."

"Sprinkles?"

The blonde made a face.

"But maybe that's it," Abby said slowly. "If they couldn't taste better, maybe what they lack is a visual punch?"

"Such as?"

"Let me think about it." Ideas began their seductive dance at the back of her brain. Some sort of surface pattern, or cut them in a fancy shape, or possibly... Abby looked up at the photos on the walls—and smiled.

"ABBY?" Kat stood at the back door, hands cupped to the screen as she peered through it. "I've come to fix supper."

"Oh..." Abby put down her pencil as Kat bounced into the room. "Is it that time already? Where're the guys?"

"Dad dropped me off and went back to finish up. Sky's helping him. What're you drawing?"

"Ideas for stencils. I'm going to paint the kitchen, then I'll stencil a pattern around the top of the walls for decoration."

On her way back from Michelle's Place, Abby had stopped in to visit Maudie Harris. Somehow she'd persuaded her elderly landlady that her cottage needed extensive refurbishing, which it certainly did. And that if Abby could barter a repainted kitchen for a second week's worth of rent, Maudie would be thrilled with the results.

More to the point, Abby had promised that other potential tenants would be charmed. Maudie had confessed that she'd been losing rentals these past few years. Bands of college kids on ski vacation didn't mind the dreary decor, but they tended to party hard and beat up the place, which then meant the cottage didn't appeal to the fussier, higher-paying end of the market.

"I like that one." Kat touched a design of a stylized

horse and cowboy chasing a cow. A whirling lariat provided the looping connection between the repeats of one rider and the next.

"How about this one?" Abby turned the page to three leaping prong-horned antelopes, like the herds she'd seen driving up from Durango.

"Oh, yeah!" Kat traced the pattern with a fingertip. "Could you show me how to do this? I saw a hawk flying today…"

"Absolutely. Or a hawk design might be simple enough to do as a potato print." It would be a pleasure to show her how. Sky was wonderfully sensitive for a boy, but he wasn't especially artistic; often Abby wished she had someone to share her joy in the visual world. She stood and closed her sketchbook. "But now let's get your leftover lasagna in the oven."

It crossed her mind to suggest that the two families eat as one tonight. She'd love to hear how their day had gone, and she had the best scoop of all—DC's sighting. But after Michelle's comments…*the King of Can't Commit?* No matter how innocent her motives, no matter how lonely she was, she really shouldn't give in to the temptation to socialize.

Because somehow she was vulnerable to Jack's flirtations, however lightly he meant them.

All the more reason to ration their time together.

BUT HER RESOLUTION hadn't taken Jack's appetite into account.

"He ate all that?" Abby frowned at the pan of lasagna, which contained a woeful three-by-five-inch serving. "That was supposed to last you guys two nights, kiddo." At least, such a pan made two meals for her and Sky.

"He said it tasted so good." Kat was both proud and dismayed.

"Well…" So much for avoidance. It was too late in the day to cook something new. "Sky and I didn't finish half our pan last night, so we could combine what we've got, then maybe add some garlic bread. And we could boost the salad with chick peas." She'd promised to teach Kat how to cook, after all, and the highest kitchen skill was how to improvise in a crisis. Abby switched into high gear. "Okay, Kat, oven at three-fifty and in this goes—covered. Then peel me, say, eight big cloves of garlic. I'll go get our pan."

So much for good intentions; tonight the Lakes and the Keltons were dining *en famille*.

CHAPTER THIRTEEN

ONCE KAT HAD BEEN GIVEN her tasks of setting the table and augmenting the salad, Abby told her she'd be back in twenty minutes, that she had a short errand to run. Borrowing Jack's Subaru, she raced down to Michelle's Place to scout the parking lot and the fenced-in area behind the kitchen, but to no avail. Perhaps DC had come earlier to dine?

Or maybe he's moved on, she worried, driving back to the house. Maybe he was just passing through on his way to New Jersey.

Or maybe the white rear end that Michelle had seen in her garbage can was connected to a piebald cat or a long-tailed skunk.

Or maybe we'll find him later. Soon. Still, Abby was reconsidering her impulse to spill the joyful news. What if she raised Skyler's hopes, then couldn't deliver? She should know; sometimes hope hurt more than accepting the blow.

Her somber mood lasted only as far as Jack's kitchen door.

"Praise the Lord, reinforcements at last!" With a grin, he caught her arm to pull her into noise and warmth and the mouthwatering aroma of baking lasagna. "I've been holding off the barbarians—but only just."

"Let's eat!" cried Kat, pulling out a chair.

THE MEAL WAS AS LIVELY as the previous one they'd shared. Kelton's construction crew was triumphant; they'd built, then raised, the first wall of the house. Skyler's face glowed as he explained in detail how they'd lifted the heavy frame with the help of jacks plus a gin stick and a contraption called a come-along. Kat chimed in with a description of the wonderful views one could now see, peering through the framed spaces that would someday hold windows overlooking the town.

"And Mr. Kelton even let me change a window when I figured out there'd be a better view if we moved it all the way over to one corner," Sky confided.

"It was a great idea," Jack affirmed, sipping his wine. "Now you can sit in the breakfast nook on the east side of the house and see a good chunk of the sunset."

Thank you, she told him silently, holding his gaze. Her ex-husband loved his son, but Steve had never gone out of his way to make Skyler feel important or accomplished. He had a boisterous, challenging approach—Mr. Top Gun himself—that might have been perfect for a less sensitive boy, but for Sky… Sometimes she felt that Steve hurt Sky's confidence or his feelings without ever intending to. *So thank you, Jack.* Who cared if he was the worst flirt in Durango, as long as he was kind to her child?

Jack's heavy brows lifted a quarter inch in wry acknowledgment and his gray eyes sparkled. *Aw, shucks, it was nothing, ma'am,* was the private message he seemed to be sending her across the table.

Abby's smile deepened. Whether he was the King of Can't Commit or not, he had…generosity. One of the qualities she most admired in a person of either sex.

"And I saw a hawk!" Kat announced, tired of all the building talk. "I'm going to catch it, Abby, and train it to come when I whistle."

"Are you?" Abby reached over to dab a smear of lasagna off the falconer's cheek with her napkin. "I can see you with a hawk riding your shoulder. Like a desert princess." In fact, she *could* see it. What a portrait that would make! Her eyes shifted to Jack's face, filled with a parent's rueful pride. *And that's the thank-you gift I could give you when I go, a portrait of Kat.* Abruptly her own mood swerved into melancholy.

Jack lowered his head as he studied her. "And how was your day?"

She rallied and said, "I've met every last cat in Trueheart, thanks to the Cooperman brothers. And I went off on an errand…" She'd decided not to speak of DC, at least not to the kids. "But when I returned, I found that Whitey had spent more time rigging up my washing machine so I could use it than he had working on the bus's radiator. We may not be able to escape this town any time soon, but when we do, by gosh, we'll do it in clean clothes!"

Jack failed to see the humor in that observation. "Yeah…" He stood abruptly. "Who besides me needs more of this astounding garlic bread?"

ON MONDAY MORNING, Jack encountered Fielding in the parking lot behind their building. "I met your neighbor at the supermarket," Alec announced, rising out of his '62 Porsche coupe. "*Sha—zam!* Why don't I ever get neighbors like that?"

"I hear you also asked her out." Jack scowled at the door of his Jeep, where Abby had dinged the paint the night they met. He needed to touch that up.

"Oh-ho, she told you?"

"Yup, and now I'm telling *you*—back off." His tone

was mild, but he underlined the message with an unblinking stare. "She's taken."

Fielding crossed his arms—a not so subtle reminder that he hit the weight machines at the gym three times a week. But he wasn't quite crass enough to flex as he smirked. "She is? I must have missed the brand, pardner. Just where on that filly is it located—flank, rump or—"

"I'm serious, Alec."

"Serious with a capital *S*?"

Jack didn't flinch, not outwardly. "Don't be ridiculous. But all the same…"

Fielding's grin only widened. "Does Abby know she's taken—temporarily, so to speak?"

"She will. So—"

"Relax, friend." Alec nodded toward the entrance. "I asked the fair Abby out from the goodness of my heart. To help you clarify your feelings."

"The only clear thing around here is an aroma of bullshit," Jack growled, matching him stride for sauntering stride. "Save it for the jury. But keep in mind, I saw her first."

Fielding opened the door and waved him through. "If seeing guaranteed scoring, we'd all be contented men. But the lady struck me as a trifle…prickly. Maybe you're jumping the gun?"

Timing was everything, Jack had to admit.

After she'd filed for her first divorce, Maura had gone for anything in pants. *Best way to drive that rat from my mind,* she'd told him with a wicked smile the first time she unzipped him, there in his office.

In the years since Maura, he'd noticed that most of the divorced women whose cases he handled—at least those in their twenties, thirties and forties—sooner or later seemed to go through that lusty stage of the Divorce Cra-

zies. A feminine declaration of independence. An irrevo-
cable sundering of the marital bond. Even the man-haters
donned their high heels and went hunting.

Could he have been unlucky enough to miss Abby's
declaration? Maybe she'd already stormed through that
stage—then out the far side—before she'd headed west?

No, Jack was almost certain not. One look in her big
green eyes, and you could see: Abby was still smarting
from her breakup. Taking it too much to heart.

"Nope, I'm not jumping the gun." He meant to make
it happen. It was high time Abby learned to laugh again—
and who better to remind her how?

"Care to bet on that?" Alec inquired. "Double the Reuben you already owe me or nothing."

To refuse the bet would be to admit his fear, to himself
and to Fielding, that Abby might not come easily into his
arms—or at all. Unthinkable. "Taken and I'll raise you—
a Reuben every week for a year," Jack countered. "With
chips."

ABBY DIDN'T FIND DC-3 Monday or Tuesday.

Wednesday, Michelle gave Doc Kerner his breakfast for
free in exchange for his setting the Havahart trap out back
by the garbage cans. At dusk its door snapped shut on a
spitting-mad orange tomcat.

Looking at his war-torn ears, Abby could guess why DC
hadn't returned to the café. Skyler's pet was about as tough
as a day-old marshmallow. No way would he battle this
furry thug for garbage rights.

But what other hope did she have? No one else had
reported a sighting of the white cat all week. Abby reset
the trap.

And found it empty Thursday at dawn.

Heavy of heart, she drove back to the cottage and

launched herself into her yoga routine. *What to do, what to do, what to do?* was her mantra as she stood on her head, gazing out across the growing lawn. Since the weekend, Sky had been asking after his pet house-to-house across Trueheart, which had to be a terrible ordeal; he was almost as shy, meeting strangers, as she was. With his hopes fading, he grew bluer and sulkier by the day, despite Kat's unflagging attempts to cheer him.

Abby couldn't bear it. He'd just been starting to regain his smile when DC vanished. Last night as she tucked him in, he'd muttered tearfully that he'd have never lost DC if they'd stayed in New Jersey. *In other words, if I hadn't divorced Steve…*

The grass blurred and wavered as if she viewed it through a rainy window. Abby swallowed the lump in her throat. *Too soon to offer him a new pet, I suppose.* Sky had the gift—or maybe the curse—of fidelity, as she had. He'd have to live with an empty and aching heart for a while, before he'd consent to let a new pet inside. Because a new cat would only seem like a trespasser until he'd gotten over the old. *Oh, DC, come home, you big white doofus!*

Her head was aching as much as her heart. She needed to wipe her eyes. She brought down one leg, the second, then sat up in kneeling position, dizzy from the reversal.

To find herself facing a long, masculine pair of legs clad in khaki—Jack's legs. That was all she needed, to be found standing on her head, crying!

"Yes?" she growled—and looked higher.

He held an armload of dirty white, owl-eyed cat—DC! "I believe this is yours?" He grinned.

"Oh!" She sprang to her feet. "Where did you—oh, *Jack!* Oh, *bless you!*" Pressing a hand to the cat's broad

back, she stood on tiptoe and leaned over him to kiss Jack's cheek. "You miraculous, *wonderful*—"

In a heartbeat, he turned his head—and caught her kiss full on the lips. She sucked in a startled breath...and tasted coffee and man. Time stopped in a moment of heat and utter astonishment.

"Abby!" he murmured fiercely against her, bringing one hand to her nape, holding her there on tiptoe.

Her lips moved, framing a mute rejection. She shook her head half an inch in stunned denial. But his mouth answered hers and somehow the movement turned to a slow waltz...liquid, enticing... Her lashes fluttered and drifted shut, the better to taste him.

The tips of their tongues touched—and her heart slammed back into motion. *What on earth am I doing?*

Squashed between them, DC growled and lashed his tail.

Oh, yes—DC... Abby set her shock aside, for later. Planted one hand on Jack's hard chest and threw back her head to break free. "W-where did you find him—Michelle's?" Borrowing the Subaru so many times this week, she'd had to tell him her reason, though she'd kept Sky and Kat in the dark.

"Yup." His hand moved restlessly down her spine to the back of her waist. Beneath her splayed fingers, his heart was hammering. "I figured since you weren't having any luck in the dawn-to-dusk watch, I'd try the night hours..." His voice was husky, dreamy, half an octave lower than usual. "About 3:00 a.m., darned if he didn't come strolling across the parking lot, smug as you please. Hopped up onto a garbage can as if he owned it."

The sound of the screen door creaking startled them both.

Abby pushed off and retreated a step, then turned. On the back stoop, Sky stood frozen, his mouth agape.

His jaw snapped shut; his eyes narrowed dangerously behind his thick lenses. His gaze moved from her pinkening face—to the cat in Jack's arms. "Oh... Oh, *DC!*" He leaped every stair to hit the ground running. Gathering the cat into a hug, he buried his face in white fur. "You luggums, spaceshot, good-for-nothing furball! Where've you *been?*"

He looked up, laughing and weeping. "W-where'd you find him, Mr. Kelton?"

While Jack explained, Abby caught a movement at the corner of her eye. Glancing aside, she spotted Kat, kneeling in the gap of the fence that was her own special passage between the yards. The girl gripped a picket on either side—and smiled.

And just how long have you been lurking? Abby wondered, warily returning her mischievous grin. Had both of their children witnessed that kiss?

"WHATCHA DOING?" Kat asked later that morning, finding Abby at her drawing table in the living room.

"Making a thank-you poster for everybody in Trueheart who helped look for DC." Abby had already completed her brushwork rendition of Sky, face radiant as he hugged his cat. She'd made dozens of sketches all morning while he washed the tomcat, scolded him, sat dotingly alongside as DC crouched over a bowl of food, then stroked his fur while he snoozed. But this particular drawing seemed to say it all. *DC's home and we're so grateful!*

"Maybe you and Sky could run it down to Hansen's for me, when I'm done?" Abby was learning to economize her efforts. One poster taped to Josie Hansen's counter would tell the world—and dash the Cooperman brothers' dreams of untold wealth and lethal weapons. While her very best sketch of her son and his pet, a quarter the size of this thank-you poster, would make a gift for Michelle as soon as she could frame it.

"Sure, we could do that." While Abby lettered her message, Kat wandered the room, fiddling with the pens and pencils on the table, then the jars of cut flowers arranged on the mantelpiece. She dropped onto the couch to open a book of Toulouse-Lautrec posters that Abby had left on the coffee table. "When's your vacation over?" Kat asked idly, turning a page.

"Hmm?" Lips pursed in concentration, Abby completed the downstroke on a *G*.

"When are you guys going home? To New Jersey?"

Abby brushed a lock of hair off her forehead with her wrist. "We're not going home. I mean, New Jersey isn't our home anymore, sweetie. We moved."

"Oh." Kat turned another page. "Then Sky's dad is flying out here? To meet you guys?"

"No-o." Surely Sky had told her? But apparently not. "No, Kat, he's not. He and I are divorced."

"Oh…" Kat sat very still. "But Sky said…"

Abby glanced around at her warily. "You know what that means, right? Divorced?"

Kat nodded vigorously. "You and Sky's daddy broke up." She smiled, closed the book and bounded to her feet. "Well, see you later!" She darted for the door.

"Don't run off, okay? I'll have this ready to go in twenty minutes."

What was that about? Abby wondered with a frown, returning to her poster. Something to do with the kiss this morning, she supposed. Kat liked everything clear and direct. She was a forthright child who needed to know precisely who was on first—and on second. *Or who's kissing her daddy—a married lady or a divorced one?*

A frisson of remembered sensation wafted down Abby's

spine. Her toes curled in her shoes. Oh, that kiss! Like a girls' boarding school dream, exactly as Michelle had said. A glimpse of wet, warm heaven. A trembling started below her navel and climbed all the way to her breasts, then rattled her shoulders. *Cut it out,* she scolded herself. That kiss had been nothing but gratitude on her part.

And on Jack's?

She punished her bottom lip with her teeth.

So the flirt copped a freebie. Turned a chaste thank-you into a cosmic meltdown. Still, embarrassing though the incident had been, she had no reason to take it seriously.

Men were inclined to grab what they could, as the ex-wife of Steven Lake should know. "That doesn't mean it's personal," Steve had protested when she'd finally confronted him with his infidelities. "Or that it means anything at all. Why shouldn't I feel good when I get the chance? You only go around once, baby, but it's got nothing to do with love—with us!"

Maybe so. Doubtless so, but it wasn't Abby's way. She wanted her kisses to have meaning, or she wanted none at all.

Right now she'd take none, thank you.

Except that a kiss once flown could never be recalled. The taste of Jack lingered on her lips like honey.

YOWZA! HOLY TOLEDO! That kiss was strobing in his brain, throbbing in all points south. Jack relived it roughly every forty seconds throughout the day, and when he grew tired of the factual replay, he spun it into a thousand fantasy versions: him kissing Abby standing on his head. Kissing her under water. Pulling her up from a tango dip to kiss her dizzy. Him kissing her all beaded with sweat and velvety naked.

Maybe he should kidnap her cat, recover it and collect another delectable reward?

Nah. There had to be some more efficient way. *Like maybe I say, "Let's kiss"? And Abby says... No, she doesn't speak; she just grabs my tie...* He was wearing a tie in this scenario. *And she—*

He looked up to find Emma Castillo standing in his office doorway, holding a sheath of papers, her eyes narrowed. "You've been playing golf again?" She blew a lock of cobalt hair off her forehead.

"Uh, no." For politic's sake he'd played a few rounds this spring with Judges Rankin and Grew, but it bored him silly. "Why do you—" *Shut up, Kelton.* The first rule of the courtroom was that you didn't ask a question if you didn't know the answer.

"That day you hit a hole in one, you— *Oh.*" Emma clapped a hand over her mouth and giggled behind it. "Oh, yikes! These are ready for your signature." She smacked the papers down on his desk and fled.

I look like that? If kissing Abby once could do that to him, what would he look like if—

When, he told himself sternly. Got to think positive, here. *When.*

This weekend, he promised himself. Today was Thursday. By Sunday at the latest he'd have another kiss to match the first.

CHAPTER FOURTEEN

"WELL, YOU TELL YOUR MAMA we're all mighty pleased that DC-3 came back." Mrs. Hansen held the new thank-you poster at arm's length to peer at it over her glasses. "Handsome cat he is, too. And this looks just like you, doesn't it?"

"Arrr-um." Sky shrugged and stared at his sneakers. He wished his mom hadn't put him in the drawing. Oh, well. "Could I please have a chocolate cone?"

Kat chose the special, which was cherry-blueberry with bits of red licorice this week, then they stood, licking solemnly, till Mrs. Hansen had taped the poster to the front of her counter.

"There!" She nodded to herself, satisfied. "Your mama ought to do portraits like your granddaddy. I knew a horse painter once who made good money."

"What color did he paint 'em?" Sky asked, picturing a man in a painter's cap, rolling blue paint on a Clydesdale. Kat giggled and elbowed him hard. Mrs. Hansen darted him a suspicious glance, then sniffed and bustled away.

"So now what?" he wondered, pausing on the walk outside the store. Kat was supposed to be sanding the last of the workbench planks for her dad. But it was too pretty a day to go straight home. DC was tucked away safe in Sky's room, catching up on his "beauty rest," as his mom had put it. All was right with the world—or as right as it could be for now, he told himself with a twinge of guilt.

"Let's go visit the fish." Kat led him down the path behind the library, then over the grass to the park.

A group of older girls were sitting on the steps to the gazebo. Kat stopped short and muttered, "Uh-oh."

"What's the matter?" Sky asked in an undertone, pausing beside her.

"It's Marylou."

The blonde who used to baby-sit Kat, Sky remembered. The one Kat claimed to have seen kissing ol' Cowboy Hat. "So?"

"So she never really liked me. It was all an act she put on for my dad, so he'd pay her. But after you and me had that—"

"He-ey, Kat. What are you, a snob?" the pretty blonde called merrily.

"Nope." Kat sighed and strolled on down the path. "Hi, Marylou."

"Ooo-ooh, would you look at that black eye? Isn't that gorgeous?" Marylou nudged the chubby brunette beside her, then leaned to whisper something in her ear.

The brunette let out a squeal of laughter.

"I hear you're fighting with boys now," continued Marylou.

Kat tipped up her chin. "*And* whippin' their skinny butts."

"Oh, right! You and who else, your little four-eyed friend?"

"You're just mad 'cause Pete's grounded for the summer," Kat said with steely calm as Sky bristled. "But he's stuck out on the Jarrett ranch, ridin' and ropin', so I bet he's not missing you at all."

The other girls giggled and poked each other while Marylou turned the color of the cherries in Sky's cone. "Oh…oh, yeah? Like you'd really know what boys want, you little weirdo! Or like you'll ever learn, collecting bugs and watching *G.I. Jane* forty-seven times in a row!''

''Come *on,*'' Sky whispered, terrified that Kat would offer to fight, and then what would he do? His mom had given him an awesome lecture after the fight with the boys. No way would she stand for it if he punched a girl.

Kat shrugged and turned on her heel. ''I'd rather watch ol' Demi Moore kick butt a *thousand* times, than watch you and Pete Sikorsky getting all mushy on the couch, with your goopy to-ongues!'' she called over her shoulder. *''Yuck!''*

''She doesn't have *one* dress in her closet!'' Marylou announced to the world. ''And a bra? Forget about a bra. What would she need that for?''

Kat stopped dead in her tracks and Sky grabbed her arm. ''No! *Don't!* Come on.''

Backs turned to the gazebo, they sat on the stepping stone, bare feet dangling in the cold water. Kat's face was pink and her eyes gleamed with unshed tears. Sky heaved a sigh. ''I'd rather fight with guys any ol' day.'' Punches hurt less than words sharp as knives.

''Me, too.'' Kat wiped her nose. ''I *hate* this stupid place! There's nobody nice here except—'' She glanced at him.

That made him feel better. He looked at her sideways and fought down a smile. He supposed Kat did look funny, with her black eye and drawn-on eyebrows, though he'd gotten so used to her, he hardly noticed. ''You really stood up to ol' Marylou. That was brave.''

''Soon as your mom and my dad marry, I'm out of here,'' Kat swore. ''I'm joining the SEALs.''

''W-what?'' The chill in Sky's feet climbed straight to his heart. ''What did you—? Why do you think—? Not *my* mom!''

"Why not?" Kat lifted her feet out of the water and clasped them as she cocked her head at him. "Somebody's got to take care of him when I go."

"Because— Because— She and my dad…" *Belong together.* Was he the only one who saw that? Was the whole world crazy?

"Are divorced," Kat said matter-of-factly. "You're not on vacation."

"So *what!*" Divorces could be undone. All they had to do was go home and forget about it. Start loving each other again. It wasn't hard.

"It's over. And anyway, she really likes my dad. Did you see her kissing him?"

"Shut *up!* Forget it!" Sky shot to his feet, snatched up his shoes and fled up the path.

THAT EVENING Abby crouched on the back stoop, drawing. Beyond the screen door she could hear Sky setting the table for supper. She jumped as he slammed a plate down, turned and started to object, then changed her mind. She sighed and got to her feet, caressing the grass with her bare toes. Dew was starting to fall, the colors fading toward violets and grays. Despite Skyler's silent rage, what a beautiful time of day.

If she wasn't going to draw, she should pick some flowers for the table. Lilacs to match the purple mood indoors.

"Hey, neighbor." Jack came sauntering around the side of the house.

Her heart gave an odd little bobble, then steadied again. "Evening. You're home late."

"Mmm." He halted beside her, so close their arms almost brushed. "Complications. I have a client—divorce case—whose ex won't let go. He was bothering her again. I had to drive out to her father's house, persuade *him* not to go ballistic. Then chat with the cops.'' He shook himself like a big dog stepping out of the water and smiled down at her. "Whatcha drawin'? Can I see?''

Steve had never asked to look at her work. A shy, small blossom of pleasure unfurled in her heart. "I suppose.'' She leafed back a page. "I'm trying to recapture—well, improve on—the moment when Chang chased DC up the tree.''

Jack laughed out loud. "Hey, that's terrific!''

"He wasn't quite snapping at his heels this way, but—''

"This is much more dramatic.'' Jack looked up from the drawing. "You're really something, you know? Talented. Maybe you can—''

She nodded excitedly. "I think maybe I *can* do it! I needed an idea for my first book and here it is. 'DC, Lost and Found.' It's very simple, but then children's books have to be, since they're short.''

"And it has a happy ending.'' His hand seemed to rise through the twilight of its own accord; one fingertip touched the corner of her smile.

For just the tiniest moment she longed to turn toward his finger, take it between her lips, explore its shape with her teeth and tongue.

A wave of heat and embarrassment washed through her, and she tossed her head, turned aside. *What is this?* This wasn't the right time in her life, nor the right man even if it had been, but still... Her eyes were watering with the blush; her breasts rising and coming alive. "Yeah...'' she managed to say, gazing off toward the bus. "Happy endings are...nice.''

And sometimes hard to find. Feeling Jack looming close behind, she changed the subject abruptly. "Whitey called a while ago. His friend brought the transmission

back from Flagstaff. So that's the last missing part.''
Soon we can go.

Jack said nothing.

Funny how one moment conversation could flow, then the next moment flounder. ''Kat should be taking her muffins out of the oven about now. You're having black bean soup and corn bread and a salad tonight. I hope you're not feeling deprived with this vegetarian menu. I thought since Kat's a—'' She started as the weight of his hand settled on her shoulder.

''It's fine. I'm eating better than I have in years.'' His fingers tightened and relaxed in a slow, seductive rhythm. ''That's why I stopped by, actually. Why don't you guys come over and eat with us tonight? Kat seems sort of blue. Could use some cheering up.''

''Yes, I know.'' Abby turned back around, swinging out from under his hand. She brought the sketchbook to her breast, a flimsy shield but all she had. ''She and Sky aren't talking. So I guess we'd better not. Come over, I mean.''

''Not talking? I thought they were best friends.''

She made a wry face. ''Well, that was this morning and this is tonight. I tried—tactfully—to inquire, but they're not talking about why they're not talking.''

''That's ridiculous! Well, whatever it is, I'll sort this out in two minutes.''

She caught his sleeve. ''Oh, no, Jack, I wish you wouldn't. I think it's better if we let them handle it themselves. They're both lonesome, so eventually...'' *And maybe that's why I'm so drawn to you. No more than that? I'm desperately lonely and here you are?*

But no other man had affected her this way, these past few aching months. He wasn't just a man, any man; he was...Jack. A little bit bigger, a little bit brighter, comforting as a six-foot teddy bear on a scary night. And he could always make her smile. *Maybe you're meant to be my best friend. That's what I'm feeling.*

Friendship might even be better than love. Uncomplicated. Unhurtful. Undemanding.

"Dammit." He swiped a big hand through his wind-ruffled hair. "I wanted to—" He blew out a breath. "Yeah... I suppose you're right. Okay. We mind our own business." He tapped his forefinger against her sketchbook, roughly over her heart. "But only for a day or two. If this nonsense continues into the weekend..."

"Then we'll figure something out," she promised. Sky needed Kat as much as Kat needed Sky.

As for herself, a weekend without a sane and intelligent adult—this adult—to talk to... She smiled and shook her head in wonder. How had it come to this? *I'd miss you.*

FRIDAY MORNING, Abby attacked the kitchen. She'd driven into Durango a few days before to choose the paint, and had returned with a pale color between ochre and butter. Desert color at sunrise, subtle but warm and cheerful. A good background for her Western-theme stencils.

Since Skyler was moping around the house, she drafted him to edge the walls and trim while she wielded the roller. He'd painted enough rooms with her these past few years to know the drill. But his mood was so savage and resentful, she changed her mind. Bad karma stirred into the paint, who needed that? She sent him to walk the cat, who was confined to a leash outdoors and therefore as cranky as his owner. Maybe they'd connect with Kat, who was sanding boards behind her cottage.

She'd finished the ceiling—in white to give it an illusion of height—when Kat poked her head in the back door.

"Stinks in here!"

"Paint fumes," Abby agreed, eyes on her roller. "What's up?"

"Can I go to the library? Check out some books?"

Take Sky along, she begged silently. "Of course. Call me if you're longer than two hours, all right?"

"Yup." The door banged shut.

Abby was completing her second wall when Sky trudged inside, DC draped over his shoulder. He glared at her handiwork. "Lousy color."

"That's why I chose it. I said to myself, what's a really revolting, putrid color to paint a kitchen and when I saw this shade, I just *knew*—"

"You're all pink, you know?"

"Well, it's pretty hot." She was feeling mildly woozy. "Would you prop open the door for me?"

"Arrr." But he did so, then stood in the middle of the floor, kicking the table legs.

"Why don't you go study your math books?" she suggested, just to be evil. His grades had nose-dived during the divorce, so she'd purchased copies of all his fifth-grade textbooks. Theoretically they were supposed to be reviewing a few pages every night. So far the resolution had been honored in the breach.

"Yuck! It's so hot. I'm gonna go down to the park."

Which was only yards from Kat's destination. "Good idea," she said gravely. "And while you're at it, would you check out a book or two for me at the library? Card's in my wallet. Anything you and Mrs. Wimbly can find on wall stenciling and on Christmas cookies, okay?"

"Ah-hh, *Mo-om!*"

"Or you could start making the salad for supper, if you prefer. Tonight's menu is—" She grinned to herself as he vanished into the living room, then stomped up the stairs.

When he clattered down a few minutes later she yelled, "Call in every two hours, okay?"

The front door slammed, hard enough to shake the house.

But, ah, the peace of it all! Just her and these walls turning the color of sunshine. A Friday hue of hope and expectation, blond and fizzy as champagne. "Oxygen break!" she muttered, and went to sit on the stoop for a minute. But she was on a roll. Rolling. Once the base color was dry, she could really start to have fun.

WHILE THE PAINT DRIED Abby remembered that she'd meant to do a load of laundry. Whitey, bless his practical, Rube Goldberg soul, had noticed her washing machine in the back of the bus. Rightly guessing that she'd be desperate for clean clothes—the closest Laundromat was down in Durango—he'd rigged the garden hose for a cold-water supply, then attached another hose to empty the machine into a garbage can back of the toolshed, where the gray water could evaporate. An extension cord ran from the house to the bus. He'd strung a clothesline using an old lariat from his truck, and voilà—she was in business.

She packed the washer with a load of sheets and towels, turned it on, then wandered back to the house to admire her paint job. Her phone rang as Kat checked in; then not three minutes later, Sky called. Both of them declared their intention of staying out another two hours. *Wonder if they were both using Hansen's phone,* she mused, picturing them licking their ice-cream cones with frigid dignity as they ignored each other. Give them a few more hours of proximity and Jack wouldn't need to rub their noses together.

Standing in the kitchen, she couldn't smell the fumes. Either they were dispersing, or she'd grown used to the odor. Another idea for a stencil sprang into her mind—columbines and bumblebees! Quickly she sketched it out on the pad.

But a distant thumping sent her rushing into the yard. "Hey, stop that!" The washer had whirled its load out of balance, with a sound like an elephant bashing its way out of the bus. She scrambled up through the vehicle's back door to switch it off. "Beast."

Rearranging the load—maybe she'd overestimated the poor thing's capacity, but it was too late now—Abby shut the lid and switched it on. The machine hummed contentedly, clothes spinning faster and faster, then—

Whump! Whumpa-whumpa-clatter-whump-whump-whump!

FRIDAY AFTERNOON, the weekend opening in front of him in all its glory, a cactus flower unfurling after the rains. And not just any weekend, Jack reminded himself as he turned into his driveway. He'd made himself a promise that this weekend—somehow, some way—he'd lay lips again on Ms. Abby Lake.

Distracted by the coming delights, he'd been useless at his office. Finally he'd set the contract he was vetting aside and called it an early day. *Let the games begin!*

Inside his house, Kat failed to answer Jack's call. On a hot beautiful day like this, he hoped she was out playing—and playing with Sky. The sooner those two mended their quarrel, the better. The last thing he wanted this weekend was a glum and bored daughter underfoot, Jack thought, as he slipped into a T-shirt and a pair of faded jeans.

Stopping by the fridge, he collected a couple of bottles of cold Negra Modelo beer. Friday deserved a proper welcome, and who better to help him toast it than...

But Abby wasn't at home. He stood in her kitchen, disappointed to an absurd degree, surveying the freshly painted walls. "Abby?" Wandering into the living room, he called up the stairs, but nobody answered.

Small wonder. In spite of the propped-open back door, the paint fumes were horrific. A few whiffs and his head was spinning. She'd been wise to flee for fresh air.

But where? He paused on the stoop and held a cold bottle to his cheek. Hot enough to swim. They should take a picnic—and a blanket!—to his favorite swimming hole along the Ribbon River. His mind served up an image of Abby in a soaked swimsuit, stretched full-length by his side. Suddenly his jeans were too tight.

This was getting ridiculous—seriously ridiculous. He liked women fine, enjoyed sex as much as any man. But for the past decade it had slipped down his list of priorities. Gone from prime preoccupation to pleasant, occasional pastime. Between his work and Kat, he'd had no inclination for more.

Yet now, with Abby next door—and the only cure for this obsession... His brows pulled together. That distant hum, where was that coming from?

From Abby's crimson bus.

CHAPTER FIFTEEN

AS JACK APPROACHED, the hum grew louder, rhythmic, hauntingly familiar. What the devil? He picked his way warily up the front steps of the bus and paused, peering back through its dusky interior, past the piles of boxes and goods toward the sound.

He sucked in a startled breath.

At the back of the bus, facing away from him, Abby sat on a milk crate. Crouched before a jiggling, rumbling washing machine, she seemed, at first glance, a humble worshiper at the altar of the great god Laundry. Light flooding through the bus's open rear door backlit her prayerfully downbent head, lending its wild wisps and tangles a halo of shimmering silver.

He'd always suspected women had mysteries men were better off not knowing. A wiser man would have backed out then and there and left her to it.

The racket of the machine drowned out his advance.

She was bent over some task that absorbed her utterly. From this angle all he could see was Abby's slender back, the sweep and jab of her right elbow, the top of her tousled head, bobbing slightly as if in self-encouragement.

A step closer and he made out the edge of the sketch pad that was balanced on her knees. *Ah.* Unwilling to intrude, too captivated to go, he stopped, smiling to himself.

A bead of sweat trickled down his temple and he rubbed one of the icy bottles he held along his cheek. Never let it be said that Abby didn't suffer for her art! With the late-afternoon sun bouncing off its steel roof and the washing machine sloshing away, the bus's interior was steamy. Sultry.

The machine vibrated and hummed. Abby sat. Jack edged nearer. Below her ragged cutoffs, her long bare legs were spread, graceful as a ballerina's at rest. One bare foot flexed, pointed and flexed to some inner tempo, a slow counterpoint to the machine's revolutions.

Whatcha drawing, Abby?

As if she'd heard his question, she straightened, turned slightly to her right to stare out a window, her wild, wistful profile edged in sunshine.

As he drank in the sight, her lips parted…curved to receive a phantom kiss… The hand that held a pencil rose slowly to her mouth. She brushed her wrist back and forth across her lips—and he felt himself jolt, then harden. Her mouth opened against her skin and the light caught a sheen of moisture. She made a tiny, desolate sound.

And kissed the back of her hand.

He wasn't dreaming; she *was* thinking about making love! But was she fantasizing—or remembering? Regretting her lost marriage?

And who was the imaginary man—lucky son of a gun? The man she was drawing. Suddenly he had to know.

The machine whirled and thumped. Abby turned to look at it, then bent to her sketch pad again.

Three more steps and he could peer over her shoulder. Whatever, whoever her subject was, this wouldn't be a painstaking portrait, judging by the way her arm was moving. More likely a whirling storm of pencil strokes. Jack's foot came down with tigerish stealth… He drew his other leg forward—and his knee brushed a stack of boxes.

Damn! Juggling the beer bottles, he made a frantic grab for the top one as it fell.

The carton landed on its edge—and a cascade of books burst forth. Abby shrieked and shot to her feet. Spinning to face him, clutching her pad to her chest, she backpedaled, stepped on something in the cluttered aisle—and toppled over a laundry basket.

"Abby!" Tossing the bottles over his shoulders, Jack lunged for her. If she fell out the back door!

His fingertips grazed her, missed. She landed with a yelp in a pile of sheets and towels, not six inches this side of the drop-off.

"God, Abby, I'm sorry! Are you okay?" He crouched beside her. "Talk to me. Where does it hurt?"

Her mouth was rounded to a perfect O. Her chest heaved, once, twice, but no words came out, just a series of soundless whoops.

The air was knocked clean out of her, and doubled over like this… "Here." He took the pad she still clutched, set it to one side, grasped her arms. "Let's have a look at you." He pulled her to her feet, but her knees wobbled and gave. She wasn't ready to stand yet.

He caught her slender waist and lifted her to the top of the washing machine. "Do you hurt anywhere?" She hadn't banged her head, but maybe he shouldn't have moved her?

"Y-y-you!" she sputtered.

Ah, temper, that was a healthy sign. "'Fraid so," he agreed, scanning her for signs of damage. She wore a white V-neck T-shirt, washed so thin it was almost translucent. Limp with sweat and spattered with buttery paint, it clung to the curves of her body. Her nipples stood up beneath it, crying mutely for a lover's caress. The machine whirled and thumped. Braced on both arms, she let out a shaking breath and gulped in a deeper one.

"Good. A few more of those…" And she'd be ready to blast him, which of course he deserved. He stooped to retrieve her pad, straightened—and froze.

On the paper, materializing out of a whirlwind of looping and curving pencil strokes, two figures stood, locked in a passionate embrace.

Behind him, Abby made a wordless sound of dismay. Absorbed in the sketch, he turned slowly to face her.

There was one question—the question that mattered. Was this an old aching memory that Abby was drawing?

Or her longing to create a new and better one?

And then he saw it, the few bold, abstracted lines that formed a cat—a disgusted cat that was leaping down and away from the lovers' embrace. Abby had improved on reality. With a few pencil strokes she'd removed the wriggling obstacle that had divided them that morning.

Which means— "May I make a suggestion?" He set the pad aside to step forward between her knees.

Face pink as a rose, she shook her head mutely.

"Imagination's wonderful, but—" Planting a hand on either side of her thighs, he leaned in till her blush seared his face. "Some things are best shared."

"Who-who said I—" She retreated in the only direction available—backward. He followed her down till she reached the last possible point of vertical equilibrium and stopped. "Wh-what are you—?"

"This." He closed the last eighth of an inch and claimed her mouth—hot, honeyed, his for the taking. Trembling with shock and desire. *I'm doing this!* No sane man could do otherwise.

Deep in her throat, Abby moaned—and kissed him back. His hands curled around her hips; he dragged her forward till their zippers clashed. He groaned in delight. Her lashes drooped, her head fell back, and he went on kissing her. Tore his lips away to suck her bottom lip, then kiss his way down the damp velvety side of her neck.

"Oh, Jack, what are you—"

Oh, no. No questions. *Don't think, just feel!* He stopped her words with another kiss—plunged deeper, caressing, seducing. *This is what we were meant to do. Fated to do.* No way could she question that.

She whimpered and laced her hands in his hair, urging him closer.

He bent to her breast. Kissed her open-mouthed through the sheer fabric, then closed his teeth lightly along the exquisite peak—she yelped and came, her legs shuddering as they wrapped around him, her body arching and leaping. The machine rumbled beneath her, its vibrations driving him wild with desire, her wavering song in his mouth.

He rode her bucking convulsions till gradually they slowed in intensity. *Oh, Abby, oh, my hot, beautiful, crazy lady!* He covered her face in kisses, licking the salt off her skin, savoring her taste, marveling at the rosiness blooming under her skin. The softness of her eyelids, the pulse at her temples. This shy, tremulous smile.

Her lashes fluttered down, shutting him out. She averted her head and murmured, "Oh!" in a tiny, stricken voice.

He had to grin. Oh, she was embarrassed, all right! Satisfied beyond any denial, but mightily embarrassed.

You won't be for long, sweetheart, I guarantee it. No shame allowed in this man's fantasy. One hand on her taut hip, he straightened, dragged a fingertip along the front zipper of her shorts. *May I?*

Her eyes flew open. She looked like Bambi under the hunter's gun—if Bambi had green eyes ringed in white.

His heart sank.

Still he slid his fingertip back up her zipper and leaned to nibble one delectably dainty earlobe. *Come on, Sweet and Shy, the party's just begun. If you think that last one was wonderful...*

Her legs clamped tighter around him; her bare feet came to rest against the backs of his thighs. She let her hands drift down his neck to his shoulders, molding and exploring their shape with her palms even as her fingers arched away in rejection. "Umm..."

This was a sound of doubt, but not yet a no. He kissed the corner of her mouth. She sighed—and parted her lips. Their tongues met like long-lost friends. Her fingertips dug in to his muscles. All hope hadn't yet faded, not by a long shot.

The machine wheezed...let out a final *whump!* And went silent, its load within coasting gradually to a halt.

The silence was as loud as a slamming door.

Abby tore her mouth away. Leaned back, panting. She planted a hand on his chest. "J-Jack?"

An immature man would have kicked the damned washer from here to Kentucky.

Jack gritted his teeth and straightened. "Well." He curved his palms to her outer thighs, so slender, so enchantingly toned; he rubbed regretfully up their silky length and down a few inches. *Woman, what you do to me.* Divorce Crazies? Much more of this and they'd be dragging *him* off, gibbering, in a straitjacket! "Well, well, well, Ms. Abby Lake..."

Meant as a teasing endearment, it was a tactical error, he saw instantly. Lake was her married name—her ex's name. Not a good time to remind her.

"Oh, golly..." She looked aside, a blush rising from somewhere south of her beautiful bosom. If he pressed his lips to a rosy curve, he'd surely be scorched. "Oh, gee..."

She gathered her tousled hair in both hands to shove it behind her ears, and he groaned out loud as her breasts rose with the movement. Arms lifted, she narrowed her eyes at him and bit her lip—was she only now realizing that she was in the presence of a thwarted male? A monumentally frustrated—

Temporarily frustrated, he amended. Because there was going to be a repeat of this. And soon, soon, sometime very soon. He smiled reassuringly and cupped the side of her face. "Glad I came home early. Wouldn't have missed this for the world."

"J-J-Jack, I…" She blew out a defeated breath, looked away, looked back warily, worriedly, from under her lashes. "Could you…um, forget this ever happened?"

His laughter just about rocked the bus. "Sure I could, when the Rocky Mountains crumble and it rains up, instead of down! By the time I'm a hundred and ten, maybe, but…" He shook his head as he rubbed his hands up and down her legs. "Till then, every last time I see a washing machine I'm going to grin like a hyena and—"

"Jack!" She flattened both hands against his stomach and shoved.

Laughing, he caught her waist and stepped back as he lifted her down. Then she was so adorably flustered, there in his arms, he had to kiss her again. But she ducked her head against his chest, so he settled for kissing her temple, then rubbing his cheek back and forth through her fragrant hair. *Oh, Abby, I want to carry you straight to my bedroom and nail the door shut!* What was it about her that got to him like this?

He sighed. "Sure you wouldn't care to, er, come clean again, before the kids get home?"

"I would not!" She twisted out of his arms, spun around to lift the washer's lid and drag out a tangle of sheets. "If you think I was sitting out here, thinking or—or wishing or… It was just that the machine was off balance. I guess it's not level here in the bus. And maybe because of the paint fumes, I was feeling…not myself? But since it wouldn't stay balanced, I had to stay out here and so I—''

"Did you ever.'' He traced the course of her spine with one fingertip. He wasn't going to be able to stop touching her now…hungering for her, not till he—

"Here.'' She swung around and thrust a load of sopping laundry into his hands. "Put that in the basket over there, will you, please? And then if you and Kat need a load done…''

SATURDAY, Sky helped them frame the new house. Well, he helped Kat's dad, but he wasn't talking to Kat, except when he had to. He wasn't talking much at all. Sky just banged in each nail as if he hated it and he hardly laughed when her dad made silly jokes, which Kat thought was very rude. She supposed he was still mad 'cause of what she'd said about their parents marrying. *Grow up and get over it,* she told him silently. But even if he was being a dork, she missed hanging around with him.

So when her dad drove off to Mo's Truckstop to buy them take-out sandwiches, she was glad Sky put down his hammer and wandered over to where she was working. "What're you making?'' He stood beside the old picnic table beneath an apple tree, where she'd spread her materials.

"Falcon trap.'' She'd formed a hoop like the rim of a huge butterfly net, out of steel rebar left over from pouring the foundation. "Dad got me some mosquito netting at the army-navy store.'' She was sewing it to the rebar with string. Making holes in the fabric with a nail, then hooking the twine through with a hook made out of coat hanger wire.

Sky measured the width of the hoop with his out-stretched arms. "What are you gonna do? Make a gigantic handle for it? You'll never be able to swing it."

She gave him a pitying look. "Wait and see."

"Haven't seen that stupid hawk all day. Bet he flew on."

"Maybe." He wanted to argue, she could tell, so just to spite him she wasn't going to take offense. "Where'd you guys eat last night?" Her dad had sent her over to invite them to share their meal of leftover macaroni and cheese, since he figured the Lake's kitchen was all fumey with paint, but they'd been gone. He'd been crabby all last night; he'd even growled at her when she tried to cheer him up, suggesting they watch *G.I. Jane*.

"We ate sandwiches down at the park. Mom called it a picnic, but it was nothing like the fancy ones she used to make when—"

She cocked her head, waiting for him to go on. But Sky stood there, turning pink for a minute, then blurted, "You were wrong about my mom! That day she—" He stooped, picked up a fallen branch and turned it over and over in his hands. "She only kissed your dad 'cause she was grate-ful when he found DC. She kisses people thank-you all the time."

"Don't you ever watch TV? Thank-you kisses don't last that long. And kissing thank-you, they wouldn't move their heads back and forth." They might even have used their tongues, though that was so disgusting Kat tried not to think about it. "Besides, they're always looking at each other, funny-like."

"Are not!"

"Are, too." She jumped as he snapped the stick in two

and threw the long half as far as he could. She marked where it landed, then added, "It wouldn't be so bad, you know. My dad's the best dad in the world."

"Huh!"

"For me, anyway," she amended. "But since your parents have broken up—"

"That's only temporary! That crummy lady he married, the stupid flight attendant, is having triplets and a gentleman couldn't let her do it alone, Dad said. But once the hard part's over and they're out of diapers, he'll come back to us. It's where he belongs."

"He said that?"

"He didn't need to! DC came back, he'll come back, too. We just have to wait and be patient, that's all." He glanced up as her dad's car bumped up the drive. "That's *all*." Off he stalked toward the foundation, his head down, his legs stiff.

Kat took a deep breath. Maybe she should offer to share her falcon, once she caught him? That would cheer Sky up.

But no, she'd be taking her bird with her when she left Trueheart. It would do fine on a ship, probably eat flying fish. Or if she joined the SEALS, instead, possibly it could be trained to attack.

"Lunch!" her dad called, waving a couple of brown paper bags as he swung up onto the flooring.

She nodded and stood, then glanced down and bent to grab another stick off the ground. Turning, she took careful aim, took two running steps, then threw it as hard as she could.

It hit the ground twenty feet short of Sky's mark. An odd little feeling, almost like a stomachache, but lonelier, swirled in her stomach. If she wasn't any good at this, what was she good for?

"Cold grilled-cheese sandwich, Kat. Yum!"

She scowled and trudged toward the house. Maybe she should start lifting weights.

STANDING ON A STEPLADDER, Abby positioned her stencil just below the ceiling, dabbed her brush in the paint—a shade of warm lavender that had taken her most of the morning to perfect—then carefully dabbed in the design. In the end she'd gone with her columbine-bumblebee idea, since she'd wanted a pattern that would appeal to renters of either sex. This one worked; the feminine, fragile flowers would be balanced by the bold black-and-gold bees, plundering nectar with the same sense of entitlement as Jack, helping himself to her mouth.

She scowled and dabbed harder. *Could we please forget that, please?*

But how did you erase a sensation—a tactile memory of motion and heat—not words at all, only drenching sweetness and desperate longing?

And absolute, utter embarrassment!

It was one thing to entertain a wistful, woozy daydream in the privacy of one's own makeshift laundry room.

But to be caught in the act of miming a kiss—by the very man whose lips she'd been conjuring?

And then to have him blithely hijack her fantasy—and the rest of her along with it!—and drive her straight past make-believe and what-if, on into outrageous, overwhelming...lip-buzzing reality?

How dare he? She felt as exposed, as mortified, as if she'd awakened from one of those dreams where suddenly you're on the stage at your own high school graduation, wearing nothing but a tassel, mortarboard and a frozen smile! If she didn't see Jack Kelton for the next hundred years, that would be too soon for her. And the passing hours since their encounter hadn't lessened her humiliation; every time Abby remembered it, it seemed to have doubled.

And how could she *not* recall it, when every ten minutes or so she found herself shaping a kiss? Or touching the dampness between her lips. *Could we please, please, please just think of something—*

"Aa-abby!" Kat sang at the screen door. "Can I come in?"

"Please," she called gratefully. Sky had petitioned that he be allowed to serve out his cooking sentence on weeknights only, so he could work late with Jack on the weekends. And perhaps to avoid kitchen chores with Kat, since they still didn't seem to be speaking. "How's the building going?"

"We got the side wall up and braced—it's a little wall. And now they're working on the third one."

While Abby continued her painting, Kat was assigned to slice red bell peppers, mushrooms, onions and garlic at the kitchen table, components of tonight's mystery menu, which Abby refused to reveal.

As she dabbed her way around the ceiling, she found herself smiling; Jack's daughter was amusing company, chattering on about the falcon trap she was building, then her own ideas for stenciling her bedroom. She might do a pattern of fish, or falcons hovering. Or maybe a big sailing ship repeated again and again.

"Perhaps a pattern of dolphins *and* ships?" Abby suggested. "You know dolphins like to play around boats? I saw them surf along the ferries' bow waves when we were stationed—" She paused. "A long time ago." In a world far, far away. It was amazing how little she thought of her old life with Steven nowadays. A month ago she wouldn't have believed it possible.

Kat's mind was like a darting perch in the park stream; she changed the subject again. "Do you think my dad's cute?"

Abby lifted a stencil and frowned at the wet design beneath it. *Um, could I pass on that?*

Apparently not. "Do you?" Kat asked insistently.

"I'm…not sure cute's the word I'd use." Try sexy. And a little breath-taking. And utterly maddening, for starters.

"What is, then?" demanded Kat, not to be derailed.

A game her own father used to play sprang to mind, and to the rescue. "Let's say…that if your dad were a member of the cat kingdom, he'd be…a lion." Sandy coloring, complete with shaggy mane. Built for power more than speed. Prone to roaring when thwarted. Tending to look mellow and a little bit lazy, but not—ever—to be underestimated.

"A lion!" Kat laughed delightedly. "And what would I be?"

"Mmm." Abby turned around to study her. "You're so graceful and restless. A leopard I'd say, but luckily, no spots."

"Really?" Kat turned a lovely shade of shell pink.

"Absolutely. You've got a complexion most women would kill for." Jack's wife—what was her name, Maura?—must be gorgeous to have produced such a child.

A familiar feeling of dismay and despair drifted across Abby's mood like a passing cloud shadow. A sense of terrible inadequacy had haunted her after she'd learned of Steve's infidelities. *If only I'd been prettier, wittier, nicer, sexier?* No, she never wanted to feel jealous in her life again. Yet here it was, the green-eyed monster. *But why would Jack want to bother with me, after having a wife like that?*

Easy, she told herself wryly. *You're available. Right*

next door, and just begging to be kissed, the last time he wandered by. Cheeks burning, she turned to the wall, loaded her brush with paint and picked up the stencil.

"Oh," Kat murmured, bringing her back to the present. She glanced around. *Don't think about Jack.* Think about this child, who needed something she could give. "In fact, we should be thinking about buying you a sun hat, kiddo." She'd yet to take Kat shopping, as she'd originally promised her father. "When you have a treasure, you ought to guard it."

Kat shrugged and looked down at her pile of vegetables, resumed her chopping. But an odd little smile came and went.

And possibly this was the best bit of art she'd created all day—all week—Abby told herself, turning back to her stenciling. Better than the best design of flowers and bees. She'd sketched a new self-image for Kat, which she could now try on and parade in front of her soul's mirror. Like a child trying on a velvet gown from the dress-up trunk.

Here's an alternative to combat fatigues, Kat. What do you think?

AFTER ABBY HAD FINISHED painting, she suggested they complete tonight's meal at Kat's house. "I'm afraid if we make the dough here, it might end up smelling of latex."

"Dough?" Kat cocked her head. "What are we cooking?"

"Oh, didn't I tell you? Home-made pizza."

Right then and there Kat decided. It wasn't just a good idea—it was a stupendous one. Her dad *needed* to marry Abby.

But how to make it happen?

Especially when Abby didn't seem to want to hang around with them as much as she had the week before.

"There," she said when they'd finished two identical piz-zas, each as big as the cookie sheet it rested on. "That's a complete meal in itself—bread, vegetables and cheese. You can always have fruit for dessert, but I don't think you'll want it."

"Aren't you and Sky going to eat with us tonight?" Kat pleaded as Abby lifted one pan. "It's Saturday night."

"I know, kiddo, but after all this painting, I'm pretty tired. And I imagine your dad would like to relax tonight and not have to entertain. So…set your oven to three-fifty degrees." Abby glanced at the wall clock. "They ought to be home any time now, so go ahead and turn it on. Then the minute your dad walks in the door, stick the pizza in the oven. That'll give him just time to take a shower…" Abby stared off into the distance, as if she'd spotted a bug on the wall or something.

"And then?" Kat prompted finally.

"Oh! Leave it in for twenty minutes. That should be long enough. Be sure to set your timer. When the timer rings, pull it out—carefully, because it'll be very hot—slice it and enjoy." Abby moved toward the exit.

Don't go! Kat begged with her eyes, but Abby gave her an odd, sad sort of smile and shouldered her way out the door, saying gently, "G'night, sweetie."

As her steps faded away, Kat stood, fists clenched, heart pounding with frustration. So close! They'd been *so* close to another really happy evening together. She stamped her foot hard enough to rock the cookie sheet on the table. She swung to glare at her masterpiece. *Your fault!* If they'd made one gigantic pizza instead of two, Abby and Sky would've had no choice but to eat with them.

Kat blinked. Did she dare? It would be almost a sin. Most certainly a shame.

On the other hand… "Soldiers have to make sacrifices

to win wars,'' she reminded herself. Think of the men in the Alamo.

With a resolute nod, she turned to the oven. Spun its knob to five hundred degrees—then past that to Broil. She listened carefully for the flame to come on, then shoved the pizza onto the lower rack, shut the door and glanced at the clock.

Six o'clock. With any luck, her dad would be late.

CHAPTER SIXTEEN

"THAT WAS A GOOD day's work," Jack said as he parked the Jeep in front of his cottage. They'd framed the west side of the house, then its first jog to the north. Sky had worked like a surly demon; what could be eating the boy? Instead of mending with time, the kids' quarrel seemed to have expanded. Jack had the uncomfortable feeling that he was now included in Sky's grudge, although he hadn't a clue why or what to do about it. Just maintain a steady, smiling course and gut it out, he supposed.

"Hang on," he said as Sky started to climb out of the Jeep. "I owe you." He was a firm believer in immediate gratification, wherever possible. "Let's see, you put in eight hours today, so that's forty bucks." He peeled off two twenties from the bills in his wallet.

"Er, thanks." Sky pocketed the cash, then turned toward the house. "Hey, do you—?"

The distant *crack!* of the back door banging open—then Kat's piercing shrieks—spun them both around. "Abby, *Abby,* fire, fire, fire! *Help!*"

"Holy Mother of—!" Jack flew around the side of the house thinking, hose, if he couldn't reach the fire extinguisher... Send Sky to phone the volunteer brigade from Abby's place... And Kat... Well, she simply had to be all right. Nothing else was allowable. Smoke billowed out the open door as he took the back steps in a bound. "God!"

He paused, inhaled a heated wave of charred cheese and burning bread, coughed it out and bellowed, *"Kat!"*

"She's here! I have her! She's fine, Jack!" Abby patted his back, then thrust a fire extinguisher into his hands.

"All of you, out of here!" The fire seemed confined to the stove. He yanked open its door—a cloud of greasy black rolled forth. He spun the temperature knob to Off, foamed the oven to kingdom come, then retreated gasping toward the door, where Abby and the kids stood goggle-eyed. "Out! Outta here. It's under control." He herded them into the dark. Paused to catch a cool breath. "Holy smoke! What was all that?"

"Supper," Kat said mournfully. "That was the very best pizza in the world."

"'Was' being the operative word," Jack noted. "What happened?"

Kat shrugged and widened her eyes. "Dunno. You were so late, I started cooking it. I was watching TV on the couch." Another broad shrug and a too innocent smile. "I guess maybe I fell asleep? Then I smelled smoke and woke up."

Jack cocked his head. Something was ringing a little funny here. She'd been up to some sort of no good. Maybe smoking cigarettes in the kitchen, then blasted their supper to cover her tracks? Nah, given her appetite for pizza, not likely. Welding again, but then where was her torch?

Kat continued the note of tragedy. "What are we gonna do now? We can't eat it, can we?"

"Of course you can't." Abby smoothed the bangs across her forehead. "You're going to come over to our house and help us eat our pizza, sweetie, while your place airs out. And maybe we'll make a salad to fill in the chinks?"

"Okay." Kat brightened immediately.

Well, whatever she'd been up to, Jack had no complaints. He'd feared Abby meant to ostracize them again this evening, as she had the night before. "Excellent," he said, seconding the notion before she could retract it. "And for dessert, I'll take us to Mo's. Apple pie à la mode." The evening was looking up.

In the end, they ate a superb pizza alfresco, out on a blanket under the stars, since Abby's kitchen still smelled of paint. Nothing like a common disaster to pull a group together. Kat's chagrin had given way with suspicious speed to smug satisfaction. Sky had actually smiled once or twice. Abby avoided Jack's gaze, but at least she laughed at his jokes.

Got to get you alone, he told her silently. If she thought she could go back to before—pretend that she'd never come in his arms—she'd better think again.

But with two watchful preteens as chaperones, that would have to wait. *Tomorrow,* he promised himself. Somehow he'd get her alone tomorrow. "So who's ready for ice cream and pie?" he inquired, trusting the kids to overwhelm any opposition from Abby.

"Me!" Kat bounced to her feet and kept on bouncing.

AT THE TRUCK STOP, their luck continued. They arrived just in time to seize Kat's favorite booth, the big round one, and Mo hadn't yet run out of pie. After a forkful of cinnamon apples and flaky crust, even Abby melted. "Oh, my!"

Remembering her moans in the bus, Jack stirred, surreptitiously caught the side seam of his jeans and pulled toward his knee. His squirming caught her attention and their eyes met for the first time that night. He gave her a wry grin. "Oh, my, indeed, ma'am. Sweeter than wine." *Your kisses are.*

Her gaze shot away, her cheeks rosy.

"You're going to have to come see what your son's been up to," Jack added, shamelessly exploiting the proud mom card. "We're about a third of the way finished with the framing, and I couldn't have done it without him."

"Oh?" Abby smiled at her son. "Hope you're taking notes, kiddo. When we get to Sedona, it's bound to come in handy for our house."

No, we don't want to hear that. Jack opened his mouth to change the subject.

Kat beat him to it. "This is fun!"

"Yeah," he agreed. *Great minds think alike.*

"Almost like being a family," she added, with studied casualness.

Sky's spoon clattered to the table. "Is not!"

"Is, *too!*" Kat raised her chin.

"How would *you* know? You never had a mother, not so's you'd remember!" Sky leaped to his feet.

Abby cried, "*Skyler!* Don't be rude."

"Well, it's the truth! Two isn't a family!" He scrambled out of the booth. "Can I use the phone?" He shoved his hand under her nose.

"That, hotshot, is over the top." Jack put some gravel in his voice. "Sit down till your mother excuses you."

"May I have the *phone?*" Sky jiggled his hand in front of her face.

Not my kid, not my kid, not my kid, Jack warned himself, biting his tongue. If he came down hard on the boy, as he would have on Kat, Abby would fly to his defense. Whether Sky knew it or not, he was playing "divide and conquer." *So sit tight and let her handle it.*

"You call your father on Tuesdays," Abby said steadily. "Saturday night, I doubt he'll—"

"*I need to talk to him!*"

"Fine! Take it." She dug in her purse for her cell phone, then thrust it at her son. "Go sit over there where I can see you."

Instead he stomped off toward the Jeep.

"Oo-oh." Abby pushed her plate away and started to rise.

Jack laid a hand over hers. "He'll be okay out there. And it is more private. You." He turned to his daughter. Miss Troublemaker. "Go hang out by the cash register and keep an eye on him, but *don't* go outside. Come get me if you need to."

"Yup." She scooted out of the booth and darted away.

Jack sighed. "He'll be okay." He was still holding Abby's hand across the table. "I'm sorry about that."

"Oh, no—I am!" Abby wiped her eyes. "And it *was* a lovely evening. If only he'd…"

"Takes time. You'll just have to wait him out."

"I keep asking myself what I could do—should've done—but…" Abby shook her head helplessly. Tears beaded in her long lashes. "But I…"

Jack stood, moved around to her side of the table, hooked an arm around her shoulders and pulled her close. "You didn't leave, Abby. You got left." By a fool who hadn't known what he had while he had it, but Jack wasted no pity on fools. Gently he stroked the side of her face. "Seems to me you're making the best of the bad situation you were handed. Doing a darned fine job of it."

She shook her head miserably.

"He's well fed, he's well loved, he's safe and secure," Jack insisted. "You've brought him to a place that most boys would think was heaven on earth. I'd say that's a good start."

"But you heard him. There's not two of me."

"There're all kinds of families, all kinds of ways to be

happy, even if Sky doesn't see it yet. Look at Kat and me. We've never lacked for anything.'' Or at least he'd have said so till Abby moved in next door.

Abby who meant to move on, build a house in Sedona. *But not yet,* he told himself fiercely. *Not till I—*

Till something was completed between them. He didn't know what, only knew that this minute—

Swooping down, he claimed her trembling mouth. Salty with tears, sweet as apple pie. What more did he need to know?

''YOU'VE GOTTA COME out here!'' Sky yelled. His dad was using his cell phone someplace noisy, people laughing and talking in the background. Sky could barely hear him.

''Hey, buddy, you're going to have to talk louder!'' his dad hollered back. ''It's happy hour around here and we're mighty damn cheerful. What's up?''

''You *need* to come out! Now!'' *Things are falling apart.*

''Come out to Colorado? Well, Sky-boy, that'd be sort of difficult. Chelsea's not feeling too spry. She's into her seventh month, you know, and 'tween you and me, if you crossed the Goodyear Blimp with a pit bull... But what can a guy do? Hey, I'll be flying right over you on my way to Phoenix next week. What if I call you from the cockpit? I can't hear you worth beans in here. You okay, son?''

''No,'' he half whispered. *I'm not.*

''Sure you are, spaceshot. And you know I'm proud of you. So catch you next week, all right? Hey, *crap,* watch what you—!'' His phone clattered against something hard. A woman let out a raucous shriek of laughter.

Sky sat with a dial tone ringing in his ear.

Big Colorado sky with stars bright as tears above.

You gotta come out here.

SUNDAY, the building crew started early. Jack set up the frame for the next western jog—that side of the house was irregular—then realized he'd forgotten something. "Can you handle these three studs alone?" he asked Sky. "I ought to run back to your place and pay Whitey."

"Sure." The kid was coolly withdrawn, but last night's explosive resentment had blown itself out, at least for the present.

"Kat's over the ridge if you need her." Setting up her hawk trap, he supposed. She'd brought along a package of frozen wieners this morning, which Jack trusted would be ignored.

Sky's shrug said it all, so Jack sighed and walked away. Trying to jolly him out of it would only backfire, something told him. "See you shortly."

Parking in Abby's drive behind Whitey's truck, he ambled back to the bus. With his Pekinese looking on, the old man was hoisting the leaky radiator out of the engine compartment, using a block and tackle hooked to the branch overhead. Jack helped him guide it to one side, bring it down on the bumper, then lift it to the ground. "Making progress, I see."

"Yep, and we picked up a good-lookin' transmission Saturday, but I lost the whole dang day. Johnnie Tso'd messed up his thumb in a lathe. Had a rush job, switchin' engines on a Chevy truck, so I stuck around. We trade chores from way back." The old man unhooked the radiator and swung the tackle over to its replacement. "Hope Abby didn't fret too much when we didn't show. Now that I've got the parts, we'll start movin'."

"That's what I wanted to talk to you about." Jack glanced toward the kitchen door. "Uh, where is she?"

"Said she had some errands."

Good enough. Jack pulled out his wallet. "What do I owe you so far?"

Whitey shifted his chaw from one grizzled cheek to the other. "Thought I was workin' fer Abby."

"We're bartering. She baby-sits Kat for me. I pay you. It evens out."

"Can't see no objections t'that. Can you, Chang?"

Apparently the dog's snort and backward kicking of his stubby hind legs meant no. Whitey named a ridiculously low figure and Jack paid it, making a mental note to give the old hand a bonus at the end. "One thing," he said casually as he put away his wallet. "There's no hurry on this job. In fact, quite the opposite. Take all the time you need."

"Huh." Whitey scratched his chin. "I kinda thought she was itchin' t'lay tracks out of Trueheart. Said something about gettin' to Sedona to build an adobe."

"Things have changed." *Don't make me say what, old man.*

"What?"

Great. Jack rubbed the back of his neck. "Well, between you and me, Abby could use some cheering up. So I need a little time."

"To cheer her up?"

"Yup," Jack said stoically.

Whitey turned to consult the Pekinese, then turned back, frowning. "She's a nice lady. A real peach. Just how far was you plannin' to cheer her?"

"As far as makes her wake up smiling," Jack admitted, throwing discretion to the winds. "She's had a tough year. What's wrong with reminding her that all men aren't rats? Teaching her how to giggle again?"

"Huh." Whitey leaned over and spat in the grass.

"Besides, she'd be smart to settle here for the winter."
Jack forged on, feeling as if he were trudging head-down
into a dust storm. "She's never built anything before and
she thinks she'll build an adobe by the fall? Ain't gonna
happen."

"Gal's pretty spunky."

"Yep, but take it from a divorce lawyer, she's smack
dab in the middle of the Divorce Crazies. She shouldn't
be making commitments till she knows where she's going.
She'll change her mind ten times in the next ten months.
Meanwhile, till she's over this phase, Trueheart's a better,
saner, safer town in which to raise a boy than Sedona'll
ever be. Last thing Abby needs this summer is to get lost
in a power vortex."

"Hmm," Whitey chewed, thought, finally said, "Sure
you know which end of the brandin' iron you're grabbing?"

Jack cocked his head. "Meaning?"

"Meanin' if anybody gets burned 'round here, it might
not be Abby. Womenfolk are always tougher than you figure. The softest woman can ride a hard man into the
ground and come back fresh as a daisy. But you, Kelton,
you might want to take a piece of advice from an old hand
at makin' the ladies smile."

Want it or not, he was going to get it.

"Look at me." As Whitelaw straightened, Jack took
another look. The old man was lean, tough as rawhide,
with plenty of humor and wisdom in those faded blue eyes.
In his pre-Pekinese days Whitey must have sat tall in the
saddle. Roped his share of hearts. "Had a wife of my own
forty years ago, but turned out she wanted a town man,
not a cowboy. Since Betsy, I've smacked a few rumps, but
I never tried to tie the knot twice. And now what've I
got?"

Jack turned up his hands. *Tell me.*

"I've got a family, thanks t'Kaley and Tripp McGraw, and reckon their young'uns'll be m'grandkids, or close enough. But I sleep with that fleabag t'keep me warm and dang if he doesn't snore. Seems t'me a man might want to think about settlin' down while he's still got his teeth and a hope of siring his own herd."

Jack had to laugh. "A few more like Kat and I'd never live to see grandkids!"

"Oh, yeah, you're laughing now, but—"

"But I'm not." Jack quelled his grin. "And I'm sure you're right. But I fell for a divorce-crazy lady once before, and believe me, once was enough. There's a time to be serious—and a time when serious will get you seriously damaged. And a wise man knows the difference."

Whitey shrugged. "Well, I can see you've set your mind, so…" He hooked a thumb at the radiator. "Give me a hand horsin' this thing into place, will you?"

They attached the replacement to the tackle. Jack swung it up above the engine, took two turns around the bumper, then lowered it inch by inch till Whitey said, "Whoa. It'll take some fiddling from here."

Jack handed him the rope's tail end. "Then I'd better run. But about taking your time?"

"Long as Abby keeps on smiling—and you're footin' the bills—you take all the rope you need."

"SO." MICHELLE PULLED a package from under the cash register. "Four rectangular cookies as big as I could possibly make them. Want to tell me what for?"

Abby smiled and shook her head. "Only when I'm sure I can deliver. Oh, and there's one thing more I need." She pointed at the far wall of the café. "Could I borrow that photograph of the cowgirl?" She'd admired it the first time she entered Michelle's Place, a woman leaning down from her horse to smack a cow with her Stetson.

"The one of Kaley McGraw on roundup?" Michelle nodded. "If you need it, of course." She threaded her way through the tables crowded with Sunday diners to return with the photo. "Let me carry it to the car for you."

Out in the parking lot, Michelle asked, "So how goes the paint job?"

"The kitchen's done and if I say so myself, it came out really well. I've invited Maudie Harris over for tea on Tuesday. If she likes the results, I'll try to persuade her to let me tackle the living room." In lieu of another two weeks' rent, Abby was hoping.

"Either you're a thwarted home decorator at heart, or that bus needs more repairs than you thought."

"Bit of both." Abby opened the door to the Subaru. "Whitey's a doll, but he's hardly Mr. Speedy Wrench. And he lost a week scrounging the parts."

"Well, when you think about it, what's your hurry?" The blonde handed her the photo. "Some people consider summer in the Rockies a vacation."

"It's just that a friend's expecting me in Sedona. I'd planned to be there two weeks ago and building an adobe by now."

"Life's what happens while we're making other plans," the blonde observed wryly. "And your studly neighbor, he's behaving himself? Oh *ho!*" she added as Abby opened her mouth, closed it again—and turned pink.

Abby shrugged. "He's made a pass or two, but nothing I couldn't handle."

"Uh-huh. Whatever you say." Michelle grinned as she backed away. "Come and tell me a-a-all about it next week, when it's not so busy around here. And if you need more cookies, Abby, just let me know."

CHAPTER SEVENTEEN

TURNING OUT of the café parking lot and toward the center of Trueheart, Abby was tempted to drive north. Jack's building site was somewhere along the far ridge that sheltered the town. It shouldn't be hard to find, and he'd invited her several times to come and take a tour.

The artist in her longed to see the place. Jack had designed the house with the help of his contractor brother, and Jack had chosen its setting. As any work of art and love, it would be a tangible expression of its builder's personality, and the more she learned about Jack, the more she wanted to learn. He was such an intriguing mix of gentle and tough. Whimsical, yet decisive. Sensitive in some ways, and utterly oblivious in others. Hopelessly male—and all the more appealing for it.

Which was why the other half of her, the woman half, was dodging all his invitations to admire his work in progress. She ought to be fighting her interest in Jack.

Just because he crashed my fantasy…

Precisely because she couldn't forget the feel of his arms around her, holding her as she came. Even though, for the first time in months, she'd felt…safe, there in his arms. Almost cherished.

She'd had such a long, dry, lonely spell these past six months or more; there was no doubt it had made her dangerously vulnerable. But only the most foolish of women would take a perfectly normal afterglow for more than it was. Mistake it for some kind of meaningful connection, an emotion with promise and future.

The last thing I need is to develop a crush on a divorced divorce lawyer! Who's dated every single woman in Durango and found not one he'd commit to? Even if she wanted him, which she did not, what chance would plain vanilla Abby Lake have if Jack was that choosy?

And to reach for him, and then fail?

Yes, that was just what she needed right now, another installment of heartache!

This is the year you stand on your own, she reminded herself—and turned south up Magpie, then left on Haley's Comet Street. Some other time, when she felt stronger and braver—and superbly self-sufficient—she'd tour Jack's new house.

But not today.

ALL THAT AFTERNOON Abby worked on her idea for Michelle's cookies. She botched her first two attempts to simplify the design, yet keep enough texture and detail. But the third effort looked promising. Regretfully she put it aside as Kat clattered up the back steps.

"What are we cooking today?"

Supper was lentil soup and grilled-cheese sandwiches, which the two families ate at their respective dinner tables, despite Jack's invitation and Kat's pleadings. Much as she would've enjoyed sharing another meal, Abby was sure it was a mistake to socialize every night. No use starting pleasant rituals that would soon be undone.

Or would be undone if Whitey ever completed his job. He'd left early on Sunday, saying he'd promised his widowed sister help with a leaky bathtub faucet. So the bus's new radiator was in place, but it wasn't hooked up.

What happens if Maudie Harris won't accept more

painting for rent? Abby worried on Monday morning while she completed her first successful cookie. At this rate, the bus wouldn't be drivable for another two weeks. If she had to fork out two more weeks of rent money...

Cross that bridge if and when, she warned herself. Meantime, she should take advantage of her splendid isolation. Jack had decided to take Monday off, since he had no appointments scheduled, so he and his half-size construction crew were busy across town. She'd deliver this cookie to Michelle, then spend the rest of the day working on her children's book. She thought about an illustration of DC, lost and hungry, rummaging through a garbage can behind the café. In fact, she should bring her drawing pad along to Michelle's, make some preliminary sketches.

When she walked into the café, she found Michelle hanging up the phone. At the sight of her, the blonde made a face.

"Problems?" Abby paused with a hand on the door. "Maybe I should come back some other time."

"Just Trueheart-type problems. Hearing all the gossip in town and wondering if it's smarter to keep my mouth shut or pass it on." Michelle nodded at the box Abby held. "Is that for me?"

"It's just a possibility." Shyness overtook Abby as it always did when it was time to show her work. "Something to jazz up your cookies?" She lifted the lid and removed a protective tissue.

Michelle clapped a hand to her mouth. "Oh, my *gosh!*"

Maybe she didn't like it? Abby hurried to explain. "Your cookies are sepia-colored, like the background of antique photographs. So I thought you might be able to come up with a dark-brown icing or glaze for the figures, which would make them look like a daguerrotype. The glaze would have to be pretty thin...."

Michelle shook her head in wonder. "This is marvelous! How did you *do* this?"

So she did like it. Abby laughed with pleasure. "Well, this, I'm afraid, is brown paint, just to show you my idea. As for the process, I made a stencil based on your photograph of Kaley McGraw. You'd place it over a cookie, then you'd dab in your icing to make the picture, and let it harden."

Michelle's gaze swung around the café. "Could you do other pictures?"

"That was the idea," Abby said. "You've got some beauties here. They look like photos of the old Wild West. That cowboy swinging his lariat, that one would work."

"Kaley's husband, Tripp. And what about this one of Rafe Montana, riding point on the herd?"

"An easy one, since it has less detail."

"Ooo-kay. Cookies. Milk. Girl, it's brainstorming time. I think you've just raised this enterprise to its next level!"

HALF AN HOUR LATER, they were giddy with cookies and ideas. Abby pushed her chair back from the table. "No, get that thing away from me! I can't eat another bite."

Michelle put the plate aside. "Okay. And I suppose I'd better get moving on supper. But I'll start experimenting with glazes tomorrow morning, and by Wednesday at the latest, I should have something for us to try."

"No hurry. I'm supposed to be working on a children's book." But was it possible that this idea could be spun into a cookie company, as Michelle was insisting? Or that Abby could be part of such a business? Most likely, this was simply an overdose of good company and powdered sugar. By morning, it would seem one more pie-in-the-sky idea, more charming than practical. Abby stood. "Give me a call whenever you're ready."

"Will do." Michelle's enthusiasm seemed to be waning as she walked Abby to the door.

So they'd gotten entirely carried away, Abby concluded. Too bad. For just a minute there, she'd pictured herself happily designing cookies, then the packaging for the cookies, plus ads to market their product on the Internet, while Michelle handled the culinary end of the business. "Well, see you later."

The blonde crossed her arms and tapped a toe restlessly. "Abby? That phone call when you first came in? That was my friend Kaley calling. I wasn't sure I should say anything, but…"

JACK SLICED ANOTHER STUD to length, shoved the whirling radial sawblade to its backstop, then glanced aside at the sound of an approaching vehicle. His own Subaru with Abby at the wheel came bucketing up the hill. He grinned and switched off the tool.

"About time you showed up for a tour!" he greeted her as she stepped from the car.

No answering smile. As she stalked to meet him, her brows were pulled together, her jaw set. Her eyes flashed cold green fire.

Uh-oh.

She came to a halt when her forefinger jabbed his bare, sweaty chest. *"You!"*

He caught her wrist and gave her a puzzled smile. "Hey, what did I do?" Her pulse was rushing like a river in snowmelt.

"You… You…!" Despairing of a word sufficiently vile to describe him, she tossed her head, glanced around. "Where are the kids?"

"Gone to Hansen's to buy us lunch." It had been voted upon and decided unanimously that today the carpenters needed to split a half gallon of ice cream and eat a large bag each of potato chips, for lunch. Lucky for him she hadn't caught them in the midst of that! "Look, Abby, what's wrong?"

"Did you—or did you not—tell Whitey to work as slowly as possible on my bus?"

Hoo-boy. When attacked by a woman on the warpath, the best tactics were stall, deny and distract. "How could you think I'd do that?" And whatever happened to the bachelor's first commandment: *thou shalt not squeal?*

"Whitey told somebody named Tripp McGraw that you asked him to work slow. Tripp told Kaley…"

Thanks, McGraw. But the rancher was newly, hopelessly, head-over-heels married. No doubt he'd told her in bed.

"Kaley told Michelle and Michelle told me. Why would you *do* such a thing?"

"Because…" Kelton's third Rule of Life covered this situation. *Let your actions speak for you.* Pulling Abby's wrist around his back, he caught the nape of her neck with his other hand as she stumbled against him—and dropped a kiss on her astonished mouth.

He savored the silky dampness inside her soft lips, then plunged inward. Heat, a hint of sugar, then after an instant of rigid immobility, came her quivering response; his eyes drifted shut. *Woman, what you do to me!*

She growled, tore her mouth away and bared her teeth. "Back off!"

"You asked." He let her go, raised his hands palm outward—*peace*—retreated a step.

"I can't believe you'd have the nerve, the sheer, unspeakable gall, to do that!"

"You can't?" He gave her his best sheepish smile, but Abby wasn't buying any. *Have you looked at yourself lately?* Even spitting mad, she was adorable. "Then you don't know me well and that was the whole point. We need some time to get to know each other." He dared to brush a stray lock off her brow. "To enjoy each other."

She smacked his hand aside. "I thought I'd made it very clear—more than clear—that I wasn't looking for any sort of…of male companionship."

"I seem to recall a recent incident that might lead a man to think…" he said, raising one brow.

"No one asked you to barge into my private life!"

"Nope. But I'm glad I did. And when you wrapped your legs around me and moaned, you seemed sort of…pleased."

"*O-oh,* you conceited, smug, son of a—" She spun away from him, folded her arms and marched away along the edge of the foundation, shaking her head. "You bastard. You *lawyer!*"

"Ouch!" he protested, following behind. Abby turned up the west side of the house and cornered herself in its first jog to the north. Before she could escape, Jack dropped a hand to either side of her and gripped the stud plate. "As an officer of the court, I suppose I should tell you, Abby, that it's no crime to lie in my bed at night, wondering what you'd do if I kissed you…*here.*" He laid a kiss in the velvety spot below her left ear.

She shuddered and squirmed around, glaring up at him, the warning plain in her eyes. *You're playing with fire, buddy!*

Didn't he know it. "Now what *is* a crime is the way you bite that bottom lip when you're worried. Or the sound of your voice, like a tiger kitten's purr." There, he'd won just the hint of a smile, which faded immediately to a frown. *Keep talking, Kelton.*

"The way you walk ought to be illegal." He lowered

his head until he could feel the heat of her face against his lips. "And when you moan? Abby, you could get arrested for moaning like that, but if you're going to do it, why not do it with me?"

She planted her hands against him, apparently to push him away, then didn't. "I told you, I don't want a relationship."

"Who's talking relationshi—*ooof!*" he grunted as she shoved him, hard, under the ribs.

He rocked on his heels, then recovered. "I'm talking a fling, woman. You're absolutely right—you don't need, don't want, shouldn't start a relationship when you're in the midst of the Divorce Crazies, but a fling is *precisely* what you need."

"With you?" Her voice dripped contempt.

"Darn right. Your pride's bruised and battered. You've been tossed when you least expected it. But sooner or later you've got to get back on the horse that threw you—well, on some horse—and ride. And here I am at your service, the perfect lady's mount. Good mouth, terrific gaits, astounding endurance. What more do you need?"

She blew out a huffing breath, ran her fingers up through her cloud of hair and shook her head at him. "You really don't know, do you?"

"Tell me," he coaxed, clenching his hands so he wouldn't reach out for her. Why was he using words to persuade, when with one more kiss they'd burst into flames?

"I need lots more—or I need nothing at all. Right now, I'm in a mood for nothing. Zip. Nada. So back *off,* Kelton!"

He backed. Followed at a respectful distance as she stalked on, inspecting his foundation with a blind scowl. Coming around to the north side, she glanced toward the top of the ridge, then headed that way, up through the gnarled old trees. He caught up with her and walked alongside. "This used to be an apple orchard," he told her. "You should've seen it last spring when the trees blossomed."

She snarled something wordless and marched on, head down.

Till they reached the top of the ridge. Abby lifted her chin and stared to the north, her breath coming slower and deeper the way his always did when he saw the mountains. "Drew wouldn't let me build up here, said we'd freeze to death in the winter. But you'll see the peaks from my bedroom." *Come share them with me.*

Except by the time the house was inhabitable late next summer, she'd be long gone, even if they'd had their fling.

No *if,* he told himself, batting that shadow aside. It had to happen. *They* had to happen.

"Lovely," she half whispered.

Eyes on her profile, he could only agree.

"Look," she said, still facing the mountains. "I would like to be friends with you. God knows I need a friend."

Jack grimaced. *Just* a friend, was what she meant. "And we are. Never doubt it. But as your friend, Abby, I strongly advise you to have a fling with me."

"Yeah, right." She spun and started down toward the house. "You're a cad and a self-serving creep if that's all you want!"

"Hey!" He caught her wrist and stopped short, hauling her around. "Easy on the insults, pal. A nice, sexy fling is all it's *safe* to want—to have—if you don't know your own mind and, Abby, you don't."

She jerked her hand, but he didn't let go. "Says who?"

"Says one who should know. Who learned the hard way. When Maura and I ran off to a wedding chapel in

Vegas, she was in the midst of the Divorce Crazies. We hadn't been married three months when she changed her mind. Decided maybe I wasn't the love of her life after all, just one more stop along the way. By Month Four she was shagging another law associate in my firm. By Month Seven she'd made it to partner. By the end of Year One she'd made senior partner, without trying a single case.''

Abby stopped pulling against his hold. Bit her lip. Looked at him, wide-eyed and troubled.

"I'm sure she'd have kept on 'finding herself' till I'd thrown her out on her pretty ear, but by then Maura was three months' pregnant. And she was getting to be a joke around my firm. I resigned to save myself further embarrassment—quit the year I would've made partner, which I'd been slaving toward for six hard years.

"But it turned out the joke was on me. She left me with the baby when Kat was eleven months old—then ran off and married her gynecologist.''

"Oh, Jack..." Abby's fingers rose toward his chest, then fell away. "I'm sorry.''

"Hey, no sorry about it. I got a dynamite kid and learned a life-long lesson. Don't marry a woman in the midst of Divorce Crazies.

"But as to messin' around while she's sorting herself out..." His eyebrows waggled in a comic leer.

"Do you *ever* quit?''

"Not when I want something. And what I want right now is a fling with you. A happy, sappy, sexy little fling.''

She gave his shoulder a condescending pat, then pushed away. "It's not what I need.''

"Who's talking need here? I'm talking *want.*''

"I don't *want* anything. You. Us.''

Liar. "Give me five minutes—three—and I'll change your mind.''

Abby hugged herself and drifted backward, shaking her head. "No, thanks. And if you're my friend? You'll stop pushing." She turned, walked off fast. Waved her hand in a wide, relieved greeting as she spotted the kids coming up the drive.

Jack jammed his hands into his pockets and swore.

THAT NIGHT Kat somehow managed to spill the pot of corn chowder she'd made all over the kitchen floor. So the families ate together in spite of Abby's misgivings. Jack behaved like a gentleman, although she detected an ungentlemanly glint in his eye each time their eyes met. He'd made no promise to stop pushing.

But he could want and want and want, and it would get him precisely nowhere. Abby had drawn the line at friendship, and though he might walk up to that line and gaze wistfully across, he wouldn't step over. He might be a sex-crazed cad or, to be charitable, maybe he was just hopelessly male, thinking sex would cure whatever ailed a woman, but he was also...Jack. She could trust him to accept her no, even when he didn't like it.

That didn't mean he wouldn't do his darnedest to tempt her or to persuade her over to his side of the line. Lawyers thrived on argument. Abby would have to ignore him, or even better, change the topic.

"Have you had Kat's eyes checked lately?" she asked after supper. Kat had proposed that she walk down to the library to get a book on falcons, and miraculously, Sky had roused himself from his blues and decided to tag along. Since the sun had set, the adults had promptly concluded that they, too, could use a good read. So here they all were, sauntering two by two down the hill through the cricket-loud dusk.

"She was twenty-twenty a year ago." Jack's hand

dropped onto Abby's far shoulder as she stumbled, then rode there, light and warm. "Why?"

"Oh, I don't know. She seems rather…clumsy lately. Spilling that soup tonight, she could've been badly burned. I thought possibly her spatial vision is off? Or…" She turned toward him, which served to break the contact, good as it felt. "How would you test a kid for coordination?"

"Take her to the nearest video arcade, where, believe me, she'd stomp us both, any game you choose from laser sabers to bop-the-dinosaur. I wouldn't worry. Kat's just going through a stage."

"But why now?"

"Beats me. Maybe her feet have outgrown the rest of her again."

He was in one of his "what, me worry?" moods, so Abby gave up. "Speaking of feet, I promised you I'd take her shopping. I was thinking about tomorrow afternoon. I have a few errands of my own to run in the city, if you don't mind my mooching your car again."

"I told you, any time you want it. It's just sitting there in the carport, getting fat and cantankerous. Needs exercise. And as for Kat, that would be terrific. Outfit her from head to toe if you like. I'll stop by the bank in the morning and get you some cash."

CHAPTER EIGHTEEN

WHEN ABBY FOLLOWED KAT into Jack's office the next day, she walked a fine line between exuberance and exasperation.

Maudie Harris had dropped by for coffee that morning and she'd loved what Abby had done with the kitchen. The landlady would be delighted to waive an additional two weeks' rent in exchange for a repainted and redecorated living room. That was the good news.

The bad news was that Skyler had pulled an unexpected snit when she'd insisted he couldn't stay home alone. He slouched in the doorway behind her, the very picture of terminal boredom.

Nothing to do but cheerfully ignore him. "So..." Abby turned slowly. Here was yet another side of Jack Kelton—the professional man. Two walls lined with legal books, a framed law degree from Stanford between the windows, a superb Turkish carpet on the floor, and Jack himself rising from a cluttered desk, looking even larger than usual in a beautifully tailored gray suit and—

She looked at his big feet and laughed. "I know I'm out west when even the lawyers wear cowboy boots!" The fanciest of boots, some sort of lizard skin; they gave him an elegantly whimsical air. And there was something indescribably sexy about that burgundy silk tie, which made her want to grab it and pull his head down for a kiss. *What's got into you?* she scolded herself. It must be his fling proposal of the previous afternoon that was giving her these ideas.

"Well, shucks, ma'am. Today's a court day." His crinkled gray eyes swept from Abby to his daughter, who was busily feeding a tank of angelfish over in the conversation area of the office. They roved on to Skyler, glowering in his doorway. Jack's shaggy brows twitched as he pulled out his wallet. "Will this cover the damages?" He handed her two hundred-dollar bills.

"That's way more than enough! We're thinking small here." Abby hadn't explained her intentions to Kat, had simply asked the kids to come along on her errands. She hoped Jack would say nothing now.

"Well, hold on to it. You can always bring me the change." He'd drifted backward as he spoke, so that now he stood almost elbow to elbow with Sky. "Looks interesting." He nodded at the library book Sky had brought along, an encyclopaedia of military aircraft.

Sky shrugged and kicked the door frame.

"If you're more in a mood to read today than run errands with the ladies, you could always hang with the fish over there." Jack nodded at his couch across the room. "I've got to walk over to the courthouse in a while. You can come along if you don't have too much metal on you."

At that, Sky looked up from the floor. "Huh?"

"Have to make it through the metal detectors. They need 'em to stop disgruntled plaintiffs from shooting the judge. Or their own lawyers."

Abby tried not to roll her eyes as Sky brightened visibly, shrugged again and allowed that he "Guessed that would be as boring as anything else." He wandered over to the couch and flopped, nose buried in his book.

They left him there as Jack escorted them to the exit. "How to charm the surly adolescent male," she murmured

admiringly, walking beside him while Kat darted ahead.
"Offer him a chance at bloodshed and he'll follow you
anywhere."

"If he knew you meant to go shopping for clothes, he'd
fall down and kiss my boots," Jack murmured. "Oh, wait
a minute!" He snapped his fingers. "Kat, I almost forgot."

Halfway down the stairs, she turned and scampered back
up. "Da-ad, *what?* We've gotta go!"

"Todd's birthday is week after next. We need to put
something in the mail. If you see anything today that you
think he'd like—buy it, okay? Abby should have enough
to cover it."

"'Kay." Kat turned and trudged off down the staircase.

"Todd?" Abby asked. Just like that, the spark of mischievous joy in Kat's eyes had faded and blinked out.

"Maura's boy by her first marriage. Kat's half brother.
He's just finished high school and joined the navy. Don't
worry if she doesn't find anything. I was thinking the first
three or four books of Patrick O'Brian's Aubrey and Ma-
turin series would do. British naval battles and all. But it's
nicer if the idea comes from her. I try to keep them connected."

"All right," Abby agreed. *But does Kat want the connection?*

She found Kat waiting by the car, as downcast and sul-
len as Skyler had been all morning. *And thank you, Jack.*
Revising her game plan, Abby decided to start with the
neutral chores. Given time, perhaps Kat's mood would re-
bound. Because to pull off any sort of image change, she'd
need Kat at her most playful and adventurous.

Kat tagged gloomily along to the hardware store while
Abby chose the paint for the living room. At her suggestion, they picked up sample cards of colors for Kat, in case
she decided to repaint and stencil her bedroom as she'd

been discussing all week. But today her enthusiasm for the project had vanished.

Todd. This all started with Todd, Abby reminded herself. "So what next?" she said briskly. "Lunch?"

Kat scuffed her tennis shoes. "I'm not hungry."

Kat was in the blackest of moods when she wouldn't eat. "Ooo-kay." Forget bras. One needed a sense of the absurd to buy one's first bra and Kat's had gone south.

"I need some fishing line for my falcon trap," she growled after a moment.

So they found a sporting goods store, where they bought the heaviest nylon line available, then a hat of Kat's choosing. Hardly the height of femininity, it could have topped the head of the most intrepid jungle explorer. Abby was beginning to regret her cockiness in assuring Jack she could affect a change. *Come back next year—or the year after,* she told herself. Whenever the estrogen tide set in. And really, she was catching Jack's panic and she shouldn't. Kat had all the time in the world. *Relax and enjoy.* That was all they should be doing today, widening Kat's scope of pleasures.

The best way was to celebrate her own. Passing a case of fly fishing gear, Abby stopped short. "Oh, wow!"

Kat bumped her elbow. "It's just fishing lures. Dad ties 'em sometimes, when he's not building."

"They're gorgeous! What jewelry they'd make! Look at those Black Ghosts. If I was a trout, I'd gobble those up." She glanced up as a salesman appeared behind the counter. "Could I please see that card of lures? Mind if I take it over to the mirror?"

She held a Yellow Marabou Streamer up to one of her ears, and something made with parrot feathers to the other, then preened, ignoring Kat's incredulous smirk. "Which do you like?"

"You'll hook your ears!"

"No, I won't. I'll glue a bead over each barb. And I'll have to find some ear wires. But which do you prefer?"

They decided on a set of Green Damsel flies for Abby. Then she chose a red-and-gold confection of pheasant feathers with a silver tinsel stripe and held it up to Kat's ear. "I thought so. With your coloring, this would be stunning."

"It would?" Kat stood very still—then scowled. "That's just stupid girl stuff, jewelry and feathers."

"Oh, I don't know. All kinds of people wear bright stuff for all kinds of reasons. Think of American Indians: I suppose it was the guys who wore the eagle-feather bonnets. All this gear is just to make you feel brave. War paint. Lipstick. Pirates with gold rings in their ears. Not much difference." Abby tilted her head to study the girl. "You know, I've been wanting to do a portrait of you for your father, a sort of thank-you gift. I was picturing you as a desert princess, with a falcon on her shoulder. How would that be?"

Kat's eyes widened. "I'd have to catch him first."

Abby shook her head. "That's the best part of being an artist. I can imagine him for you, show you just what he'd look like. I was thinking a sparrow hawk, with those wonderful spotted wings and you wearing a burnoose like a Bedouin?"

Kat giggled. "You're crazy, Abby."

"Ha! You haven't begun to see crazy."

They left the sporting goods store with twenty dollars' worth of fishing lures and a much improved attitude. Abby grinned to herself. Poor Jack. No doubt he was sitting at his desk about now, smugly patting himself on the back for solving the Kat Problem. *He's probably picturing us all girlish shrieks and giggles—up to our ears in silk stock-*

ings and lace bustiers and push-up bras right now! Instead of trout line and fishing lures and pith helmets.

"The next stop is for ice cream," she declared. No girl could pass through the arcane rites of American womanhood till she'd developed a wholesome respect for chocolate and carbohydrates.

Half an hour later, floating on a cloud of whipped cream and fudge sauce, they sailed out of the ice-cream parlor and simply strolled, window-shopping and idly chatting. *So this is what it would be like to have a daughter,* Abby mused. To have an ally in your pocket. Someone with whom you shared instant rapport. Much as she loved Skyler, she often had to struggle to comprehend his moods and needs. While Kat was as clear to her as a mountain stream.

They came to a consignment store and Abby stopped abruptly. "Oh, I love antique clothes!"

In short order, she'd picked out a two-dollar costume jewelry necklace that could be cannibalized for its glass beads; she'd use them to complete their earrings. Also some simple brass clip-on studs, from which to dangle Kat's fish lure finery, since her ears weren't pierced.

Abby turned next to the belt rack. "Would you look at this!" She held up a small beaded leather belt, imitation Zuni work, but charming all the same with its geometric patterns in turquoise and corals and creams. "Now this would work for my portrait of you. It's very desert-looking, isn't it? Try it on," she suggested casually, then turned back to the rack.

"Oh, and this is nice!" An embossed concho belt from the fifties, also made for the tourist trade and definitely not silver, but still very pretty. She threaded it through the loops of her own dark blue slacks, then turned to inspect Kat. "Oh, yes!"

Hooking her thumbs in the beaded belt, Kat gave an offhanded shrug.

Abby intended to draw a close view of Kat, probably from the shoulders up. But for now, she'd found the back door into Kat's wardrobe. "That's perfect for your Bedouin costume. And once we're done, you could always use it for blue jeans." Kat's favorite attire. "And I'm going to splurge and get this concho belt." It took two to make a shopping spree.

"Now we need to find you a burnoose." Pulling Kat over to a rack of accessories, Abby chose an Indian silk scarf in luscious stripes of ruby and scarlet and purple, spangled with gold thread. Standing behind Kat at the mirror, she draped it over her shoulders and around her head and throat to create a soft hood. When Kat made a doubtful face, she added quickly, "These colors would go well with a sparrow hawk, wouldn't they?"

Instant smile.

You are so easy, lovey. She had a sudden urge to stoop and kiss the top of Kat's head. But better not. Not today.

So when? wondered a small ironic voice in her mind. Two weeks, and the bus would be ready. She and Sky would have no excuse left to stay in Trueheart and every sane reason to go. Her happiness wavered. Her smile wobbled.

Live in the now, not later, she reminded herself and rallied. "This scarf is gorgeous." Kat was gorgeous, but she would be courting a tomboy backlash to say so. Today's task was much more modest. Simply to instill the notion that Kat could enjoy lovely, sensual things without betraying her own fierce sense of self.

"And feel how soft it is." Abby brushed the sheer silk along Kat's cheek. "Nice? Now let's look at this gold one." She whisked the scarf away and substituted another.

"This one would complement the russets and blacks on the sparrow hawk's wings. And imagine this mustardy-gold in the foreground, if I made the background a deep Prussian blue. As if you and your falcon were up on a mountainside, near sundown."

Abby tipped her head, considering. Maybe here was a topic for another children's book? Like butterflies spreading their wings to the sun, pictures unfolded in her mind. "I think I'd better get you both of these scarves, then decide which one works best for your portrait later on."

IT HADN'T TURNED OUT to be such a boring day after all, Sky admitted to himself as he and Jack walked back to his office. They'd gone out to lunch with Jack's friend, Mr. Fielding, the lawyer Sky and his mom had met at the grocery store. The men had treated him just like one of the guys. They'd talked about cars and skiing and going fishing, and a case of Mr. Fielding's, where he was defending a man accused of stealing some cows. A real-live cattle rustler!

Then he'd gone to court with Jack—Sky still called him Mr. Kelton, but he thought of him as Jack—and watched while he asked the judge for something called a restraining order. "Why was that man so mad?" he asked now. "He was really yelling."

"Mmm." Jack frowned. "That was the tail end of a divorce case, kiddo. Mr. Murphy and his wife—my client—split up. But he's been bothering her since then. Scaring her, which of course he shouldn't. So I asked the judge to tell him he couldn't go near her or her family. And the judge did. Finally."

Sky pushed his glasses up his nose. "But if the man wants to get back together with her? Not be divorced anymore?" He blinked as Jack's hand came to rest on his shoulder, silently bidding him to stop as they came to a corner. The light changed and they walked across the street. Jack's hand stayed in place, warm and heavy and making him feel funny inside—sad and happy and as if he belonged somewhere for the first time in months and months.

"It's hard," Jack said in his rumbly voice. "But it takes two people to want to be married. If only one of a couple wants it, it doesn't work."

"But what if somebody—one of them—*really* wants it. Loves the other—"

"Even then, Sky, that's not enough. Sometimes you have to learn to take a no. Let go of something you wanted and loved. It isn't easy, and Lord knows it hurts. But it's part of growing up."

"Mr. Murphy was a grown-up." Bigger than Jack, even.

"On the outside, maybe. His insides haven't quite caught up with the rest of him. You're not all the way grown till you can take a no and come back at least trying to smile. Pretending to smile."

"Pretending isn't honest, is it?"

"Well, if you pretend to smile, sometimes it turns into the real thing—and then it's honest." Jack pulled him to a halt. "Mind if we cruise the hardware store for a minute? I could use a five-eighths-inch drill bit."

AFTER THEY'D RANSACKED the consignment store, they lugged their bags of goodies to the car. "We've got to grocery shop at some point," Abby reminded them both. "But first, you know what I need? Some lingerie."

"What's that?"

"Wait and see. Where can we find a nice department store in this town?"

"Now that is really pretty," she said a short while later,

fingering a low-cut brassiere made of a sheer sparkly lilac fabric.

Kat wrinkled her nose. *"Eeuw!"*

"Girl stuff, absolutely," Abby admitted. "But I've *got* to try it on. This one would make me feel like a superhero."

"Huh?" Kat cocked her head, looking so much like her father that Abby almost laughed out loud.

"You know. I walk around in a shirt and a pair of slacks and the world sees plain, shy, everyday Abby Lake. But beneath this humdrum disguise lurks—" Abby held the sparkly brassiere to her chest and shimmied her shoulders "—ta-dah! Lilac Lady! Ready to leap tall buildings and battle monsters whenever and wherever I hear the call. As long as I can find a phone booth to change in."

Kat giggled and shook her head. "You're nuts!"

"Probably, but it's kind of nice to be two people at once. A private person and a public one. So…I'm going to go try on this brassiere, and while I do that, why don't you look around? See if your inner lady needs anything." Abby had already spotted precisely what Kat needed, but that would take some tactful maneuvering. First step was simply to be a role model.

Once they'd made their choices in the lingerie department, Abby insisted they change into their purchases, to feel like superheroes all the sooner. Seeing the glow on Kat's face as she came out of the dressing room, buttoning her shirt over a demure cotton camisole with pink satin shoulder straps and edging, Abby considered her mission complete.

Still, when they passed the perfume counter on their way out, she couldn't resist pushing her luck. Kat consented to sniff—then warily accepted a dab of this behind her ears and a spray of that in the crook of her elbow. Abby explained about pulse points and how a woman's body heat would alter a scent, make it her own. But today was a day to appreciate rather than buy; they left the counter empty-handed, blithely reeking of roses and orange blossoms and jasmine.

With the exit in sight, they passed through the men's accessory section. Abby touched Kat's shoulder. "I'd forgotten about your brother. Todd. Should we be shopping for him while we're here? Maybe he could use a new wallet? Or some aftershave?"

Kat scowled and looked at her feet. "Dunno."

"Well, then, let's not worry about it today." She'd tell Jack to buy and mail those books he'd mentioned. "But tell me about Todd," Abby coaxed, brushing a wisp of bangs off Kat's forehead. "What's he like?"

"Dunno. He's just a guy. Conceited. And he's not as tough as he thinks he is. Once when he was visiting us, he fell off his bike and cried."

"Did he? Still, it must be nice to have a big brother."

"Dad thinks it is."

Ah. "Why do you say that?" Casually she hooked a hand through Kat's elbow to pull her along. "Todd's related to you, not your dad."

Kat heaved a sigh that must have come up from her toes. "Dad said once…to my uncle Drew…that sometimes he thought it would've made more sense if my mom had given him Todd—and taken me instead."

Oh, Kat! Abby's heart contracted. She moved her hand from the girl's elbow to her shoulders, half hugging her as they walked. "He said that in front of you? When?" *Jack, how could you?*

"I was hiding behind a curtain. He'd tucked me into bed, but I couldn't sleep. And I wanted to listen to him and Uncle Drew talking."

Sometime years ago, then. But oh, it was the wounds of early childhood that cut the deepest, left the worst scars. *So you've been trying to out-boy the boys ever since, my poor sweetie. To prove yourself a keeper.* "I wonder if maybe he meant something different than you heard?"

Kat frowned. "What d'you mean?"

"I mean sometimes we take things wrong. Not how they were really intended. I wonder if your dad wasn't simply saying that he was scared about being able to raise a daughter."

"Scared?" Kat snorted. "Dad's not scared of anything!"

"Oh, you'd be surprised, kiddo. I'll bet maybe he was scared that he couldn't do a good job, bringing up a little girl. Though it sure turns out he was wrong. He's done a super job. You are *so* special."

"Me?" Kat's eyes were shiny with tears as Abby stopped and turned to grasp her shoulders.

"You, Katkin. Extra-super special. Your dad is the luckiest guy in the world to have you in his life—and believe me, he knows it." *I wish I had a daughter like you.* Abby brushed the back of one knuckle playfully along the girl's brow. "All you need to be absolutely, completely perfect is eyebrows, and they're on the way." There, that had won a smile.

Meantime, you and I have something to talk about, Jack Kelton! "Well…" She glanced around. "You know, it's getting late. I think we'd better head straight for the grocery store, then go find the guys."

CHAPTER NINETEEN

BY THE TIME they reached Jack's office, it was nearly sundown. Too late to go home and cook, he insisted, when they walked in his door. "And I'd say it's my turn to provide a meal. Let's eat out.

"Any success?" he inquired, guiding Abby along with a hand at her back while Kat and Sky raced ahead to the Subaru. "I half expected you two to show up in dresses and heels."

"I'm afraid I left my fairy godmother wand at home. So, no—no ball gowns and glass slippers this trip, but we do have a few things to show you." And secret talismans he'd never see, like the lilac brassiere and bikini set Abby was wearing, which did make her feel superhero-sexy. "And I suppose it's okay to tell you that she's wearing a Calvin Klein camisole that should carry her most elegantly through any sixth-grade gym class."

"A camisole! This calls for champagne."

He took them to a wonderful Mexican restaurant where they ordered margaritas instead of champagne, and the evening was delightful. Sky was full of his day's adventures: he'd watched a real trial in court, helped Jack's secretary Emma clean the fish tank, then listened to her sing the latest song she'd written, which was better than anything on the radio.

Sounds like a crush in the making to me, Abby mused with a smile. And Jack had bought Sky a special hammer, with a perfect balance and swing. She flashed him a warm look across the table. *Thank you!* His kindness and generosity to her son were almost reason alone to love him. Almost.

"I bought some fishing lures," Kat bragged, not to be outdone. "And a jungle hat."

"And you smell," Sky noted, leaning over to sniff her. "Oh, yuck!"

"He's just jealous," Abby said quickly as Kat's brows flew together. "Guys aren't as free as we are. We can wear anything they can—and dresses besides. And no matter how much they'd love to, guys can't ever smell like flowers. Or wear certain colors, like shocking pink."

"*I* always wanted to wear mauve and dance around with a rose between my teeth," Jack said mournfully. "But alas, it was not to be."

"Oh, gross!"

"Daddy, you did *not!*"

Closing ranks in the face of adult insanity, Sky and Kat shuddered with disgust. While above their heads, Abby and Jack shared a moment of silent laughter across the table.

And whatever this feeling was, it didn't feel like friendship.

"So," Jack said a short while later as they drove into his office parking lot. "Who wants to ride home with me?"

Sky opened his mouth to volunteer—then remembered. Today was Tuesday! He called his dad every Tuesday at eight; he was late already. His mom was carrying her cell phone as usual, but it would feel weird to make the call from Jack's car, with Jack listening in.

He slunk low in the back seat as Jack looked behind. "Um," he muttered, confused and miserable.

"Hey, the Katkin's asleep," Jack noted, lowering his voice.

She was. She'd curled up in the crack between seat and door and was smiling in her sleep.

"Then you'd better take care of them both," Jack decided, turning back to the boy, "and I'll catch you later." He thumped his knee. "Great day, Sky."

So his feelings weren't hurt by Sky's desertion. Sky felt a surge of relief as he nodded. "Thanks for my hammer." He was holding it in his lap. It was a most excellent tool, with a steel handle—not a wooden one—that should last forever.

Jack got out of the car and strolled around its front. He stopped by the driver's window, looking down at Sky's mom. "You're not too sleepy to drive?"

"Oh, no," she murmured. "I'm fine."

"Well, catch you later, too."

He touched her face with the backs of his fingers—Sky stiffened and sat up straight. *Don't do that!* He rolled down his window and leaned out. "'Night, Mr. Kelton," he said loudly.

Jack straightened, gave him a lopsided smile. "Goodnight, Sky." He swung away and strode off toward his Jeep.

Across the parking lot, a car switched on its headlights and Jack put up a hand to shield his face from the glare. Tires squealed, the engine roared—the car rushed right at him!

As Sky's mother cried out, it screeched to a halt and the driver's door burst open. A man staggered out. *"Kelton!"*

"He's got a gun!" Skyler cried. It was Mr. Murphy, the big, angry guy from court, and he was waving a gun!

"Hands up, you bastard, and get over here! Where's my damn wife?"

"Beats me." Jack stood with his hands raised on the far side of Murphy's car. "You tried her father's?"

"You know *damn well* they've cleared out of there! You think setting timers on their damn lights was gonna fool me? Now *where is she?*"

Jack's voice was very, very calm, almost cheerful. "Well...why don't we talk about that? And thanks for the ride, Ms. Lake," he added in a flatter tone. "G'night." His head moved the tiniest bit toward the road.

Mr. Murphy spun around and pointed the gun at Sky's mom. "You drive anywhere and I'll shoot him! Got that? Stay where you are. Yeah, and give me your keys! Throw 'em out here where I can see 'em!"

"Don't," Jack said in that calm, toneless voice. "Drive on. Murphy and I will stay here and talk."

"You shut up or you're dead and she throws me the keys—*now!*"

"Of course," Sky's mom said softly, then softer yet, "Get down on the floorboard, Skyler, and get Kat down." The keys jangled as they hit the pavement.

Sky couldn't believe it, but Kat was still sleeping. She'd slid down even farther, where she couldn't be seen.

"Now get in the car!" Murphy screamed. "*Do* it!"

Sky peeked over the edge of his door. Jack was climbing into Murphy's car! His mom made a tiny moaning sound and leaned to grab something below her seat. Things thudded onto the floorboard. She was hunting for the phone, Sky realized, which was always at the bottom of her purse, under all her junk. But even if she called the police, the man was about to drive away with Jack and that would be awful!

As Murphy's car started rolling past them, Sky sat up—and threw his hammer as hard as he could.

He'd meant to smash the windshield. Instead it clattered

across the hood with a terrible racket. The car bounced to
a halt—

And kept on bouncing.

Sky could see Jack and the guy moving behind the glass,
arms swinging, bodies shoving, things thumping and
cracking. Somebody yelped. The car was *really* rocking on
its springs! His mom was telling somebody on the phone
that it was an emergency, an assault, please, please, please,
come quick!

The horn blared on Murphy's car—and kept on blaring.

Kat sat up. "Whuh?"

The horn continued to honk, and the far door of the car
banged open. Jack stood up and rushed around its hood.

"Oh, *thank* you, God!" Sky's mom whispered.

"What's going on?" Kat punched Sky's back. "Let *me*
see!"

Jack yanked open the driver's door, hauled Mr. Murphy
out from behind the wheel, and the horn stopped. He
dumped him facedown on the pavement—then knelt on
top of him. Panting, he glanced up at them. "Every...
body...okay there?"

"Oh, Jack, we're fine," his mom cried. "Should I—?"

"Don't get out, sweetheart. You called 9-1-1?"

But they could all hear the sirens coming.

Jack's mouth was bleeding as he glanced up at Sky and
grinned. "Now *that's* the way to swing a hammer."

HOURS LATER Abby saw the headlights turn into Jack's
driveway—at last! She scrambled up from her front steps
and ran. Flew through the old gate between the yards,
across the grass to reach him just as he stepped out of the
Jeep and turned. "Oh, *Jack!*"

"*Ooof!*" His arms closed around her as they collided,
fell back against the vehicle's side. "Hey...hey, easy!"

"Oh, *God,* Jack!" Her arms locked around his waist, Abby buried her face against his chest. "I..." *Was so frightened. He almost killed you right there in front of us.* "If anything had happened to you!" Jack with his strength and his kindness and his wonderful silliness, to be swept away from her all in a senseless second? *Before I ever had a chance to*— Every time she pictured it, her stomach turned over.

"*Hey,* it's okay." He lifted her chin. Smiled down at her.

But it so nearly wasn't! She hugged him tighter, glorying in the hard solidity of him—safe—there in her arms.

"I'm not even scratched," he insisted. Framing her face with one big hand, he kissed her.

She shuddered, arched up against him on tiptoe and kissed him back, tears welling. *Oh, Jack.* She'd known that she cared for him, but not till that night, helplessly watching that struggle in the car, not knowing who'd win it... She'd been reliving her terror ever since.

Only now with their mouths hungrily fusing, their tongues caressing and gliding, her arms sliding up around his neck and her breasts against his hammering heart, could she begin to really believe that she hadn't lost him. That Jack was still here in her world, where he ought to be.

His lips trailed up her cheek, to brush back and forth through her lashes. "Tears? No tears, sweetheart. No need for 'em."

"S-sorry." She tried to laugh through her sniffles. "I was just so scared."

"I'm sorry you were scared. I'll go back and thump the creep again for scaring you."

"*No,* don't—" But he swallowed her refusal, turning them both with dreamy slowness as he kissed her—till she found her backside pressed against the car. His hardness nestled snugly against her belly. She shivered and moved closer, her hips rocking to meet him.

"Whew!" Jack lifted his head. "Or maybe I should thank him." He angled his head to nibble her ear. Laid a string of hot, open-mouthed kisses down the side of her neck. She gasped with sheer pleasure—gasped again as his hands closed around her waist and he lifted her up to the hood of the Jeep.

She opened her thighs and he slid between them. "Oh, Abby!"

She'd only meant to satisfy herself that he was unharmed, but in satisfying that need she'd awakened further needs, deeper hungers, in them both. She moaned with impatience as he surged rhythmically against her, sharing his arousal, driving hers higher and higher. Their tongues twined, danced... He raised his head, breathing hard. "Heck of a time to be asking, but the kids, are they out of the way?"

"I put them to bed at my place." It had taken hours to calm them down. Sky had talked a blue streak, gloating over every minute of the fight, telling her again and again what might have been, how close they'd come to tragedy, till she'd wanted to scream. And Kat had been cranky, furious that she'd missed the excitement, jealous that Sky claimed to have saved the day. Badly frightened under her petulance.

"They should be fine there, for a while." He rubbed his cheek back and forth against hers and something scratched.

She tilted her head far enough back to focus. "Oh!" In the dark, she'd missed the flesh-colored bandage on his cheek. "You *are* hurt."

"Just a gash. The paramedic patched me up." He smiled

as she cradled his face in both hands, scanning him critically for more damage. "Nothing to speak of."

"Nothing!"

His hands curled around her hips and he pulled her
close, closer; they moved as one, yearning for that final
melting release. "All I could think of," he said in a whisper, "before I got hold of the gun, was that it couldn't end
this way, before I'd loved you."

What I was thinking, too. Bracing her arms behind her,
she dropped her head back for his slowly descending kiss.

And a small querulous voice called, "Daddy?"

"Aggggh!" Jack took one swift step backward, still
holding on to her. Made a rueful face. Turned to call over
his shoulder, "Yeah, Kat?" He smoothed his hands down
Abby's thighs, then swung around, blocking Kat's view of
her for a moment.

Abby ran her hands through her tangled hair. She
hopped down from the hood, then slipped out from behind
Jack to see Kat trudging across the grass.

"Hey, kiddo, I thought you'd gone to bed." He went
to meet her. Knelt and hugged her hard. "Couldn't sleep?"

"Uh-huh. You shouldn't have sent us back."

"Well, I had to chat with the police for a while. They
wanted to know things. Fill out some forms. I figured
you'd be bored."

"Did that man really have a gun? Sky said he did, but
I didn't see it."

"Wasn't much to see. Just a silly argument, no big
deal." He rose stiffly to his feet. "Well, bedtime, Kat. I'm
beat. You look pretty sleepy, too. And I bet Abby's tired."
He glanced at her apologetically. "Let's call it a night."

"Did he have a gun? What kind?"

"Kat, you'll be a prosecutor when you grow up, for

sure." Jack herded her toward his front door. "Say good-night to Abby."

Kat looked back, obviously surprised to find her there. "G'night, Abby."

Empty and aching, she stood barefoot in the wet grass. Watched them troop up the stairs, a family of two, complete in itself. "'Night," she called wistfully.

And went home to her lonely bed.

BY MORNING Abby's frustration had turned to gratitude. Kat had saved her from a bad mistake. *What happened last night changes nothing,* she scolded herself while she washed the breakfast dishes.

She'd known before that Jack was wonderful.

And now she knew that her heart would break if he ever came to harm.

But that didn't mean it would be wise to love him.

Even if it was already too late to call back her foolish heart, it was still safer to love him from a distance than to fall into his arms.

Into his bed.

He may be braver than brave, sexy enough to make me go weak in the knees, but he's still the King of Can't Commit. Wanting a fling. Willing to risk nothing.

At least now she understood why, after he'd told her about Maura.

And knowing about Maura, how could Abby blame him if he was wary of involvement—especially involvement with a woman newly divorced? It was part of the man's essential toughness that he'd decline to be burned a second time. That he'd take a clear-eyed, unsentimental approach to his own sexual needs.

And maybe he's right when he warns me about—what

*did he call them?—the Divorce Crazies. How it's not safe
for me to have anything right now, but a fling…*

Three weeks ago Abby would've said she knew *precisely* what she wanted from life.

Now she hadn't a clue.

To stay here and risk her heart again—especially on Jack's temporary terms—would be truly insane.

But to continue with her original plans, to go on to Sedona…when Trueheart now felt like home, full of friends and a future?

Turning off the water, she could suddenly hear voices in the backyard. Sky was out there walking DC. Probably Kat had joined him. Abby wiped her hands on a dish towel and prowled into the living room, where she stood staring down at the latest sketches on her drawing board. *This is what I should be thinking about. Focusing on.* A career that would feed her soul and pay her bills, not a short-term romance with no possible happy ending.

"Abby?" Jack darkened the kitchen doorway. "I knocked, but I guess you didn't hear. May I come in?"

Why ask when he was in already? In her house. Under her skin. And it was all very well for her to fret about what *she* wanted, but here came Jack with his own agenda—finishing what she'd started the night before.

He stopped so close to her, his big boots overlapped her bare feet. "I've been thinking…" His hand drifted up, and his knuckles brushed along the line of her jaw, sending a wave of hot pleasure rushing across her skin. "What if I hired a sitter for tonight to watch the kids while we go out on a date?"

"A date?" That sounded entirely too innocent for the wicked promise in his dancing gray eyes.

"Well…" He dragged his forefinger across her lips.

"Out for supper? Someplace where they bring it up to your room on a rolling cart?"

That's what I thought. She smiled. Sighed regretfully. Stepped into his arms as they slid around her and pulled her close. *How can I ever, ever, resist you?*

If she didn't, she'd live to regret it.

And she'd already racked up too many regrets this year.

"Or I s'pose, if you prefer your dates alfresco..." His voice had dropped to an intimate rumble. "We could pack a picnic...drive up into the mountains?"

Take each other under the stars, on the hood of his Jeep. She'd been imagining that all night long, and, clearly, so had he. She shivered with longing.

He kissed the side of her neck and whispered huskily, hopefully, "Yes?"

"No." She flattened her hands on his chest. "I'd love to, but."

"But?"

"But." He knew the reasons. *Last thing I need is a fling—and with a man who only needs flings.* She pushed and he let her go.

"Ooo-kay. Not tonight. I'm a guy, I can take it."

"Not—" She paused as he pressed a finger to her lips.

"Uh-uh. Don't say anything you'd only have to take back. I've gotta run. Wouldn't miss Murphy's arraignment for the world." Swooping down, he replaced his finger with his mouth. Kissed her briskly but thoroughly—then strode out the door, calling over his shoulder, "Catch you later, Abby."

And that was as fair a warning as she'd get.

CHAPTER TWENTY

"THERE'S NO JUSTICE!" Alec Fielding complained on Monday at the deli, once Jack had finished the tale of his encounter with Murphy. "I leave town for one measly week, looking for excitement, and all hell starts a'popping the minute I turn my back! I even worked late last Tuesday. Must've missed the rumpus by minutes." He sighed disconsolately. "Would have loved to give you a hand."

"Abby's kid was all the help I needed."

"Spunky little devil," Alec agreed. "And Sky's sexy mom? How did Abby cope with the situation? She keep her cool?"

"Absolutely." She'd saved her heat for afterward. Jack's heart rate spiked with the memory. Abby on the hood of his car, his for the taking. If Kat hadn't wandered by, they might have melted the Jeep.

"Cool is good," Alec said. "Can't stand a hysterical woman."

Cool was lousy. The morning after, Abby had given him the cold shoulder, and the weather had been distinctly chilly ever since. Try as he might, Jack couldn't thaw her. At least not with the kids looking on. And so far she'd dodged his every attempt to cut her out of the herd.

Also handicapping him was Kat's sudden insecurity. Even though she'd missed the fight, Sky's ghoulish recounting had clearly scared her; she'd been Daddy's Little Girl ever since, climbing into his lap, wriggling in between him and Abby on the couch or whenever they walked. All in all, Jack had suffered a frustrating, strictly PG-rated weekend.

"How's the bus repair coming?" Alec inquired. "Must be about done by now."

"Moving along." That was another problem. Abby had confronted poor Whitey on Saturday, telling him that contrary to whatever he might have heard, from whatever unsavory source, she wanted her bus repaired sooner—*very* soon—not later.

Conveniently forgetting that it was his gossip that had started the trouble, Whitey had sulked all weekend, spending most of his time under the bus, communing strictly with Chang and the exhaust system, crawling out only to spit tobacco and to scowl. Jack hadn't dared ask him how much progress he'd made, but the old man had worked nonstop and stayed late.

"She still headed for Sedona once it's done?" Alec questioned.

"Far as I know." Jack shoved his plate with its half-eaten sandwich aside. Abby gone. The cottage next door empty, where there had been laughter and warmth. Its welcoming back door locked. Kat would miss them badly. His heart hurt, just imagining his kid's coming loneliness.

"You're going to let her go?"

What the heck am I supposed to do? Handcuff her to my bed? He was just about that desperate. He stood abruptly. "Got an appointment at two."

Alec grinned up at him, keen-eyed and unrepentant. "I suppose if she does go, she'll still have to come back for the trial."

Previously too lenient, Judge Hutchins had considered Murphy's stunt a personal insult. He'd denied him bail. Fast-tracked his trial for assault and attempted kidnapping.

"Uh-huh." Jack didn't like it, Abby testifying, drawing Murphy's malice her way. But the D.A. had already taken her statement, telling her she'd be called. And Abby was quietly determined to do her part, to put the man away for years.

"Divorce Crazies or no, hadn't you better ask her out on a date?" Alec prodded.

He'd asked her out five times in the past six days! "Thanks, Mom, but I know what I'm doing."

Going cross-eyed with frustration.

"PLEASE, PLEASE, PLEASE?" Abby prayed as she lifted the stencil. Finding an icing of the proper consistency had been harder than she'd expected. Today's recipe was version four in a week.

"*Yes!*" Michelle cried as the cookie was revealed. The design of a woman on horseback, whacking a cow on the rump with her Stetson, was picture-perfect. "It's beautiful. You're a genius!" She hugged Abby, let her go to twirl around her big kitchen in her apartment above the restaurant. "The very Remington of Cookies!"

"Hey, you're the one who came up with the icing." It was a butter-and-caramelized brown-sugar glaze. Stiff enough to stencil, thin enough to show detail, hardening nicely when it cooled.

"And who came up with the idea to cut it in four?"

The cookie was as large as four normal cookies, so why not take a razor-thin wire and score the dough before baking, Abby had reasoned. The cookie could be stenciled in one piece, then broken later, like four parts to a jigsaw puzzle. Michelle planned to introduce them to her customers by serving a complimentary quarter cookie to each diner at the end of a meal. Children would have fun putting

the picture back together. Later on, when they had more
than one design, Michelle could mix and match.

"I wish I could serve them tonight." Michelle pulled a
gallon of milk from her fridge. She placed two crystal
goblets on the table and poured, then set one in front of
Abby. "But there's no time to make more, and this one is
ours." She broke the cookie in two—nodded her approval
at the clean break. Divided it again. They saluted each
other solemnly with a piece and nibbled.

Lemony, melt-in-your-mouth buttery, eye appeal. "It's
a winner," Abby murmured.

"Mmm. I was thinking we should debut it next week,
a week from tonight." Thursday was always El Rancho
Night at Michelle's Place. She limited her menu to a few
Mexican and Western dishes—enchiladas, fajitas, cowboy
baked beans, barbecue, chili—and the locals came in
droves. "Speaking of which, are you coming tonight?
You're comped all the way, of course. Bring your hunky
neighbor."

Abby grimaced. "Actually, Jack invited us to supper
here tonight, but Kat pulled an anti-cowboy fit. We made
the mistake of watching a film on TV last night. A Western, with a very detailed branding scene. Apparently she
saw a real branding this spring, out at some ranch, and was
utterly scandalized. The film brought it all back."

"The Suntop branding party, yes, I heard about that.
Anse Kirby says she bares her teeth at him every time they
cross paths. He thinks it's cute."

Abby raised her head. "Anse Kirby?" Michelle's smile
seemed rather wistful.

"Rafe Montana's right-hand man, which is half a step
down from ranch foreman, as I understand it. If you ever
want to lasso a long, tall cowboy…"

"Nope. Not in the market." Not for cowhands, anyway,

though she'd developed an alarming weakness for lizard-skin boots.

"And speaking of that, how goes the siege?"

Under the influence of too much sugar last week—they'd been licking the icing bowl—Abby had found herself confessing, telling Michelle about her terror watching Jack in that fight. Also of his continuing insistence that what she needed was a lighthearted fling.

Contrary to her expectations, Michelle hadn't shared her indignation. She'd been wryly amused. "A divorced divorce lawyer, what did you expect? Who's less likely to believe in marriage?"

"He's still pushing," Abby admitted now.

Pushing back was getting harder and harder. She'd actually been disappointed last night, when Kat had wriggled between them on the couch. Still, resourceful Jack had draped his arm along the backrest, reaching past his oblivious daughter. His slow, work-hardened fingers had stroked the far side of Abby's neck, played with her ear, then the corner of her smile throughout the movie. His touch had turned her bones to warm taffy. Had they been alone, Abby would have found herself on her back before the cattle drive crossed its first river.

Face it, the only way she was resisting his relentless advance these days was through avoidance. *And how long can I keep dodging?* "I have to get out of here," she said on a note of desperation. "And soon. I spoke with my friend Lark in Sedona. She's still offering me a building site on her ranch. I'd be a dope not to accept."

"But you can't go away now," Michelle protested. "How will we ever become cookie tycoons if you let Jack Kelton run you out of Trueheart?"

"I'm not *running*. This was my original plan. And you aren't ready to start a company anyhow." They'd agreed it would be wise to begin slow. Test the market first through Michelle's café, later by selling boxes of cookies at her counter. Then, if there truly was a growing demand...

"Yes, but I know they'll catch on. By this time next year..."

By then she'd be gone. Long gone. Give her some functional wheels and she was gone yesterday.

Better than hanging around, waiting for heartache to happen.

"YES, JUST LIKE THAT. As if you're looking at the sunset over to your left," Abby said from her place at the easel. If Kat's portrait was to be a farewell and thank-you present to Jack, then it was high time she started it. Whitey couldn't promise that he'd finish the bus this weekend, but for sure he'd finish it the next. The Lake's final days in Trueheart were flying past, with so much still to do.

"Or maybe I've spotted a caravan coming over the hill?" Kat suggested, staring intently into the distance.

"Exactly. Now can you find something to fix your eyes on, sweetie, so you won't move?"

"That stain above the window," Kat agreed.

Reaching for her pencil, Abby made a face. "That's the next project, painting this room." She'd start on the living room this weekend—tomorrow—while the kids were out of the way, helping Jack build.

With a few flowing strokes, she began to block in Kat's head, the drape of the mustard-colored burnoose that framed her face, the graceful lines of her throat and shoulders, the fanciful fish-lure earring that dangled from her right ear.

"I still wish I'd caught my falcon," Kat grumbled.

"And I wish I'd been there, drawing you trying to catch

a falcon.'' Really, Kat could've been the subject for a
dozen children's books. Yesterday she'd spent her entire
day crouched in the brush on the far side of Jack's building
site, hoping to tempt a falcon into her net. Her lure had
been a once-beloved stuffed rabbit with badly frayed ears,
to which Kat had fastened a length of fishing line. Each
time a hawk flew over, she'd twitch the line to animate
the bunny, in the growing conviction that hawks preferred
living prey.

Theoretically the hawk would dive on the "rabbit"—
and Kat would yank a second line, which would bring her
net pivoting out of the bushes to trap the bird.

All she'd caught in a day of patient lurking was a sun-
burn, since she'd forgotten to wear her jungle hat. Abby
hoped to complete her underlying pencil sketch today, then
take up her oil pastels next Monday or Tuesday, when
Kat's complexion wasn't quite so fiery.

Kat squirmed in her chair and wriggled her pink nose.

"Just a few more minutes, then we'll take a short break,"
Abby said soothingly.

"Are you drawing my hawk yet?"

"Not yet." She'd made several thumbnail sketches,
both from books and a nature show she'd been lucky to
catch on TV the other night, till she'd settled on the image
she meant to use.

"Are his wings going to be spread like he's about to fly
off my shoulder?"

"Wait and see." Actually the sparrow hawk would be
leaning in to admire the brass and feather lure dangling
from his mistress's ear, while Kat stared like a young falcon off into the distance. But Abby preferred to surprise
her.

Kat rolled her eyes toward the front windows. "Here
comes a blue pickup. I think it's Mrs. Harris."

"Oh, darn, I forgot! She wants her elk head." Once Abby had convinced her landlady that the cottage needed a fresh new look and that some of her potential renters might even be anti-hunting, Maudie had decided to reclaim her father's trophy. "Oh, no, you don't," she said now as Kat stirred eagerly. "It took us too long to arrange that burnoose. You can shift position a tiny bit if you're stiff, but don't get up, okay? I'll be back in a minute."

ABBY HADN'T BEEN GONE for more than a minute when a phone rang. Kat craned her head slowly around and spotted it as it rang again—Abby's cell phone, sitting on her drawing table.

Surely she wouldn't want to miss a call? Clutching her burnoose with one hand, Kat stood and walked on eggshells across the room, grabbed it and said, "Hello?"

"And who's this?" demanded an old lady's voice, sounding like Maudie Harris, except she was out in the yard.

"I'm Kat Kelton. Who's this?"

"Abby Lake's mother, dear, calling from Maryland. Is she around?"

"She's helping Mrs. Harris with her elk head."

"Oh." There came a pause while this was digested, then, "Would your father be the lawyer who lives next door?"

Kat giggled as she wandered over to the mantel. "He would be."

"Ah. Well, in that case, perhaps you could tell me about him. Abby never tells me anything."

"Like what?"

"Well, let's see. For starters, is he handsome?"

Abby's mom had all kinds of questions and she was easy to talk to. And Kat had been dying to discuss her plans with somebody, but this was the one subject she couldn't share with Sky. "I think Daddy and Abby love each other, but they don't know it yet," she confided. "Every time I look at Daddy, he's staring all funny at Abby, and she's staring back."

"That is a good sign," Abby's mom agreed. "What else do they do?"

"Oh, I dunno. Weird stuff. Last night Dad taped a picture of a washing machine to our refrigerator, and when Abby came over to supper, she turned red, ripped it off the door and chased him out of our house. Dad couldn't stop laughing."

"That does sound promising! And how would you feel, dear, if they did marry? Would you like that?"

"Absolutely. I'm going to be leaving soon... Well, pretty soon." Somehow her leaving Trueheart hadn't seemed quite so urgent this past week or two. "To be a captain on a tall ship. I was going to be a SEAL in the navy, but I don't think they can wear camisoles, can they?"

"Probably not."

"And they *definitely* can't wear earrings and I'm thinking about getting my ears pierced so I can buy more fish lures. But a ship's captain could wear earrings, even pirates do, so that would be okay. But when I leave, Daddy's going to need somebody to take care of him and Abby's perfect." Kat had been pacing around the living room as she talked. Something crashed to the floor behind her and she spun around.

Sky stood in the kitchen doorway, glaring at her, a pile of library books scattered around his feet.

"I think she's perfect, too, if I say so myself," chuckled Abby's mom in Kat's ear. "And how do you think Sky would feel if they married?"

"Um...well, actually, he just came back from the library. Maybe you should ask him—er, well..."

"Skyler's there? Oh, yes, dear, please do put him on."

"Well, actually...he's gone again." She winced as the back door banged, so loud it shook the house.

"THE PARTY that you've called is not available at this time. Please leave a message at the tone."

"Dad, I've got to *talk* to you! I know you said you were busy this month, but this is *important!* You've *gotta* come out here! Will you please, please, please call me? Oh, it's...uh, Friday. Friday night. I'll stay up late, so it's okay to call me late if you need to. Bye-I-love-you. And *call* me."

Sky shut the phone and flopped back on his pillow. "Darn, darn, oh *darn.*" He'd phoned twice, earlier in the day, and gotten the same stupid recording and hung up each time without leaving a message. But now he was getting desperate.

The mattress bounced as something heavy landed on it, then jiggled under deliberate padding steps. Eyes black in the dusk, DC-3 stared down at him, then sniffed his hair. "Why doesn't he *call?*" Sky rolled to his side, grabbed the cat and rolled back.

DC settled onto his chest, and a deep, satisfying rumble, like a big old plane warming up, shook them both. Sky filled his hands with thick fur. "Maybe he's flying and he shut it off? Or his battery's low."

The cat kneaded his shirt and settled into an even deeper drone, a DC-3 climbing through night-time clouds.

"He's gotta come out here!"

CHAPTER TWENTY-ONE

AT LUNCHTIME Jack remembered something he needed back at the house. "Why don't you guys go down to Hansen's and grab a sandwich, my treat?"

Kat looked up from where she sat cross-legged, doodling on the plywood flooring with a carpenter's pencil. "Abby packed us tuna fish sandwiches, remember? You put them in the cooler."

"Oh…right. Well, here, take some money anyway and don't wait lunch for me. If I'm late coming back, go get ice-cream cones and cool off in the park. It's hot as blazes today."

After he'd driven away, Sky fetched some more studs from the stack in the basement, then looked around. Kat was gone.

Gone over the ridge to search for hawks? He turned slowly—and spotted her coming out of the metal shed where they locked up the tools during the week.

He caught up with her at the picnic table, where she was laying out some copper tubing and Jack's butane torch. He hadn't spoken to her since yesterday; he'd been too angry.

His dad had finally phoned this morning, so Sky was feeling better, but there were still things she had to understand. Things he couldn't say in front of Jack. "My mom is not gonna marry your dad," he said, standing over her.

Kat cocked her head the same way her dad did, her eyes

gleaming from the shadow of her jungle hat. "How do you know?"

"I just know. Mom doesn't love him."

"Did you ask her?"

"No, but I don't have to. And you shouldn't have said that to my grandmom. That was *really* stupid."

Kat's chin rose as she scowled. "What's stupid is you thinking they'll get back together. If they loved each other, then why'd they ever get a divorce?"

"Because—" That she could put her finger *precisely* where it hurt, on the one question he'd asked himself again and again and again—he wanted to smack her. "Because stupid Chelsea liked my dad, but how could he help that? Then Mom got mad. It was all a mistake." A terrible, terrible mistake, but it could be taken back. *All Mom has to do is forgive him. She always says that people should forgive each other. So why won't she?*

Kat shook her head pityingly. "How long does it take to make a puppy?"

What was she changing the subject for? "I dunno."

"Eight weeks. And how long does a kitten take?"

"Seven?"

"Nine weeks." She took off her hat and frowned down at its brim, then hooked it on a finger and spun it around and around. "Sooo...how long does a baby take?"

He shrugged, and she said, "Nine months."

As if that meant something. Something to him. Sometimes she was such a prissy know-it-all. Such a *girl.* "Yeah, like you'd know."

"I do know. I looked it up in a really icky book with yucky pictures at the library. Mrs. Wimbly said I was too young and she grabbed it away, but that's exactly what it said. Nine months."

"So?"

"So...think about it."

The way she said that made him decide he shouldn't. He shrugged, kicked the dirt. "Anyway, you're wrong about my parents. I told Dad he needed to come to Trueheart and he's coming. Thursday. He's gonna fly in to the airport and take me with him. He said maybe we'd fly to Disneyland and stay overnight, then he's gonna come back and visit Mom."

"Oh," Kat said in a very small voice. She gazed down at her hands, twiddled her thumbs, then said in an even tinier voice, "Disneyland?"

He felt half good for winning, and half bad for the same reason. "Yup," he said loftily, looking away over the orchard. *Bet you've never been there.*

"Well, big deal." Kat scrounged in one sagging pocket of her shorts and pulled out several objects that made a clunk as they hit the table.

Now that he'd won, Sky was happy to help her change the subject. He picked up a cube of metal, roughly an inch on a side. "What's this?" It had a backward *R* carved on one face.

"Something."

"Come on, what?" he wheedled. She was like DC when he got mad and sat there lashing his tail. You had to tickle his throat just so before he'd calm down. "Tell me."

She pouted for a minute, then said in a rush, "It's a letter, like they used in the old days to make newspaper headlines. I bought 'em in Durango, in the antique clothes store, when your mom and I went shopping."

It had the pleasing heft and polish of a fine tool. He picked up another, turned it over, found a backward *E*. "Cool. What are you doing with 'em?"

She pulled a box of matches out of her other pocket and

turned the knob on the torch. Struck a match and held it
to the hissing gas. "I'm making a brand."

She looked at him over the blue flame, daring him to
say what they both knew; that her dad would skin her for
messing with his torch. "Of your name?" Sky said instead.

"Nope. They didn't have a *K* or an *A*. But this'll be
almost as good."

JACK COULDN'T WORK, couldn't sleep, was almost walking
into doors with wanting her. Not since he'd turned fourteen
and lost an entire year, thinking about nothing but *sex* with
wild, wicked, wanton fifteen-year-old women had he had
it so bad.

Abby, Abby, his green-eyed Abby. Slipping away from
him day by day. His hands clenched on the steering wheel
as he bucketed up Magpie Street, then left on Haley's
Comet. *What am I going to do about you, Abby?* They'd
crossed over some river—at least he had—and burned the
boats on the far shore. There was no going back. No way
to stop wanting her now.

Yet she was leaving. Whitey would finish the bus any
day now.

I could steal the lug nuts off all its tires.

Nah, too obvious.

Disconnect the timing chain? Because that was the problem here, timing. Timing was everything. The difference
between heartbreak and bliss was always measured in
minutes, days, weeks. You caught the train—and sat down
next to a woman who'd change your life.

Or you missed it by ten seconds and stood panting on
the platform, watching an unforgettable face in a window
sliding past you and gone forever.

Timing. You met her too soon—and she wasn't ready.

Or you weren't.

Or you both were, but then some idiot declared a war and you were drafted. Or—

Why the heck does this have to be so hard? If she'd only let me kiss her... A nonstop, no interruptions, meltdown cosmic kiss—then everything else would become instantly simple and clear. They needed to fall into bed and be nice to each other. Exceedingly nice for a very long time. That was as far as he'd figured things, but at least this was the start of a plan.

Bounding up her front steps—Whitey would spot him if he went around to the back—Jack found the door propped open, paint fumes drifting out. He stepped through, glanced around—and jumped violently as Abby, standing on a ladder not a foot to his right, let out a startled shriek. "Jack, oh, *look* what you—"

A slash of bold yellow-orange marred the snowy ceiling. "Oops," he muttered as she dropped her edging brush into the roller pan and glared at him. "Sorry."

"Oh, that's *all* I needed, you popping up like jack-in-the-box!"

Timing again; God was a joker. "Sorry." He scanned the dropcloth that covered the floor. "Is there a rag?"

"Never mind." She backed down the ladder, practically into his arms, planted a hand on his chest and moved him aside. "*I'll* do it." She snatched up a cloth and a bucket of water, turned back and tried to smile. "It's latex, not the end of the world. I just..."

She wasn't far from tears, he saw, as she climbed up to the ceiling to dab at his mistake. "Hey..." He curled a hand around her ankle. "Are you okay?"

"Yes..." The streak widened to a smear. "No." She gave a harried sigh. "I've had better days... Months... Years."

She was wearing raggedy blue jeans cutoffs, which made her look like a teenager. He slid his hand up the back of her calf, warm and silky and wonderfully slender. "I'm sorry. Let me do it?" *Do everything—anything—to make you smile again.* He thumbed the velvety skin at the back of her knee and felt her tremble. *Oh, Abby.* She could pretend, but he wasn't alone; she was feeling this, too.

"Fine," she snapped as the paint smeared further. "Here, take it." She stomped down to the floor, then shoved the bucket and cloth into his hands.

And smiling down at her, Jack noticed her T-shirt for the first time. *A Woman Needs A Man Like A Fish Needs A Bicycle.* He wanted to rip it off her and use it for his paint rag. Every time she wore that thing, it felt like a slap in the face. Why was that?

Because needing was what he craved from her. *I'd rather be needed than loved,* he realized, turning away. Needed by Abby. Somehow that felt safer than love.

Than loving her.

Needed, you were in control.

Loving, you were lost, just one more poor sucker blundering through life with a sign taped to his back, reading Kick Me, I've Got Something To Lose.

He stepped up onto the ladder and scrubbed grimly at the stain, which gradually lightened, but it sure didn't whiten. "I'll have to repaint this for you."

"Don't worry about it." She touched the back of his calf with a fingertip, so lightly she probably thought he didn't feel it—and he sucked in his breath.

Felt himself stir and harden. *Tell me you don't want me, too!* Looking over his shoulder, he opened his mouth to say something, anything like, "How about a date?" or "Want to roll around on the dropcloth?"

But she beat him to it. "Steven called."

Steven… Focused on her lips—on that delectable bottom lip—it took him a second. Steve. Ah, the contemptible ex. "He did?" *And this is why I find you practically in tears? That rat could still move her?*

He'd been right from the start. She was still in the first stage of the Divorce Crazies, or possibly the second. Much too soon for a man to take her seriously, or to take her at all.

Unless he was half crazed himself. Driven mad by lust. And a longing that cut much deeper than lust. Jack reached down to brush the backs of his knuckles along her cheek—and left a smudge of yellow behind. "What did he want?" *And what do you want? Your rat or me?*

"He's renting a plane, flying out here. On Thursday. Wants to take Sky to—" Her mouth quivered, her eyes filled. "To Disneyland."

That was bad? In fact, with Sky out of the way… "Disneyland," he repeated, carefully neutral.

"Disneyland! If that isn't *just* like him! How am I supposed to match that? Here I'm Ogre Mom who does all the dirty work. Makes Sky brush his teeth, go to bed by ten, do his homework, take out the trash—then once or twice a year, Steve drops out of the heavens in a Cessna and whisks him off to *Disneyland.*"

"Doesn't seem quite fair," Jack agreed, trying not to smile.

"Fair? It stinks! Steve was too busy to take half custody, but when it comes to playtime? Oh, he knows how to do that! Always has time for the fun stuff."

"But you're the one who's there for Sky."

"There to ground him when he needs it."

"And hug him when he needs that, too." *All that soft stuff we pretend not to want, and would slowly wither and starve without. Telling our jokes, pretending not to care, growing harder and lonelier by the year.*

She tried to smile. "You think?"

"Sweetheart, I know."

"Well...I sure hope you're right." She brushed at a tear trickling down from her lashes, left more streaks of yellow. "And another thing, Steve said he wanted to talk to me. About Sky. I don't know what he's up to, he wouldn't say, but whatever it is, I don't like it."

"Well, if you need any legal backing..." *Or I could just whomp him for you, which would be much more satisfying.*

"Oh, thanks, but..."

"But?"

"I owe you for so much already."

Jack groaned, shook his head. "I thought we were past that. You dressed my daughter in a camisole and taught her to cook. We're more than even."

But so much for his fantasy of a quick lunchtime seduction while the kids were safely occupied across town. Timing was everything, and this time Abby wasn't in the mood.

But soon, soon, it's got to be soon. If she'd only let him love her, maybe she'd give up her notion of running. Stay in Trueheart through the winter.

By spring, surely these crazy longings would have faded. He'd be sensible and sane. Able to think again, sort out just what he was feeling and what to do about it. He glanced at his watch. "Ouch, look at the time! Guess I'd better run. The kids..."

She gave him a puzzled smile. "What was it you needed?"

"A quick word with Whitey. I was just cutting through to the back."

SUNDAY Jack tried to get her alone again, late in the day, after he and his crew had raised and braced the fourth wall of his house. Next weekend they could start on the ceiling joists.

Next weekend he'd very likely be working alone, Jack reminded himself with a pang as he turned onto Haley's Comet Street. He'd miss his cantankerous and conscientious little carpenter's apprentice almost as much as he'd miss Skyler's mom.

If he couldn't persuade her to stay.

Which was why he'd dumped the kids at the park with money for ice cream, and a promise that he and Abby would pick them up in ninety minutes at the library. Then they'd all go for burgers at Mo's.

That left him a scant hour for some hot and heavy persuasion. It was time to take the gloves off. Make her see. Well, at least, make her feel. How else was he ever going to learn how deep her feelings went? Whether he should simply throw out his rules and risk it all?

Please, he prayed in case God was tuning in as he swung into her driveway. *This time, give me a break?*

His foot came off the gas and he coasted, blinking, unable to credit his eyes. At the back of the drive, where it had glowed in the shadows beneath the trees for weeks now, there should have stood a crimson bus.

No bus. Only Whitey's old feed truck, pulled off to one side.

She's gone.

The Jeep rolled to a halt as he shook his head to clear it. Couldn't be, not without Sky.

Gone for a test drive, he realized.

Testing her wings.

With the transmission in place, Abby was ready to fly.

"IT'S ONLY HALF FINISHED, but I thought you might like to see it." Abby pulled a stencil sheet from her folder and set it on Michelle's kitchen table.

"Looks good so far." The blonde glanced up from the half-cut picture of Tripp McGraw riding a hard-charging horse while he spun a lariat over his head. "Looks better than you do, if you don't mind my saying."

"I haven't slept much these past few nights," Abby admitted. "In fact, I guess I really came over for some tea and sympathy. I can't make up my mind what to do."

"Forget tea." Michelle turned to her fridge, pulled out a bottle of Chardonnay. "Hard choices call for the hard stuff." Filling two wineglasses, she set one in front of Abby and sat across from her. "So…you're reconsidering? Thinking about staying?"

"Oh, no." Abby shook her head mournfully. "There's no choice there. I've finished painting the living room and finished Kat's portrait. We're just about packed, except for the cat and our toothbrushes. Sky flies off on his adventure tomorrow. He'll be back late Friday. Then Saturday…" Her eyes slowly filled with tears. "Oh, *damn!*" She snatched up her glass and gulped.

"Sounds like you're just dyin' to leave Trueheart," Michelle said dryly.

"It's the right decision. I thought my heart was broken when Steve told me about Chelsea, but *this*… This is…" Abby shrugged helplessly. "Jack Kelton could hurt me so much worse, if I let him. If I got seriously involved with him."

"Seems like you might be there already."

"No-oo…not really. Just…wishing. But all he wants is a fling, and if I stayed, I'd want more. Give more. More than he wants or would take. He's been very frank about that from the start." She sniffed, rubbed her nose, smiled through her tears. "So I don't know what all the confusion is about. Gotta go."

"Girl's gotta do what she's gotta do," Michelle agreed, refilling her glass. "Then if that's all decided, why are you sitting up nights worrying?"

"I just…" Abby turned her glass around and around on the table. "Call me idiotic, but I can't *stand* leaving unfinished business behind. I'm so afraid Jack'll be like one of those songs, you know, the one you can't stop singing? It drives you absolutely crazy, but it just keeps spinning around and around in your brain.

"Now…if that's bad, then imagine—what if I didn't know the end of the song?"

Michelle made a face.

"What if I get stuck on him—on his memory—before the song's finished? Maybe get stuck all the worse because it *isn't* complete?"

Michelle smiled and sipped. "So you're saying the cure for all this is…?"

"I'm not saying anything! I'm just…wondering. Worrying." Abby tugged on a lock of hair till it hurt. Took in a breath and let it go. "And I feel like *such* a scaredy-cat, running away. My goal for this year was to become a strong woman. I got so burned, playing faithful little wife to Steven. I decided if I didn't want to be hurt again, it was time I learned how to stand alone. Make my own life. Find my own satisfactions. Depend on nobody but myself. Like you."

Michelle let out a yelp of amusement. "Yeah, right! Don't underrate yourself, Abby. You're plenty strong."

"I wish. But what if this—if Jack—is some sort of test? What if he's a stepping stone on my way to becoming my own woman? A truly strong woman should be able to take sex where and when she needs it, shouldn't she? Choose her own pleasures without apology?"

Michelle lifted her glass. "Bliss on her own terms!"

"Or…then again, maybe not," Abby said dejectedly, and drank.

"Mmm. Or maybe so."

"And then I think, well, he'd be so…*sexy.*"

"Oh, ye-e-ah, he'd be that, for sure."

"So what if Jack's right? What if this is precisely what I need after my divorce—to get back on the horse and ride?"

"And here's a ready and willing stallion, just rarin' to go?"

Abby giggled as she brushed a tear away. "Something like that."

"Then why not go for it? Yippie-yiii-cowgirl!"

"Well, aside from my own cowardice, there's Skyler. He'd never forgive me."

"You're planning to be an old maid all your life to please your son?"

"No, of course not. But this is too soon… Isn't it?"

"Far as I can tell, happiness follows its own schedule. You either hop on the train as it passes—or you don't."

"Yes, but. Sky's called his father four times this week. I'm afraid he still hasn't accepted our divorce."

"Maybe your taking a lover would help him see that it's over. That there's no going back."

"Or maybe he'd flip out." Abby shook her head. "See what I mean? Around and around and around? Where do I get off?"

"Someplace that makes you smile," Michelle advised, picking up their empty glasses and placing them in the sink, a signal that it was time for the restaurateur to start her supper prep. They walked down the stairs together.

"Or look at it this way," she said as they parted. "What would you do if you were single?"

"But I'm not," Abby pointed out, looking back over her shoulder.

"*Well...*" Michelle gave her a wide, wicked grin. "You are tomorrow."

CHAPTER TWENTY-TWO

"YOU DID REMEMBER to write down Jack's home phone number, didn't you? And his office number?" Abby fretted on Thursday morning as she and Skyler drove west out of Trueheart toward the airfield. "Just in case?"

"I know 'em by heart," Sky said patiently, and recited them both.

"You won't forget them? Maybe you should—"

"Mo-om!"

"Right. And you have our phone?" She hadn't realized it would be this hard to let him go.

"Arrrr." He unzipped the top of his backpack, pulled the phone out for her to see, then shoved it back.

"Be sure to zip that so it doesn't fall—"

"Mom! It's just overnight. Will you calm *down?*"

"I'm perfectly calm," she said with dignity, and managed to hold her tongue for almost a mile. All the while her panicked thoughts scurried and darted. *What if the plane Steve rented isn't safe. It's not as if he's maintained it himself. Or if the weather turns bad—a twin-engine plane in a thunderstorm?*

But if there was one thing she could still trust about Steven, it was his flying skill. Sky would be as safe flying with his father as he was driving with her in a car. Not that she wouldn't worry.

And even if she could've let go of her flying concerns, below them prowled the deeper, darker fears that had haunted her sleep last night. *What if Sky decides he'd rather live with Steven, and Steve decides he wants him? What if Sky never comes back to me?*

"Don't forget to feed DC tonight," Sky reminded her, and for a moment she was comforted. DC. He'd have to come back for his cat.

But if he decides he loves Steven more than me?

Her hands tightened on the wheel. *Get a grip. He's right. It's only one night away from home.*

His first, since the divorce. And his first with his father. "I won't forget. Or if I do, he'll sit by his bowl and yell."

Sky straightened in his seat and pointed. "There it is!"

As Jack had promised, the small airfield couldn't be missed. Far off to the left of the highway, its two runways made a gigantic X, oriented toward the prevailing winds. A few private planes were parked along the edge of the field and inside the open hangar. Abby turned down a long dirt road. Only minutes now. She should put a brave face on it. "Well, you've got a lovely day for flying. Kat and I will think about you while we're poking around True-heart. I thought I might take her shop—"

"Kat's gone."

"What?" Abby parked in one of the four designated spaces in front of the tiny terminal, its jaunty little glassed-in control tower flying a windsock. She turned to frown at him. "Gone?" Jack had said nothing last night when the four of them had eaten supper together.

"She's gonna hang around her dad's office all day. She stopped by and told me while you were upstairs. Anyway…" Sky paused, gripping his door handle. "Are you gonna be okay?"

All alone. *All day and tonight, too.* For a ridiculous moment Abby wanted to cry, *"No!"* But who was the grown-up here and what was her alternative? Even if she'd been invited along, she had no desire to see Steve. If there was a great echoing hole in her heart these days, he wasn't the man to fill it.

And the man who could wasn't interested in filling any woman's heart for long. Because a fling, by definition, was finite. Limited. With the end in sight even as you entered it.

She gulped and smiled. "I'll be okay. Probably work on my book. Or maybe that cookie stencil for Michelle. And I'll go to her place for lunch."

But she could tell that Sky didn't care about the details, he just wanted her off his conscience. "Great." He scrambled out of the car. "See you tomorrow!"

"Oh, no, not so fast! I'm coming, too." Despite his groans, she followed him into the terminal. Steve wasn't due to fly in for another twenty minutes, but Abby *really* didn't want to risk meeting him if he was early. Jack had assured her last night that Bret Halliday, the pilot who owned and ran the airport, would be happy to keep an eye on Sky, and that he was entirely trustworthy to do so.

Quickly she introduced herself and her son, explained that Steve would be arriving to collect him at any moment, then pulled Skyler aside.

"Have a wonderful time, sweetie. Be sure to call me tonight. I'll be waiting by Jack's phone till you do. And say hi to your father for me, okay?"

"He's gonna visit you tomorrow," Sky pointed out. "We'll be back about suppertime. I was thinking maybe we could have barbecue chicken? And corn bread and coleslaw. And chocolate ice cream."

Steve's favorite meal. *Oh, sweetie, the old times are gone.* Abby sighed. "We'll see." She was thinking more along the lines of taking her ex to a loud and neutral spot, like Mo's Truckstop. "Well, goodbye, sweetheart." She reached for his shoulders.

"Mo-om!" Sky glanced frantically across the room to where Halliday stood talking with a tall, weatherbeaten cowboy.

But moms had a right to the mushy stuff. She gave him a smacking kiss on the cheek and let him go. "Be good." Her eyes were tearing up—he'd be mortified if he realized she was crying. She turned and hurried out of the building, back to her car. Drove toward Trueheart as if forty devils were on her tail. *Come back to me, sweetie. Oh, you've got to come back!*

Without even Kat for company, it was going to be a long, long, lonely day.

WITH ALL THE TIME in the world to fill, what was a woman to do?

Abby took a bubble bath, sunk down amid citrus-scented fizzy islands of foam, while DC crouched in the bathroom doorway, surveying this unusual event with round-eyed disdain.

After that she considered doing a second session of yoga—she'd done her first at dawn—but settled instead for sitting on the back steps in the sunshine while her hair dried, trying to be as focused on the moment as the cat, who sat grooming himself beside her. *Don't think about Sky, flying away from me. Don't think about Jack, who'll be out of my life the day after tomorrow.*

Almost unthinkable.

So she wouldn't think it. *Be mindless as a cat, watching the leaves blow, the clouds move across a blue sky.*

Listen to your heart beating, like a slow drum in the desert. A-lone… A-lone… A-lone.

Abby bolted to her feet and into the kitchen. Carbohydrates and something creative, that would shake these blues! She laid out her latest cookie stencil on the table, then set two cups of Michelle's icing to warm on the stove in a double boiler.

By the time the icing was heated to its proper consistency, she'd finished cutting the last few gaps into the stencil. She placed one of the cookies Michelle had given her on a paper towel and set to work, dabbing the glaze carefully into the openings of the design.

"Whatcha doing?" Jack inquired behind her.

"*Aaaah!*" Luckily she'd just raised her brush, so it wasn't a repeat of the ceiling disaster. She released her breath and stared straight up, since he was standing directly behind her chair, leaning over. "What are *you* doing here?"

"Ran out of clients, so I came home."

Even upside down he looked wonderful. And just like that, the day had gone from empty and aching blue to shimmering gold. If laughter had a color… "I see." She glanced down, dipped her brush into the icing, twirled off the excess. "Where's Kat?"

"Stayed in Durango. I thought she needed a consolation prize to make up for Disneyland. So I asked Emma, my paralegal, to take her to a movie matinee, do some mall crawling, then out to supper. Girls' night out."

Her brush had paused in midair. *So here we are, alone at last.* And hardly by accident! "That was nice of you," she said, biting her bottom lip to stop the smile.

"Wasn't it just?" He pulled out the chair beside her and sat. Their eyes met. Danced together.

What if you were single? Michelle had asked her.

And here she was. Single for a day. Feeling shy and terrified—and utterly happy. Without any idea how to get from here to where they were going.

But Jack would know the way. She looked at her cookie. Dipped her brush and daubed in more icing.

"New design?" he asked idly, apparently in no hurry at all, content to bask in her company.

She could feel his gaze celebrating her bare arms. Under that caress, the pale fine hairs rose on tiny goose bumps. Her breasts came alive. Excitement feathered down her spine. "Mmm," she agreed. "A roper." She set the brush back in her bowl of icing and lifted the stencil. "See?"

He leaned so close, his shaggy hair brushed her temple. "Dynamite!" He turned so that his lips hovered not an inch from the corner of her smile. "Downright…irresistible. Can I make one?"

"Well, I dunno," she teased, shifting back half an inch. "It's not that easy."

"Try me."

I will. All in good time. She knew it. He knew it. She was done running, for this one special day.

She swallowed, nodded, set a cookie in front of him. Wiped off the stencil. Then, standing behind him, resting one hand on his broad, hard shoulder, she showed him how to lay in the icing. "Just a little at a time. Like that. Very good." His hands were steady and deliberate. She sat again and watched, ripples of anticipation sliding up from her bare feet, along the backs of her thighs. She crossed her legs, rubbed one calf sensuously along the other, uncrossed them.

"Don't distract me," he growled, eyes on the cookie. "This is a delicate procedure."

"Oh, sorry." She arched her spine and stretched, this time on purpose, glad she'd shaved her legs, glad she was wearing her favorite pair of cutoffs—ragged, but somehow they always made her feel sexy. So very, very glad that she had the power to distract him. Her outstretched foot brushed across the top of his. She sighed with pure pleasure.

"You…are asking for it," he warned, setting his brush back in the bowl. "But that's okay, because I've got it rii-iiight here." His voice had dropped to a dangerous purr. He lifted the stencil aside.

"By gosh, you did it!"

"I'm a talented man," he agreed, eyes filled with laughter. "And now, could I offer you a bite?"

He picked up the cookie as she cried, "Wait!"

And it broke in two. He'd bent it slightly as he'd lifted.

For an instant he looked not a day older than Skyler as his jaw dropped in dismay. Crushed, mid-seduction. "Well, *blast!* Shoot. And it was a masterpiece!" Ruefully laughing, he looked up and, as Abby laughed with him, the realization hit her, clear and perfect as a dewdrop fallen on her hand: whatever happened, she'd love this man forever.

"My fault. I forgot to tell you they're perforated." She ran a soothing finger down his arm, glorying in his hardness, the crisply curling golden hairs. "It'll taste just as good."

"No way. I'm aiming for perfection here. Can I try again?" He wiped off the stencil and looked around the table.

"Sorry." She shook her head. "That was my last cookie."

"Oh? Then I'll just have to improvise." He scanned the kitchen with a frown, glanced back at her—and grinned. "Ah." Lifting the stencil, he laid it on her bare thigh. "This'll do."

"Jack!" If he'd plugged her toes into a socket, she couldn't have felt a stronger jolt. Crackling heat sizzled up her leg from where his hand moulded the stencil to her curves. "You're out of your mind!"

"Certifiable," he agreed, moving the icing bowl between them on the table. "Round the bend and headed for home." He picked up the brush, dripped off the excess, dabbed it onto her skin. "And loving every minute of it. Sanity is sadly overrated, I'm finding."

That she could believe as he brushed hot icing delicately across her thigh. Beneath her skin, the blood surged like a moon-drawn tide. Her hips lifted in a slow wave, yearning toward his touch.

His fingers tightened on her leg and the stencil. "Easy there."

"Easy for you to say," she protested in a voice gone breathy and low. Giggles danced inside her like champagne bubbles. "Ow, that tickles!"

"If you wiggle, I'm gonna smear it. Then I'd just have to start all over," he warned. Raising his head for a moment, Jack considered her T-shirt. "Though curves *are* a problem. Maybe I chose the wrong canvas? You have such a nice…flat…stomach."

"Don't even think about it!"

"Too late. The thoughts are out of the barn, rampaging across the scenery. Can't you feel 'em?"

"Ah," she gasped as another brushload of hot icing defined the wider parts of her design—the roper's horse, his shoulders, his face and hat. And yes, she could feel Jack's thoughts running wild across her body, everywhere he meant to touch her and would. *And soon,* she prayed. *Please, soon.* Before she melted.

His brush lifted away and her hips rose again, an instinctive offering. Turned toward the icing bowl, Jack glanced over his shoulder. His eyes seemed to darken. "Hang on.

Almost done.'' He swung back to dab more icing, glazing the horse's galloping legs, the whirling lines of the lariat.

This was heaven, this was hell. He was deliberately going slow, torturing her!

But at last he was done. He set the brush aside. ''So. Shall we have a look?''

''It'll never come out. I'm too hot.''

''Your lips to God's ear.''

''I…mean, the icing will have melted.'' Her tongue felt lazy and slow in her mouth. Her skin was on fire, hot tides surging from her breasts to her toes, swirling behind her navel.

''Then I'll just have to cool it and try again.'' Jack lifted the stencil away. ''But wait!''

The design was picture-perfect, a sugary horseman galloping toward the ragged hem of her shorts. ''And now what?'' She laughed, delighted, embarrassed. ''Do we take a photo?''

''You have to ask?'' Jack dropped to his knees beside her. ''You never wrecked a sandcastle before?'' Dipping his head, he licked the outer edge of the design. ''Um, ye*sss*…''

''Ohhhhhh.'' She fell forward to support herself on his hard, warm shoulders. *Oh, no…yes…oh, please!*

Hot and supple, wet and rough, his tongue traveled her thigh, sending a tidal wave of sensations ahead of it.

''Sweet!'' he murmured fiercely against her, kissing and licking. ''*So* sweet… Oh, sugar, oh, Abby, oh, sweetheart, have I died and gone to heaven?''

Bending over him, laughing, she traced the shape of his shaggy head, the wide strong lines of his face and jaw. ''You.'' Crazy man, gentle man, clever man, her man. *You. No one but you!* She tugged on his ears, bringing him up for air and a kiss—their tongues swirling brown sugar…

caramel…traces of butter and exquisite tastes of each other.

"I can't get enough of you!" He leaned away, grabbed the legs of her chair and spun it around to face him. Settled between her knees, he addressed himself to her inner thigh—lapping and nibbling till she yelped and giggled and squirmed. Then he licked her clean in three long swipes and looked up, appalled. "That can't be all. I'm starving!"

"Oh, we can't have that." Abby dipped a forefinger into the icing bowl, let him suck it greedily off her fingertip, while she ruffled his hair with her free hand. Leaned down for another caramel kiss.

"Hey." Jack caught her waist. "Come down here, I'm getting lonesome." He pulled her off the chair, and she landed with a laughing yelp, kneeling astride his folded legs. His hand on her bottom kept her from sliding away. "Ah, that's more like it. But…" He groped across the table, found the icing bowl, brought it down to their level. "Supplies. Might be here awhile."

Scooping up a fingerful, he smeared a line of burnt sugar across her lower lip, cocked his head to admire the effect, then sucked it off. Swept his tongue into her, growling wordless delight, sipping sweetness while he curled his hands around her hips to urge her closer…closer…closer in a rhythm as slow and dreamy as their languid kiss, slower than their thundering heartbeats.

When they pulled apart, they were gasping for breath. "What's…under here?" Jack plucked at her T-shirt.

"Haven't a clue." Another kiss like that last one and she wouldn't know her own name!

He smoothed the hem an inch up her stomach. "Then maybe I should check?"

"Mmm." She smiled, too shy to say yes, and she

couldn't say no. Lifted her arms like a child while he
tugged it slowly up her body, then tossed it across the
room.

"For sure I'm in heaven!" he whispered, sliding a fingertip back and forth along the rim of her lilac brassiere.
"A double serving of heaven."

What he was *doing* was heavenly, and now his fingertip
was circling her nipple. Desire spiraled higher and higher.
With a tiny whimper, she arched her back. *Take more.*
Take all of me.

His hands found the clasp between her breasts and he
unclipped it with shaking fingers—slipped the brassiere off
her shoulders, his eyes never leaving her. "*So* beautiful.
Abby, you're so beautiful!" He cupped her with one hand,
shook his head, marveling, then bent to tongue her
slowly...then even slower.

"*Ohhhh!*" She rocked against him, wet and needy and
trembling. Closed her eyes. *Do with me anything you will.*
His mouth moved away and she whimpered. *Only do it!*

Heat and grittiness circled one nipple then the other as
he glazed her with icing. "Gilding the lily, I know," he
admitted huskily, "still..."

He dipped his head and sucked it off her, his eyes darkening when she whimpered, "I can't take much more of
this!"

"Oh I'll bet you can." He iced her again. Ate it off her,
bending her backward over the hard bow of his arm.

"Please, oh, *please*..." she whispered—and he closed
his teeth delicately over one throbbing peak.

"*O-oh!*" The room blossomed into darkness as she shut
her eyes. A kaleidoscope of colors expanded behind her
eyelids, exploding out from the wet, sucking heat of his
mouth. Arms locked around his neck, she hung on, shud-

dering, crying out, while the rest of her sailed a short tour around the starry cosmos.

And returned at last to her own kitchen to find him roughly murmuring, "Abby, Abby, oh, Abby…" Jack brushed his face back and forth through her hair, kissed her temple, rubbed her shoulders. "Sweetheart?"

She managed to laugh. Opened her eyes. "I'm f-fine. It's just—" *Like nothing I've ever felt before.* Too rich, too powerful for words.

"Overdose of icing?"

"Something like that." But much, much scarier. If Jack could do that to her, half trying, on a kitchen floor…with only his mouth…

He stood, bringing her up effortlessly along with him. "I'd say you need to lie down, but I'd be lying. *I* need to."

She smiled, swayed against him, hooked her fingers over his belt. "Sounds good to me, too." She backed toward the doorway, pulling him after her. "There's something upstairs called a bed."

They made it as far as the living room couch.

THERE WERE ALL KINDS of reasons for his dad to be late, Skyler told himself for the first half hour as he sat outside the terminal on a bench that overlooked the runways. Eyes fixed on the horizon, he recited them one by one. His dad could've hit headwinds. Or bad visibility. Or storm clouds to fly around. Or maybe the plane had needed something on inspection. His dad was a stickler when it came to maintenance. If he'd made them change the oil…

Or maybe he'd overslept? He'd hitched a ride on one of his airline's jets to Denver last night and was planning to rent a plane there. But if he'd stayed up late last night, hanging out with the flight crew…

He jumped violently as the phone in his backpack rang. He scrabbled for it as it rang again. "Dad!"

"Sky-boy, guess where I am?"

He squinted eagerly toward the east. "Almost here?"

"Nah, I'm still on the ground in Denver, looking up the tail of a mighty fine little Albatros jet. They've got a string of us backed up for a mile or more, cussin' and fussin', waiting our turns to take off. Whole darned field is locked down. Line squalls rumbling through, just one storm after the other. Bad chance of wind shear. They take that seriously out here."

"Oh." Sky felt his face going hot. "Can you— When will you—" It was over two hundred miles to Denver. By the time he reached Trueheart...

"Soon as I can, partner. Shouldn't be long now. I can see a patch of blue opening up, over the front range. Once conditions clear, they'll be glad to get rid of us. Reckon I'm ninth or tenth in line."

"So when—"

"Maybe you should go on back to the house. Have some lunch, and I'll call you when I hit the halfway mark."

"Mmm." His mom had fussed so much the first time, he didn't want to go through that again. And something about a Real Adventure required that you set your face from home and kept moving away, growing freer and braver and more capable with every mile you traveled. If he had to turn around and go back, somehow the magic would be spoiled. "I'd rather stay here. There's a soda machine, and Mom packed me a snack. Packed us a snack." He'd wanted his dad to remember the sandwiches she made for special occasions, chicken salad with walnuts and celery on sourdough.

"Well, okay, but it's gonna be a while. You go ahead and chow down."

"I will."

"Conditions still clear there?"

"Not a cloud in the sky."

"Then I'll call you soon as I'm up and on course. Can't imagine this'll last much longer."

CHAPTER TWENTY-THREE

THEIR FIRST TIME wasn't tender. It was all tumbling bodies and caressing limbs and giddy laughter on a barely wide enough couch—riven by one moment of motionless astonishment. *Jack, oh, Jack!*—bigger, heavier, hotter, harder than Abby could ever have hoped or imagined. In her, over her, his heart hammering against hers, his weight pinning her deliciously down. Shock waves of delight shivering out from their point of contact.

Slowly he shook his head, brushing her lips with his own. "Tell me I'm not dreaming! I've dreamed this so many times."

She arched up against him, bringing him even deeper— and shuddered from her toes to her chin. "Does that...feel like a dream?"

"Dream of an earthquake, nine on the Richter scale."

"Or...*this?*" She hugged him internally, her breath feathering out with the effort it took to keep the rest of her from moving.

"Oh... I think California just fell into the ocean. I'd better go...check...it...out." Somehow he eased a half inch farther into her.

Thrusting toward ecstasy.

"Ah-hh-hh!" She sang one note of dawning delight and could hold still no longer. Wrapped her legs around him and they were off again—flying, swooping, surging, teasing. Chasing each other higher and higher, laughing and incredulous that anything could possibly feel this good. That they were here, together, at last. Astounded that such excitement had no apparent end, that it could peak and rise and peak and climb and—

"Oh—*ahhh*—!" Abby pressed her open mouth to his shoulder and muffled her cries against him.

If he'd been holding back, Jack held back no longer. He came with a ragged shout, driving her down and down and down into swooning darkness. Their mouths clung; he groaned inside her—murmured her name, Abby thought— and she took that sound with her, like a trophy, off into smiling sleep.

SHE WOKE—minutes later? Hours?—when Jack shifted his weight onto his elbows, started to pull away. "No!" Curling her hands around his hard buttocks, she shook her head fiercely. "Oh, don't go!" *I've been empty and aching for so long, lonely for years, and now*—

"I'm not going far," he promised her huskily. "But sometime or other you might want to breathe, so—" Carefully he turned them both till they lay side by side, still joined, legs entangled, her breasts flattened to his chest. "Better?" He framed her face with a big hand, brushed his smile over the tip of her nose, her cheeks, her eyebrows, her lashes. "Abby, oh, Abby…" He shook his head. "I've got no words for this. Off the charts… Ten thousand on a scale of ten."

"Iridescent, like a peacock feather," she agreed drowsily, hooking an arm around his neck and snuggling closer. "Opalescent, like the inside of a shell." Rainbow trouts. Neon. Butterfly wings. He was so wonderfully big; she'd known it visually, but to fill her arms with him, to be so joyously, bountifully filled.

He caught her bottom lip between both of his, tugged

on it gently, sucked it thoughtfully. "Mmm." Pulled back an inch at last to say, "But we've got this problem..."

"No." She squinched shut her eyes. *No problems, please.* She felt as if he'd solved all her problems forever. *Don't tell me this is only a fling. I know it. You know it. But please, please, let's pretend for a little while longer. Just for the day.*

"'Fraid so. Something tells me we'll be needing another one of those happy raincoats—and soon."

"You only brought one!"

His silent amusement rocked them both. "Oh, no. I came determined and I came prepared, with pockets crammed. But where did we lose my jeans?"

Pockets full of joy! When had she last been this happy? *Not for years and years.* She smoothed a hand down the damp, hard planes of his sculpted back. "Haven't a clue. Shall we find 'em on the way to the shower?"

JOINING EMMA at the cash register, Kat set her book bag down with an audible clank.

"So...what've you got in the bag?" Emma inquired with a grin while the saleslady folded Kat's selections. She'd picked three more camisoles, just like the ones Abby had helped her choose. Except these were yellow, pale green and blue.

"In my bag?" Kat rounded her eyes and shrugged. "Oh...stuff."

"A Lego set?" Emma guessed.

Kat snorted. "That was back when I was a kid!"

"Rock hammer and rocks?"

Time for a distraction. Kat shook her head, then stood on tiptoe to touch one of her camisoles. "Don't these ever come in camouflage?"

After the department store, they bought fish lures for

Kat, then a pair of black lace-up boots with high-stacked heels for Emma. They passed a tattoo parlor and Kat begged for a Mickey Mouse tattoo—now *that* would show Sky—but Emma said, "No way," not without her dad's permission. Then they headed for the movies. "I thought we'd have supper there, afterward." Emma nodded at a restaurant they were driving past.

"I want to eat in Trueheart. At Mo's Truckstop."

"Really? But your dad said we should— Um, that we *could* eat anywhere in Durango we like. And that place has terrific vegetarian dishes. Desserts to die for."

"I've gotta eat at Mo's. And Dad said today's *my* choice."

Emma sighed. "No accounting for taste, but sure, Kat-teroo, you're Princess for a Day. You going to bust out and have a steak burger?"

"Steak burgers are made of cows, who have feelings just like anybody else. They're sacred in India. I'll get a grilled-cheese sandwich and a double order of fries."

"Yum! And for dessert?" Emma parked outside the movie theater.

"It's El Rancho Night at Michelle's Place. We can have chuckwagon brownies." Kat scrambled out her door, then leaned back in to snatch up the book bag she'd almost forgotten.

"Hey, you don't have to lug that around. I'm locking up."

"No. I'd rather carry it."

SKY HAD CHECKED the phone so many times, making sure he hadn't accidentally shut if off, that he'd grown tired of putting it away. It sat ready on his lap. He rubbed it with one finger while he stared at the only cloud in the sky.

Please, let his dad be coming up fast behind it. Any minute now his plane would burst into view…

The door to the terminal opened and Mr. Halliday leaned out. "No sign of him yet?"

Silently, Sky shook his head.

"You tried to phone him?"

"Dad doesn't like to be called when he's flying. It messes up his concentration. He said he'd call me."

"Good enough. Well, if you feel like company, come on up to the tower. Nice view from there, and I've got the radio on. You can monitor the traffic."

"Um, thanks. Yeah. Maybe later."

The cloud turned gradually from snowy-white to hazy purple, then oozed off over the rim of the earth. Another twenty minutes crept by, then the phone rang and he snatched it up. "Dad?"

"Nobody else. I'm finally blowin' this joint and headed your way. But, Sky, I've been thinking…"

"I know." It was nearly three. And after all his bragging to Kat.

"We could fly after dark, but the traffic on the coast is fierce. And we'd arrive pretty late. Tuckered out. So what would you say to Las Vegas instead? Swim in one of their big ol' pools, then catch a magic show? Tigers and babes and stuff."

Not half as good as Disneyland, but then, Disneyland had never been the point. Still, he'd begun to picture them there, and it was hard to let the picture go: he and his dad, happy together, riding all the rides. It would have been such an excellent trip. And somehow the distance and the trouble and the cost and the time would've been proof that his dad still cared. "It's okay. We don't have to do anything. I just wanted to…" *To tell you that we've got to put it all back together. You've got to hurry, before it's too late.* "To talk. Maybe you could stay here tonight? We could go out to supper. Mom could come."

"She's probably made other plans, buddy."

"No, she hasn't. She's just moping around the house. She was sad that we were going without her."

"Was she?" His dad sighed heavily. "Well, tell you what, Sky. Let's think about Vegas. I'll be there in an hour, tops, and then we'll decide, okay?"

He hadn't said no, Sky told himself, switching off the phone. His dad hadn't said no or even "We'll see," which was another way of saying no. So they were still at "maybe"? And if he could turn that "maybe" to yes...

THEIR SECOND TIME started as joyfully frolicsome as the first, in Abby's claw-footed bathtub. But its sloping sides made vertical lovemaking perilous, and they'd run through so much hot water in their soapy foreplay there wasn't enough left to fill the tub. Besides, Jack's legs were too long.

He laughed, scooped her up and stood. "Hey, mermaid, what's wrong with a bed?"

"Thought you'd never ask!" She hooked an arm around his neck, its muscles agleam with water.

"I've been asking for weeks," he pointed out, maneuvering her dangling feet past the doorjamb and into the hall. "Wanting to ask since the first night I met you."

"Really? Even back then? That first night I thought you were domineering. Bossy."

"I thought you were crazy, but drop-dead beautiful." He bent his head; she lifted hers. Their lips touched. He groaned, leaned against the wall; the kiss deepened. She reached down with her free hand and grasped him—all silky heated skin, sculptured desire—and he groaned again, thrust against her encircling fingers, tore his mouth away. ''Oh, *woman*...''

He walked on down the hall, slowly, but his breathing was ragged by the time they reached her bed. He lowered her—then rolled her onto her stomach. Came down over her like a predator taking his prey. He slid between her thighs, cupped her breasts as she cried out and pressed back against him. Catching the top of her shoulder between his teeth, he bit down just hard enough to claim her—a primitive, wordless demand for submission.

Instinctively granted. Every nerve in that most sensitive spot exploded—she gasped out loud, spread her legs wide and arched her neck as he laid a chain of hot, wet kisses up to her ear. ''I want to be *in* you,'' he whispered savagely.

''Please...oh, *please*...''

It was all the invitation he needed.

THE LAST TIME they'd shared their lovemaking. This time Jack controlled it. Giving and giving and giving till she could take no more, till she was nearly limp with surrender.

Then he wanted that, too.

''*Say you need me!*'' he whispered hoarsely, his fingers twined with hers, their arms stretched back beyond her head, his mouth hovering over hers, tauntingly just out of reach, their panting breaths loud in the dusky stillness.

''I...I-I-I...'' *Love* you. But Jack hadn't asked for that, didn't want that from her.

His mouth came down over hers as he surged into her like a big, breaking wave. She closed her eyes, spent. She could swim against him no more, was drowning in passion, sinking deeper and deeper beneath its surface.

He kissed the corner of her kiss-swollen mouth, then her lashes, too heavy to lift now. "You need me?"

I need you to love me. But if he wouldn't give his heart…

He pinned her hands with one of his, as if it was she who was dangerous. Cupping her breast with the other, he rolled its turgid peak between thumb and forefinger as he stroked into her, deeper and harder and longer and slower, the tide rising, inevitably rising… "Say it, Abby. Do you need me?"

If this was all he could or would give her, still it was breathtaking. Not to be resisted. Too late to refuse. Undeniable. She came and came again as his mouth took hers and, tears streaming, she cried into him, *"I do, oh, I do need you. Yes, yes, oh, yes!"*

And with her surrender, he was released. He came with a triumphant roar, wrapped his arms around her and rolled them both through a welter of sheets, till finally she lay cradled atop him. "Abby, Abby, oh, Abby…"

Long after she'd shuddered and sighed and rubbed her tears dry against the curls on his chest, then drifted away into sleep, Jack lay there. Stroking her tangled hair, soothing her velvety curves with shaking fingers, staring up at the ceiling.

She said it. She needs me.

So why didn't he feel satisfied? Safe at last? He'd pushed for everything he'd wanted and in the end she'd given it, so why…

Because he was a lawyer as well as a man.

Contracts made under duress aren't legally binding.

AROUND FOUR, the phone rang again and Sky snatched it up. "'Lo?"

"Sky-boy, do you see me?"

He leaped to his feet, eagerly scanned the eastern horizon. "No-o-o. Not yet. Are you—"

"Almost there, but we've got a problem. Just got off the phone with Chelsea. Her water's— Her babies are coming, a whole damn month too early. Neighbor's driving her in to the hospital."

"Oh." Had she done this on purpose? He hated her, hated her. She always spoiled everything!

"I promised her, Sky, that I'd be there for her—be there when they came. If I turn back now, I won't have to refuel. I should just land in Denver in time to catch the evening flight. Might still make it if the babies come slow. At least I'd be there for the mopping up."

"But... B-but..." *We've got to talk! You were supposed to talk to Mom—make up with her!* That was the whole reason...

"I know, son. It's rough. But what can a guy do?"

But... Time was running out. The world was slipping and sliding through his fingers, just when he'd thought he had a chance to stop it. Fix it. Put it back the way it belonged. Skyler stood, blinking back the tears.

"And Disneyland'll always be there, buddy. You and me, we'll do it soon. And do it right. Soon as I get Chelsea and company straightened out."

"Yeah..."

"So...do you see me yet?"

Far, far, far to the east, at the very edge of the world, he spotted a tiny shape, no bigger than a bird. Or maybe it was a speck on his glasses. "Um..."

"I'm wagging my wings at you, buddy. That doesn't mean 'g'bye,' it means 'I love you. See you soon.' And you give your mom a big hug for me, too, you hear? Over and out, son."

CUDDLED IN JACK'S ARMS, forehead pressed to the pulse beating in his throat, Abby lay, pretending to sleep. Satisfied in body, terrified of soul. And with nobody to blame but herself.

Jack had warned her about the Divorce Crazies—and he'd been right. She'd been utterly crazy, certifiably insane, to think she could love him even once, without consequences.

Oh, what have I done?

She'd told herself that maybe Jack was a test. That loving him, then driving away would prove she was strong—a woman who could stand alone, take her own pleasure. That the best way to forget him would be to have him. That if a lighthearted, no-consequences, frivolous fling was all he offered, then a fling would be enough.

What a liar you are!

She'd wanted him. There was the simple truth of the matter.

And whatever lies she'd needed to tell herself to find her way into his arms, she'd been willing to tell.

Happy to believe.

But after today, after loving Jack, she could believe them no longer.

There would be consequences. The pain she'd felt on arriving in Trueheart would be nothing to the pain she'd carry away.

But what other choice was there? No way could she stay here now. While they were in touching distance, she'd touch him. Come whenever he smiled and beckoned. And each time they were together, her love for Jack would only grow.

Better to yank it up by the roots while the tree was still young.

"HEY, POSSUM, you're awake," he noted huskily, smoothing a hand over her hair.

"Mmm." She kissed his throat.

"So come on up here." He gripped her arms and dragged her gently up his body, till they lay nose to nose. "Missed you," he said, eyes crinkling.

"And you." *I'm not even gone yet and, oh, I'm missing you!*

They kissed and this time it was like falling down a well; darker, deeper, indisputable as gravity... "No!" She tore her mouth away.

He frowned. "What's the matter?"

"I just...I..." If she told him of her decision right now, he'd only try to change it. And in bed, where Jack could bring all his powers of persuasion to bear... "I need to check your answering machine. Sky has that number. If anything goes wrong..." He wasn't supposed to call her till later that night, but the excuse was a good one.

"Right. And I suppose there's always a chance Kat might've called." Jack rolled apart from her and stood.

For a moment all she could do was lie there, drinking him in, in all his naked magnificence.

He paused and smiled down at her. "Keep looking at me like that, and I'll never make the door."

"Sorry." She covered her eyes with her palm.

"Don't say sorry, say later. Soon."

"Mmm." How long was a fling by Jack's definition? She'd never thought to ask. *Do you imagine we'll be doing this a week from today? A month? On through the fall?*

In actuality, they had only hours left. Emma had been instructed to deliver Kat at ten, and not a minute before, Jack had confessed. Once Kat was home, there'd be no sharing beds.

Then tomorrow... Whether Jack went in to work or not,

somehow she'd have to find the strength to pull back, start pulling away. By the afternoon, when Sky and Steven—oh, God, Steven—returned from their adventure…

No, the next few hours was all the time that remained. She could start mourning now—or she could cherish every last precious second. Live vividly in the moment, storing up a lifetime of memories to treasure.

"You coming?" Jack called from the foot of the stairs. He must be looking for the rest of his clothes.

"Be over in a minute. I'm going to change." And take Kat's portrait, her goodbye gift, from its hiding place. Because tonight was her farewell, even if Jack didn't know it.

"YOU SURE your mom's home?" Mr. Halliday drummed his fingers on his steering wheel while he frowned at the cottage. "Don't see any lights."

"She's probably taking a nap. But she's here. There's the car." Sky nodded at the Subaru, parked in the drive, then opened his door. "Thanks for the ride, Mr. Halliday."

"My pleasure. And if you get a hankering for a flight before your dad makes it back this way, come on out. Experienced copilots are hard to find."

After Mr. Halliday had driven off, Sky tiptoed through the living room, then up to the second floor. He didn't want to talk to anybody. Halfway down the hall, he halted at the sound of rhythmic thumping. DC galloped up the last step, spotted him—then turned his back and sat to busily lick his flank. "Yeah, I know, you didn't miss me for a minute." Somebody cared about him anyway. Sky scooped up the tom, draped him over his shoulder and went on to his room. He looked at the bed, sighed and wandered out again.

All day he'd been forced to sit still while he craved

movement, flight. Sad as he was, he couldn't go to bed. It wasn't even quite dark yet.

One ear pressed to the cat's purring body, he trudged into the kitchen. Stood frowning at the table. "Wow, and Mom tells *me* not to leave messes!" And she'd put a bowl of icing down on the floor for DC, though she never let *him* feed the cat from people dishes.

His stomach rumbled at the thought of food. "Mom?"

He wandered into the backyard. Checked the bus, which she'd been packing for days. "Where'd she go, luggums?"

Next door, he concluded. She'd probably been sitting by Jack's phone all afternoon, worrying and waiting for him to call her. His dad might come and go, but his mom was always there. Sometimes that drove him crazy, but to-night...

Still stroking the cat, he headed for the garden gate.

CHAPTER TWENTY-FOUR

"It's—" Holding her portrait of Kat, Jack shook his head. "Abby, it's beyond wonderful. You've caught her. What she's going to be someday."

"You think?" Abby laughed delightedly, pushing the hair back behind her ears. "You really like it?"

"She's a falcon. A flyer. And you're some kind of talented artist. Maybe you're going to end up a portrait painter like your father." He could see that had pleased her, the way her face glowed.

He propped the portrait on the mantel and backed away from it, coming to stand beside her, his arm around her waist. "I can't get over the colors!" How could anyone as gentle and shy as Abby be so bold with her colors, so bold in bed? "Even the sparrowhawk—you've trapped one for her. Has Kat seen this yet?"

Abby shook her head against his shoulder. "I wouldn't let her look."

"She's going to love it. I'll have to get it framed for her."

"Oh, no. I mean, frame it, of course, but this is for you, Jack."

"It's mine?" He glanced down at her. "What's the occasion? My birthday isn't till—"

He paused as she blinked rapidly. Her eyes glittered with gathering tears. "Wait a minute." He hooked a knuckle under her chin. "Why did you—"

She bit her lip and twisted away. "It's just to say…thank you. For everything you've done."

A farewell gift, she meant. A kiss-off. "Hold on." He grasped her chin, brought her gaze up to his with the tip of a thumb. "You're still planning on…going?" A fiery thread of pain was wrapping around and around his heart, making it hard to take a breath. "What do you think I've been telling you all afternoon?"

Tears were dripping and her smile wavered. "That you like sex?"

"Dammit!" He caught her waist and dragged her against him, consciously looming over her, willing to intimidate if that was what it took to get through to her. "Yes, sure. Absolutely. But you think that's *all* I was saying?"

She shrugged, her eyes darkening with emotion. "And that you…want me to need you?"

Constantly. *Need me and use me and let me serve you. Depend on me always. Need me so badly you'll never, ever be able to leave.* "Well, you got that right at least," he growled. He slid his hands around to her hips, pressing her against his rising arousal. Words weren't the way to say this.

"Well, here's what I don't need. I don't need a fling! I mean, I've flung today, but…"

They were maybe ten thousand miles past a fling, didn't she realize?

"And just what's my needing you supposed to do for *me?*" Abby shoved at his chest, but since he wouldn't let go, that only served to bend her backward. She scowled as his eyes flicked down to her breasts. "I've been needing all year—no, for years now! Needing somebody to really see me for who and what I am and love *me,* not because

I'm a pretty-enough woman, which is the only thing Steven cared about, but because I'm Abby. Me.''

"That's all you want?'' He couldn't help laughing for sheer relief. And for joy. Because he could do that—couldn't help doing that! Doing was easy. It was the admitting. Confessing his own need—love—whatever she cared to call it—that scared him silly.

"All!'' She looked ready to punch him.

She was too mad for a declaration of love. And he was too hot. Too hot to think through what needed to be said, or how to say it. "Look…'' He traced her eyebrow back and forth with his lips. "Let's back up a few steps. Calm down.''

She shivered in his arms. "I'm *perfectly* calm.''

"Uh-huh.'' He brushed his mouth slowly down the bridge of her nose. "Then let's start with this.'' He kissed the tip of her nose, felt her body soften ever so slightly against his. "First, this isn't a fling, not to me. Not if by fling you mean it doesn't matter.''

"But you said—''

Sometimes I talk too much. He captured her mouth. This was one place, at least, where agreement between them was guaranteed. She moaned and opened to him. He soothed, courted, caressed. Tongues were most eloquent when they didn't speak. *Abby, I do see you. I couldn't look at another woman if I wanted to and I don't. Can't you feel that? Feel this?*

She moaned again and her arms came up around his neck—at last.

He was breathing faster when he lifted his head. "Second. You aren't going anywhere till we figure out what this is.'' *Till I find a way to tell you. Because I know what this is already.* He was ten thousand miles past what he'd ever felt for Maura.

Which made this more dangerous. The potential for damage infinitely greater. But still, he was ready to risk it. Risk whatever it took to keep her in his life. Could no longer even imagine why it had taken him so long. One part of him had known from the very start.

She shook her head and frowned. "But—"

"No buts. I'll steal all the tires off your damned bus if I have to, but *don't go.*"

"You really don't want me to go?"

"*Argh!* What does it take to get through to you, woman?" He lifted her off her toes, and as he'd hoped, she brought her legs up, graceful as a dancer, to wrap them around his waist, bringing them into exquisite contact. Sending the rest of his blood south, and all coherent thought with it.

Finally she was starting to smile. "Three little words, that's all it would take."

"Please don't go?"

She tipped back her head and laughed. He kissed her throat. "What's so funny?"

"You! You're so big and so strong it's hard to believe, but you're scared, aren't you?"

Terrified. Teetering on tiptoe on the edge of the highest cliff in the world, with a hard wind blowing. "Me? Come upstairs and see how scared I am."

And miracle of miracles, Abby smiled, let him kiss her. He'd started walking even before she said, softly, sunnily, the sexiest word in the universe. "Okay."

THE LIGHTS WERE ON at Jack's house and Sky paused, seeing movement through the living room window.

Jack was carrying his mom. She was all wrapped around him and he was hugging her hard. They were kissing even as Jack moved, slow as a sleepwalker. They vanished in the direction of the stairs.

He stood, thunderstruck, his heart thumping hard enough to break ribs. DC let out a yowl; he'd been holding him too tight. Claws stabbed into his shoulder. He gasped, knelt, let the cat squirm away and flounce off, tail lashing.

Sky stayed down, hands pressed to the earth. Had he really *seen* that?

Desperately hoping, he glanced back at the house—and a light came on upstairs. In the room he knew was Jack's. His bedroom.

So he was too late.

Everything was broken.

It was too late to ever put it back together again.

"I DON'T KNOW WHY we didn't just stay at the truck stop," Emma complained as they waited to be seated. Every table, every chair in Michelle's Place was filled for El Rancho Night. "Mo's apple pie à la mode looked scrumptious. In fact, why don't we go back there?"

"Uh-uh," murmured Kat, her eyes fixed on one particular cowboy hat at a far table, though she'd already seen his truck parked out in the lot, as it always was Thursday nights. "I had to come here." She'd promised the calves she'd do this—well, do *something*—months ago, and her dad had always taught her to keep her promises. Tonight was the best chance she'd ever get. Still, she was feeling sort of sick. Or maybe that was the double order of French fries, which she really should've split with Emma. Or the cherry Coke.

"Though I've gotta say the scenery's awfully…scenic," Emma admitted as they stepped to one side to let three cowboys stride past them. They all slowed down to bestow wide grins on Kat's companion, ignoring her completely.

She stood on tiptoes to hiss in Emma's ear. "I gotta run to the Ladies'! Go ahead and get us a table."

"Sure do like your blue streak," one of the cowboys was drawling as Kat hurried away, holding her book bag close to her side. "Danged if you don't look like one of those bluebirds, flyin' low and fast."

In the Ladies', Kat locked the door, then turned to the small, high window that overlooked the parking lot. It was open already and its screen raised easily.

She threw her book bag out first. It made a dreadful clank, but there was no one out there to notice. Hoisting herself up so she balanced on her stomach on the sill, she squirmed out into the dark. Commando on a Mission.

THIS MUCH HAPPINESS was almost scary, Abby told herself, seated at Jack's kitchen table while he cooked an omelette. She'd become a soap bubble floating up toward the sun, colors sliding across her in rainbow hues. But such a lovely feeling, how could it possibly last? Sooner or later something was bound to pop.

Still, on and on she floated. There had been no discussions since their brief one in the living room. Nothing had been spelled out or defined between them, not in words, but that last time they'd made love…oh, if tenderness counted for anything… Sighing with contentment, she leaned back in her chair.

Jack turned at the sound, cocked his head as he studied her. No smile, but the look that passed between them curled her toes.

"Kat should be arriving any minute," he noted, lowering the flame beneath his skillet. "Can't tell you how I'm going to miss you tonight." Crossing the room, he bent, raised up her chin, claimed her mouth. "Miss…

doing…*this*. If you hear somebody howling below your window 'round midnight…it's not a coyote.''

"I'll be the one howling back.'' They jerked apart as the phone rang in the living room.

"Blast! I wish the world would leave us alone, just for one night. If that's one of my clients, I'm gonna fire him.''

"It's probably Sky reporting in,'' Abby guessed, following him toward the sound. "I asked him to call here, since he has our cell phone.''

There'd been no messages from Sky on Jack's machine when she'd looked earlier. If this wasn't her son now, she'd give him one more hour to check in, then she'd do the calling.

But a woman's voice rattled forth in response to Jack's greeting.

His eyebrows climbed. "What's she done? *When?* Tonight?''

Another brief, passionate avowal and a distant phone slammed down.

Jack slammed down his own and lunged toward the door.

"What?" Abby cried, snatching at his sleeve.

"Kat, of course. Michelle wouldn't or couldn't explain. She said this one we have to see for ourselves.'' He patted his pockets. "My keys? Oh, right.'' He headed for the kitchen.

"And turn off your eggs!'' she cried, searching for her shoes.

IN THE FAR CORNER of the parking lot at Michelle's Place, a half dozen onlookers surrounded a big gray Ford pickup. Jack braked beside it and stepped out of the Jeep. Abby hurried around to join him as the crowd grinned, muttered and shuffled aside.

His back turned to the ring of spectators, a tall cowboy stood, arms tightly folded across his chest, head bent down, contemplating the right rear flank of the truck.

Standing by his side, Michelle turned with an expression halfway between laughter and despair. "Behold."

For a moment Abby thought the emblem marring the truck's sleek surface was paint—grafitti printed with black precision. But as she moved closer and stooped, she sucked in a breath.

The letters T-R-U-E, surrounded by a lopsided heart, were burned—*branded*—into the glossy gray enamel, surrounded by a smoky haze. "Trueheart," she murmured, comprehension dawning.

Dazedly, Jack touched the heart. "You're certain Kat…did this?"

"Oh-hh, yeah," Michelle assured him. "When Anse came out, she was standing there bold as you please, holding her brand and the torch she used to heat it. Said she'd done it for the calves. So he'd know what it felt like. And maybe next time he'd think twice."

Jack groaned and glanced wildly around. "Where is she?"

"A woman who said she works for you has her. I told her they should wait in her car. They're parked out front."

Jack swung to face the truck's owner, who still stood, unmoving, eyes locked on the brand. "Of course I'll pay for it, Anse. Whatever it takes to put it right—*exactly* the way it was. Just send me the bills."

Eyes shadowed by the brim of his Stetson, Anse Kirby slowly shook his head. "It ain't the paint job…"

"Well, as for Kat, by the time I'm done with *her*—"

Kirby's head kept on shaking. "She might as well've branded *me*. I live to be a hundred, I won't live this one down. Every brandin' day for the rest of my life, somebody's going to elbow somebody else and snigger and say, 'Remember the time that little girl branded Anse Kirby's truck?'"

He sighed, resettled his hat. "Lately I've been thinkin' about Wyoming, finding some land of m'own up there. Dunno. Maybe this is a sign. Maybe it's time I headed on down the road."

"Well, before you pack your saddlebags, there's time for a good stiff drink." Michelle caught his arm. "Come on, Anse, I've got this bottle of Scotch upstairs that needs opening…" Sending Abby a glance of wry laughter, she silently shaped the word, *Later!* and towed him toward the café, calling, "Show's over, folks!" to her other customers.

"It's illegal to strangle your offspring in Colorado," Jack muttered, staring at the brand. "Still…" He shrugged. "I was figuring someday she'd end up a biologist. Or possibly a veterinarian. But I don't know…maybe a master criminal?"

"Or how about an activist? A political crusader? Or just a spirited and passionate young woman with the courage of her convictions?"

"Keep talking. I'd give a lot to be convinced. Meantime, what do I do to her that's horrible enough to make an impression?"

Abby laughed helplessly and turned up her palms. "Cook your meals for a solid year to pay you back for Kirby's paint job? Or—" She hooked a hand through the crook of his elbow. "Why don't you sleep on it and let *her* worry tonight. Tell her it has to be so awesomely awful, it'll take you a while to devise a suitable punishment, which it will."

"Yeah…sounds good. Good enough." Jack walked

with her toward the Jeep. "Poor Kirby. He was shook. Wish there was some way to make it up to him."

"Well, I had a thought about that," Abby said as he helped her up onto the seat. "Would a portrait make him feel any better, do you think?"

"Portrait by you?" When she nodded, Jack added, "Of what?"

"Whatever he loves. A sweetheart?"

"Far as I know, he's a loner."

"Ah." Abby glanced up at the lights that had been switched on in the apartment above the restaurant and smiled to herself. "Then…does he have a horse he's proud of, or—"

"Well, he certainly rides. And he hangs with this big Airedale."

She laughed. "I could do a dog easily. Or what about his truck? I could show it just the way it was, in all its glory—even better. Super Truck." Posed heroically on a hilltop, with a red sunset silhouetting its gun racks?

Lifting her hand, Jack kissed her knuckles. "Bless you. That just might cheer him up. It'd give him a way to claim he got the last laugh whenever the other hands rag him. But for now…want to wait here while I go collar the Katster?"

Watching him walk away—body by Michelangelo on his very best day, heart to match—Abby leaned wearily back in her seat and smiled. A proper portrait would take a week or more, what with the preliminary sketches. One more excuse to stay, not that she needed excuses now.

She sighed happily. *I hope Anse wants his horse done.* If she did a bang-up job, and then word got around… Because how many cowboys lived around Trueheart? If they all cherished their horses—and their trucks—why, there was a livelihood right there, whether she ever suc ceeded in selling a children's book or not. She glanced up at the stars. *What do you think, Dad? Want another portrait painter in the family?*

To think that only a month ago she'd come limping into Trueheart without a job, without a home, without a love to call her own. Yet now, here was happiness blooming, unfurling itself petal by gorgeous petal.

She jumped as a man's voice called, "Ms. Lake? I thought that was you. Evening."

Bret Halliday, owner of the airfield, had just stepped out of the café. He stood near the Jeep, fishing a ring of keys out of his pocket.

"Oh, hello." She smiled, too tired to make conversation.

"That was too bad, about today," the man went on, opening the door to his car. "Nice kid you've got there. And patient, too. Hated to see him so disappointed."

"Excuse me?" Abby sat up in her seat. "What are you saying?"

One foot inside his car, Halliday paused. Frowned. "Then you weren't home when I dropped Sky off. You haven't been back yet?"

"I..." Slowly Abby's hand crept to her throat. "You..." *Oh, no, please, no.* "Why did you drop him off? And what time?"

And what, dear God, had Skyler seen?

CHAPTER TWENTY-FIVE

DAWN OF THE LONGEST NIGHT he'd ever known. Jack steered his Jeep slowly up the northern slope of the valley, zigging up bird streets and zagging down stars, covering every possible route through the town that a sad and angry and bewildered boy might have taken. Scanning the bushes and side yards through strained and gritty eyes. *Sky, Skyler, you contrary kid, where are you?*

"Abby, I'll find him for you. I swear I will," he muttered with a glance toward the east. Maybe an hour left before the sun rose above the low range of mountains known as the Trueheart Hills, and they'd been hunting since midnight. *You'd think by now somebody would've spotted him.*

But only if Sky wanted to be found, and clearly he didn't. He could be crouched down behind any fence or garbage can and they'd never see him. *Sky, you poor little surly beggar!* Running and sulking never helped anything.

How much had he seen to make him run?

Nothing too shocking, Jack was fairly certain, given the time Halliday had fixed for his drop-off. Possibly Sky had seen nothing at all. Only heard them laughing upstairs in Jack's bedroom, then put two and two together. But stack that revelation on top of his father's letting him down…

And why did the rat stand him up? Sky had only told Halliday there'd been a change of plans, but not why. Throughout the long night, Abby had tried reaching her ex, but for some reason Lake wasn't answering his cell phone. *Damn the man! And if there's anybody really to blame for this, I'd place it squarely in his lap.* If Lake had made good on his promised visit to Sky, this never would've happened. Sky wouldn't have witnessed something he wasn't yet ready to accept.

Blame. Jack gritted his teeth, swung the wheel again at the end of a block. Abby was blaming herself. Half-hysterical, near collapse with exhaustion, she just wasn't being reasonable. *If I'd been looking out for my son's happiness, instead of my own!* she'd cried, shoving against his chest when Jack had first tried to hold her, to comfort her.

But Abby had wanted no comforting, at least not from him. She wasn't blaming him, thank God. Abby wasn't a blamer, or not of others, anyway. But clearly she thought their day of bliss had brought this punishment down from above.

And so she wanted nothing more to do with him.

Whether she realized it or not, she was bargaining with God. Proving to Him that she'd be willing to trade all chance of happiness to have Skyler back. Give it up forever, if need be. *Give me up. Throw us—what we could be to each other—right out the window.* Out of her life.

Jack braked the Jeep at a crossroad and sat, staring down over the rooftops, seeking any sign of movement between the houses. God, to go from such shining hope and happiness yesterday—to this?

Off to the west, something moved. He swung around and squinted, then made out a blue car, creeping eastward along the road past the white spire of the little Lutheran church, then down the hill into town. Halliday's car, returning. He'd agreed with Jack that the airfield was a possible destination for Skyler. The last point of contact with his father, it was also a symbol of the kid's dreams and ambitions. Of happier days. Halliday had volunteered to search the hangars, the planes, the outbuildings, and if that didn't prove fruitful, to prowl on west toward Cortez, though it seemed unlikely the kid would run west.

Abby was convinced Sky had headed east. That his running meant a complete rejection of everything she'd brought him to—Trueheart, this new life she'd been building here. Her relationship with Jack. She was sure her son was on his way back to New Jersey, either to the home she'd sold this spring, or to the house Lake had bought in a nearby town for his new family. Conceivably to Sky's grandmother in Maryland. But east, definitely east. Back to his world before the divorce.

Sky, you poor crazy kid. You can't go back. You have to square your shoulders and set your face to the future, no matter how it hurts. I should've been teaching you that instead of carpentry. Would've been honored to teach you.

Jack rubbed his hand across his face. *Don't give up.* Not yet. This was just exhaustion talking. And blues.

And aching loneliness. *Abby, could you really throw us away? Leave me now, just when I've handed over my heart?*

Once they'd searched their two cottages and yards, finding only DC, crouched on the kitchen stoop, they'd scoured the town itself—the school buildings and streets, the shops on Main, the library grounds, the park. Anse Kirby, Michelle and Halliday had helped in that first round of searching, while Emma had stayed at Jack's cottage, in charge of home base communications and Kat, who, in spite of her protests, had been sent, sleepy and chastened, off to bed.

When they'd combed Trueheart and failed to find the runaway, they'd called in reinforcements. Whitey and Tripp McGraw were covering the roads to the northeast, out toward Suntop and the Circle C; Rafe Montana, the back roads northwest toward the Jarrett ranch. Sheriff Noonan had returned from some unspecified investigation out of town to join the search.

He'd shown up just in time to head off a major blowup. Abby had been insisting that she and Jack should drive separately to cover more ground. But Jack refused to let her go alone, exhausted and upset as she was. He'd threatened to confiscate her keys to the Subaru if he had to, and she'd been crying, insisting that she'd drive her own bus, when Noonan arrived to break the impasse.

So Abby had gone east in the sheriff's car, helping him scan the highways, since her greatest fear was that Sky was hitchhiking. By now he might be wandering through the truck stops on the outskirts of Durango, seeking a ride.

God, don't let her be right. The kid was too smart for that. Basically sensible, even if he was outraged and upset.

With Abby in good hands, Jack had opted to reexamine the town. *Sky didn't take his cat.* That was part of Jack's reasoning for sticking close to Trueheart. *And his dad let him down.* Wouldn't that have given him pause?

If it was me, I'd look for refuge somewhere I'd been happy. If I felt little and lost and scared, then I'd go where I'd last felt competent. In control. So Jack was working his way uphill, toward his building site, where this summer Sky had learned the satisfaction of working with his hands. Of building something, in this changing world, that would last. Abby might call this guy-think, but then maybe it took one to know one.

To find one.

Not that he hadn't searched here once already. It was the first place he'd looked after Haley's Comet Street. Still it would've been easy for Sky to hide if he didn't care to be found. But by now? *He's had a whole long, cold night to feel sorry for himself. Without a bite to eat.*

Parking at the base of the drive, Jack walked up, scanning the gaps between the gnarly old apple trees. *Or I suppose he could be up on a branch.* He'd wait for better light to search the grounds, then go on over the ridge.

He reached his house and stood, surveying the plywood floors in hope of fresh sneaker tracks in the dew. But found nothing, not a sign.

He sighed wearily and trudged on, checking the picnic table out back, then the metal shed where they locked up their tools. But the combination padlock hung in place, so Sky couldn't be inside. So much for his theory.

Maybe he should call Abby, see if she'd had any luck. Emma had lent Jack her cell phone for the search and Abby had recovered her own. She'd found it in Sky's bedroom, in his backpack.

One more reason I don't think he's hitchhiking. Surely he'd have taken his pack?

Unless the kid had seen something that had so shaken him he'd fled without thought or plan.

He blew out a breath, turned toward the ridge. No. It wasn't light enough for bushwhacking yet. Turned back—and frowned.

The foundation enclosed a full-size cellar, dug into the slope. His future workshop, but right now it was where they stored the lumber and more valuable supplies, such as the finished windows waiting to be installed. Someday the walk-out door to the basement would be covered by a set of steel bulkhead doors. At present, Jack tacked a sheet of plywood to the door frame at the end of each weekend. Hardly an unbreachable seal, but at least it hid the contents from view.

Hours ago, when he'd circled the foundation, that rectangle had been securely nailed. Now it stood in place, but at a slight slant.

The boy must have pried it off—taken a hammer from the shed to do so. Then propped it back up to cover the doorway.

Heart pounding with hope, Jack lifted the sheet aside. Scanned the gloom. Small windows high up in the foundation walls let in faint rays of early light. If Sky lurked within, the boy could surely see him silhouetted in the doorway. ''Sky?''

No answer, but had that been a stirring, over there along the east wall, on top of that stack of two-by-sixes? He eased into the space, trying not to think about rattlesnakes, which might find this a cozy den. *Skyler?*

Another movement in the dark, there below the window, and somebody sighed.

Thank you, God!

His eyes were growing accustomed to the available light. Sky sat with knees drawn up, slumped back against the concrete wall. Jack settled beside him. ''Hey.''

Poor little devil, the temperature had dropped steeply overnight. The chill and damp down here must have crept to his bones. Jack longed to place an arm around him and to pull him close.

Too soon. Go slow. Easy does it. He leaned against the cold wall, their shoulders not quite touching, hoping his body would radiate some heat. He fished in his jacket and found a sports bar, one he'd brought from his cache in the Jeep. ''Long time since supper.'' *Which you didn't get.* He balanced the bar on Sky's knee.

It rested there for one minute. Two. A stomach snarled in the dark, and Jack smiled. Waited some more.

Sky ripped it open. Ate with slow dignity.

As proud as his mother. *Oh, Sky, let me do this right.*

But before he could find the words, the kid blurted, "I saw you kissing her."

Jack winced at the tone of accusation. Raw betrayal. *I was supposed to be your friend, then I did that to you?* "Ah. Thought you might have." He sighed; how to soften it? *Or do I just plunge straight through?* "Yeah...I hope to be kissing your mom a lot, from now on."

"But she and my dad—" Sky stopped, made a small inarticulate sound of frustration and misery.

Jack dropped an arm around his shoulders—felt him stiffen, start to jerk away...then give up. A long, despairing sigh blew out into the darkness. "Yeah," Jack said simply, and pulled him back against his side. *They're divorced. It's finally starting to sink in, isn't it?* "Must hurt something awful."

Sky nodded fiercely and Jack tightened his arm, broadcasting heat, solidarity. A caring, masculine presence. *Oh, Sky, how to do this...* "Your mom's pretty special, you know?"

A nod, silky hair brushing his chin.

"Everybody deserves to be special to somebody. *Needs* to be special. And kissing, that's one way a man tells a woman he finds her very, very special. So I was telling her that."

"But my *dad*—" He stopped again, defeated.

"Used to kiss her," Jack agreed. "And think she was special. But, Sky, looks like your dad changed his mind. Or lost his way for a little while, got to thinking maybe somebody else was more special?"

"Stupid ol' Chelsea!" Sky growled, leaning into his warmth.

Takes two to tango, kiddo.

"She's having her babies. She wanted Dad to be there,

is why he didn't— Couldn't— She's *always* spoiling things!''

''She's having them, you mean now? Or yesterday?'' So that was why Lake hadn't shown, not a despicable reason at all, Jack realized as Sky nodded. *Though if he'd kept his pants zipped in the first place, he'd never have had to choose.* ''I see. So by now, maybe you have some brothers or sisters?''

Sky shook his head, emphatically disclaiming any such. Jack smiled to himself. Waited.

''But when they're older, Dad said once they're house-broken and Chelsea can handle them, maybe someday he'd...''

Come back? Many a jerk longed to have his cake and eat it, too— Jack had seen plenty of that kind of thinking in his profession. But surely Lake hadn't promised him that? Tried to weasel past his son's pain by pretending it was only temporary? Revocable? ''He said he'd come back to your mom?'' *To you?*

''Well...sort of. Yeah. He didn't exactly *say* it, but I know.'' Sky looked up at him defiantly. ''So-you-shouldn't-be-kissing-my-mom.''

Hmm. Jack rubbed his chin, grimaced at the sound of bristles. Whatever had originally been said or not said, clearly Sky's wish had been repeated so often, like a spell to banish the bad times, bring back the good, that it had achieved the weight of truth.

How to shake it? ''Tell you what. Why don't we ask your dad what he thinks? And see how ol' Chelsea's doing?''

OUTSIDE, the day had dawned bright and clear. They scrambled up onto the decking and Jack paced, hands in his pockets, while Sky punched in his father's number.

Maybe this was the worst possible idea. Maybe he should grab back the phone. Maybe Lake was still at the hospital and he wouldn't—

"Dad?" Sky's face lit up.

Jack sauntered over. It was his life on the line here, too. Cocking his head, he could hear Lake's tiny, booming, jubilant voice, one of those *Right Stuff* kind of pilot's drawls.

"*Three* of 'em?" Sky's mouth fell open.

And had anyone ever told him what the word "triplets" actually meant, Jack wondered, smiling in spite of himself.

"Yeah, and beauties every one! Your sisters are doing great, Sky-boy. And Chelsea, too. They had to do a cesarean, but she came through like a champ. And everybody's got ten fingers, ten toes and a pair of lungs like you wouldn't believe. So I'll be sending you three cigars, buddy—that's three—to help me celebrate." The happy, relieved voice rambled on and on, recounting the event's perils and victories, while Sky listened, blinking behind his thick lenses, gulping and nodding automatically.

Gradually, Lake wound down; he would've had a long night, too. And at last he thought to ask, "How about you, buddy? You find something interestin' to do after I couldn't make it?"

Sky nodded again, as if his father stood in front of him. "I saw Mom and Jack kissing."

There came a long silence, then Lake said, "Jack? Who's—"

Jack lifted his brows in command and held out his hand. Sky plunked the phone into his palm. "Jack Kelton here." He turned his back and strolled off a few long strides and lowered his voice. "The man who's going to marry Abby and take care of your son as best he can, whenever you're not there to do it."

"Hey…well, this is pretty damn sudden!"

"Not as sudden as *your* family, sport. March to July, that's goin' some. But it's no less sincere. And since it sounds like you may be needing some help in the college tuition department and since I'm not going anywhere, let's see if we can get along, shall we? Now…" He drew in a breath and forged on. "Sky seems to have gotten a notion somewhere that this divorce isn't permanent. That some-day you're coming back. You want to tell him where you really stand on that?" He turned, handed the phone back to Sky and stalked off to wait at the far end of the house, fists clenched.

Another man who'd held Abby. He'd just as soon have punched him as talked to him, and doubtless Lake felt the same. Still…*I could've been more tactful.* But it had been a long, cold night with too many things that mattered hang-ing in the balance.

The balance hadn't tipped yet. *Tell him. Come on, tell him.*

Behind him, he could hear Sky's soft mumbled re-sponses, coming at longer and longer intervals. Fi-nally…silence.

Jack glanced over his shoulder, then turned. Sky sat cross-legged, phone clutched in both hands, head down, slowly rocking.

Kat he could have pulled into his lap and cuddled, but not a boy of ten. Jack settled stiffly beside him. Sat looking down at his own hands, wishing he had a knife to whittle with or something—anything. Scrounging in his pocket, he found a stub of a pencil. Pulled it out and turned it end over end over end.

"Dad…said he wished what happened…hadn't hap-pened, but now he's stuck. That he couldn't come back for years and years. And that wouldn't be fair to Mom.

That she's too special. She shouldn't have to wait. Oughta have somebody to take care of her now.'' Sky rubbed his knuckles across his nose.

Thank God. And thank you, Lake. ''Your dad's right. She's very special. And even better, she comes with a bonus.''

''Whazzat?'' Tears dripped onto the plywood and Sky wiped an arm across his face.

''You.'' He waited for that to sink in. ''I never realized till you came along how much I needed a son.''

''Arrrr.'' Sky sat very still, looking down.

''I know you've got a perfectly good dad already. But what I'm hoping is, one of these days, maybe you'll find you could also use a…whatever you want to call it. Friend? Part-time consultant in the guy department?''

Sky shot him a look that wasn't entirely discouraging, then looked down again. Shrugged. ''Dunno.''

''I suppose if that doesn't work for you, you could always go back to New Jersey, help your dad with the diapering. Three of 'em, *whew!* That's going to be a truckload of stinky diapers for the next few years. And all those bottles to warm? And pushing a triple-wide stroller everywhere they go.'' *Think about it, pardner.*

''On the other hand, I'd be grateful for some help out here. I'm going to have to expand the house, and now's the time to do it, while it's still warm enough to pour foundations.''

''Expand it?'' Sky looked up, looked around critically at all the fine work they'd done. ''Why?''

''Well, whether you decide to live here with us or just choose to visit, you're going to want your own bedroom. And your mom will need some sort of studio.'' Jack tapped the pencil's eraser on the plywood a few times, then sketched some quick lines. ''I was thinking if we bumped

it out…here. The studio would go back of the garage…
Then your room above that? Good view of the mountains
up there.''

Sky blew out a long shaky breath, then gazed all around,
taking his time. ''Or…you could take another jog out to
the west.''

Heads almost touching, they sketched in that idea, re-
vised, scratched out, tried again, shaping it better and better.

''And then there's the matter of a cat door,'' Jack reminded him. ''Shouldn't be on the north side—drafts.
Maybe over here in the mudroom?''

ONCE JACK HAD PHONED HER, Abby came home on
wings—eighty miles an hour down the highways with the
sheriff at the wheel. Still, it had taken them almost an hour.
Time enough for her to cry for sheer joy and relief—
mightily embarrassing her companion—then to fall fast
asleep, lulled by the hum of the speeding tires.

She woke when he pulled into her driveway. Hastily she
brushed her tousled hair behind her ears, gathered up her
purse and sweater. ''Thank you *so* much! I don't know
how to—''

''Entirely my pleasure, ma'am.'' Sheriff Noonan
touched his hat brim and the car pulled away.

Leaving her standing in front of her cottage. Looking
up at Jack, who sat on her steps, slouched against a porch
post. He gave her a tentative smile. Its watchful wariness
pierced through her numbness. She swallowed around the
lump rising in her throat. Yesterday he'd trusted her entirely. She'd held his heart in her hands. But now…

*All the things I said to him last night. Or should have
said!* Tears welled again. But what could she do if Sky

wouldn't accept him? *Doesn't matter how much I love you if Sky can't be happy.* "Where is he?"

"Upstairs asleep."

She had to see for herself.

She stood for a long time in her son's doorway, drinking in the sight of a pale toss of hair on the pillow, one pink ear, infinitely precious. His face was out of sight, buried in the flank of his purring cat. Yes, it was really Sky, really home and safe. She could start to believe it now. Sighing, Abby came back down the stairs, holding hard to the banister.

Jack hadn't budged. She sank down beside him. "Has he eaten?"

"Two sports bars and a Mo's egg sandwich on the way home."

"Oh, Jack!" His arm came around her and she turned into his shoulder, curling into his hard, solid warmth, shivering with emotion. *"Oh,* if he'd…"

"But he didn't. He's safe. He's fine now."

"Yes, but…" She lifted her face to tell him that, much as she wanted it to, maybe this wasn't going to work. Not if Sky couldn't be happy.

Jack claimed her mouth—thoroughly, ruthlessly. At length.

"Oh," she said when she could breathe again. She rested her forehead against his throat. At peace. How could she move from here? Ever? When this was where she belonged?

"Maybe now's the time to tell you," Jack said, brushing his face through her hair. "The three men in your life have consulted and we seem to have reached an agreement."

Three! She lifted her head again to meet his eyes. "You spoke with *Steven?*"

"Mmm. And much more importantly, with Sky." Jack

smoothed his knuckles across her parted lips. "I have his permission to court you."

"You…" Hours after daybreak, but only now was the sun rising inside her. Or maybe this was her heart rising up, turning from shades of break-heart blue to rosy red…gold the color of laughter…hope bright as new spring leaves… "You do?"

"Yup." He nodded, and the wariness and worry were gone. This was Jack at his smuggest. Jack with triumph dancing in his gray eyes, inviting her to dance with him.

But she was a woman who'd sworn she'd stand on her own two feet, even while she was falling head over heels. "How nice that you three agreed, but do *I* get any say in this?"

"Oh, absolutely." Jack's voice was husky with laughter as he traced her lips with his finger. "As long as you say yes."

"Don't you ever, *ever* quit?" she demanded as he gathered her in to kiss her eyes, her cheeks, her arms as they wrapped around his neck. Then he returned to her smile.

"Well…of course I do. After I've won. That's Kelton's Rule Number Four."

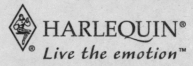

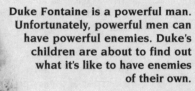
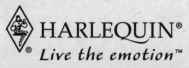

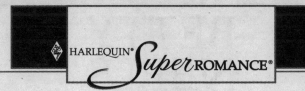

Cowgirl, Say Yes
by Brenda Mott,
author of _Sarah's Legacy_

Widowed rancher Wade Darland and his children have never met a cowgirl like Tess Vega, who has just set up a horse sanctuary for abused and abandoned horses. They all want more of her in their lives. Now they have to get Tess to say yes!

On sale starting April 2003

Buffalo Summer
by Nadia Nichols,
author of _Montana Dreaming_

Caleb McCutcheon is living his dream—owning a large Rocky Mountain West ranch and a herd of magnificent buffalo. Now if only the woman he's beginning to love would agree to share his dream…

On sale starting June 2003

Heartwarming stories with a sense of humor,
genuine charm and emotion and lots of family!

Available wherever Harlequin books are sold.

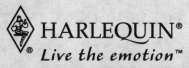